TO LOVE
AGAIN

TO LOVE AGAIN

DODY MYERS

BellaRosaBooks

TO LOVE AGAIN
ISBN 978-1-933523-67-5

First printed December 2009

Library of Congress Control Number: 2009941691

Printed in the United States of America on acid-free paper.

Cover painting by Joyce Wright – www.artbyjoyce.com
Book design by Bella Rosa Books

BellaRosaBooks and logo are trademarks of Bella Rosa Books.

10   9   8   7   6   5   4   3   2

Dedicated to my husband Ainslee (Doc) Gruen with love.
For all the things you do . . . this one's for you.

Acknowledgments

Dr. Jane M. Thibault, PD.D, Clinical Gerontologist, University of Louisville, who graciously shared her lecture notes on Senior Sexuality.

Connie Daley, friend and story editor, for her constant reminder to avoid the 'ick' factor.

Margaret Sponsler for her lovely poem 'What is This Love'.

My thanks to the ladies of the Northgate/Northfield Reading Club who read and critiqued the rough draft of this book.

Note from the Author

Although I personally have been fortunate enough to find love again, this novel is not autobiographical. The idea for the story was born while en route from Denali Wilderness Park to Fairbanks, Alaska on a tour. The narrating guide in our railcar was a gray-haired woman, probably in her late sixties, with a distinct New England accent. Ever the storyteller, I began to hypothesize how she might have come to Alaska, at her age, to work as a tour guide. The title came naturally when, several years after losing our spouses, Dr. Gruen and I married. And the joys and sorrows of seniors in second marriages came alive after years of living in a retirement community.

BOOK ONE

PROLOGUE

It was over.

Grace Maguire stood in the doorway and watched the last of the mourners head for their cars. The fall air of western Pennsylvania had a bite and she pulled the black jacket of her suit tightly against her chest. Her best friend, Shirley, fluttered her hand. Grace raised hers in acknowledgment.

She walked back into the empty house, eerily empty, and silent. She shivered. It had begun to rain, softly at first, now swelling into a substantial downpour. Like a wayward branch it slapped the windowpanes and splashed out of the down spouts with a vengeance.

Thank heavens it didn't rain during the ceremony at the cemetery, she thought wearily settling into the loveseat before the fireplace. Her son, Ben, had laid a small fire before taking his leave and it crackled and danced in the darkening room. She closed her eyes remembering all the evenings she and Peter had sat here, side by side, listening to a favorite CD—the gravely voice of Rod Stewart, Frank Sinatra crooning "My Way," or Christopher Smith at the piano. No words were ever necessary, just the warmth of his shoulder touching hers, just his presence.

Now Peter was gone and she was a *widow.* The very word made her shudder.

She and Peter had had the real thing; the golden years, the joyfulness of creating new life, the gratification of blending their lives together. Was it only last year that they celebrated their fiftieth anniversary; only last year they began to plan for retirement in earnest?

"Which would you rather do," Peter had asked jokingly as he led her through the aisles of the New England Sportsmen's Show, "live on a houseboat in the Florida Keys or spend each season in a different part of the country in one of these handsome motor homes?"

A houseboat in the Keys? What an intriguing idea. Her mind flashed forward to John D. McDonald's books about life on the Busted Flush on Marathon Key. Then, just as quickly, she remembered standing on a dock in the Florida Everglades looking down at marsh grass alive with sunning water snakes. Snakes terrified her. She had asked a bystander if they ever climbed aboard the boats. He just smiled.

"I think I'd opt for a motor home," she said looking at Peter with a grin. "Let's look at that colorfully painted Montana with all the slide-outs."

Peter squeezed her hand. "That's my girl," he said happily.

That was then—this was now. Grace turned her head toward the window that faced their garage. There in the driveway sat the Montana, once waxed and polished, ready for flight, now dingy from neglect during Peter's long illness. The motor home listed slightly on one low tire, dejected and abandoned as if it knew, as she did, that it would never follow the seasons. Peter, her companion and lover for half a century, was gone.

A log dropped into the grate with a hiss, sending off brief sparks that slowly settled and faded. The storm had intensified, pewter water pummeled the windows. Grace closed her eyes and settled herself on the soft cushions of the love seat.

It felt good to be alone. To be able to abandon the brave smile, to stop being a hostess to the friends that milled about her living room, to stack the last well-meant casserole into the freezer, to return the last hug of compassion with a kiss on the cheek. She simply wanted to let down her guard and to grieve in her own way, in her own space. No thoughts about the future.

Not yet.

CHAPTER ONE
Pittsburgh, Pennsylvania
Two years later

Grace Maguire's announcement hit her children with unexpected suddenness.

"Alaska. Did you say you want to move to Alaska?" Her son, Ben, stared at his recently widowed mother, his jaw slack, his eyes blinking.

"I did."

"That's a crazy idea."

"Excuse me." Her chin jutted defiantly.

"I . . . I mean . . ."

"You meant exactly what you said. I am not a crazy old woman."

Ben looked at his mother and she looked back at him. Grace had not meant to upset her son. When he arrived today, a roll of blueprints in hand and his sister in tow, to announce plans to build her an apartment above his garage she simply rebelled by making known an idea she had been toying with for several weeks.

Recently she had received a letter from an old friend, Lois Yost, now living in Alaska. Like Grace, Lois had lost her husband. She wrote that with the help of her daughter and a Tlingit Indian guide she was continuing to operate Eagles Nest Lodge but she did need to hire additional help. They were closed until next spring and she had an apartment in Seward, Alaska. She wondered if Grace might consider coming up for a visit. They would have lots of time to relax and renew their friendship.

Susan stared at her mother dumbfounded. "You don't mean move, do you? You mean go for a visit, don't you?"

"No, actually I do mean move, or at least temporarily until I see how I like it."

"But leave Pittsburgh? Move to Alaska?" Susan sputtered.

"Whatever would you do there?"

"I don't have a firm plan. Lois Yost invited me up for a visit and dropped a hint that she might have a job for me at her lodge. I don't know that I would want to work for her, she and I often clashed, but the idea of leaving Pittsburgh and all its memories is appealing." She looked into her daughter's bewildered eyes. "Honey, I am a senior citizen—not a crazy old woman, as your brother intimated. I want to maintain my independence—not curl up in the fetal position and await the inevitable." She glanced at Ben. "I know you want me to sell this big house and move closer to you and Amy. It's just something I'm not ready to do—I don't want to be dependent on my kids. I want to try something new."

"But, God Almighty, Mom . . . Alaska! Why Alaska of all places?" Ben stammered.

Grace turned her head toward the living room window and looked out at the motor home sitting in the driveway. Why indeed? She and Peter had planned enthusiastically for their retirement, spent hours planning the motor home's maiden trip—destination Alaska. She was glad they had had the time together to share those dreams. So many couples embark on retirement with fear and trepidation, suddenly aware of their mortality, afraid to try new things. But she and Peter looked to their future with excitement. A tear escaped the corner of her eye. "Because it was a place your Dad and I dreamed of going," she answered simply. "And Lois's letter has suggested a way I might fulfill that dream."

"Mom, I think you're acting out of grief," Susan said. "Wait. It's way too soon to make life changing decisions. Give yourself more time to adjust to Dad's death. It's only been two years."

"Honey, I know I am still grieving . . . that never really ends. But I'm too old to sit around waiting for life. Life is what happens while you're waiting for something to happen."

Ben seemed to regain his composure and strode over to stand in front of the fireplace with his hand resting on the mantle. At forty-eight, he was slightly overweight, with hazel eyes and ginger hair that had begun a swift retreat from his high forehead. He looked so like his father it jolted her. Grace felt a surge of emotion coupled with a vague foreboding. How many times had she seen Peter strike that same pose when he had something of importance to announce.

"You can't strike out on your own. You need to be with your children and grandchildren. Be sensible, mom."

She dug her nails into the palms of her hands. Her son's inference was that without his father she was already old and infirm, unable to make decisions for herself. Ben let out a deep sigh and his eyes bored into hers. "I've already talked to the zoning commissioner and he feels certain we can get a variance." For several minutes Ben rattled on, outlining a floor plan and ideas for an enclosed entrance that would accommodate a chair lift should she ever need it. Grace felt her face grow warm. *A chair lift?* What in God's name were her children thinking?

"No!" she said. "Absolutely not."

Susan jumped to her feet. "Well, if you're looking for change, how about Englewood, the new retirement center west of town. On and on she went about the attributes of a retirement community, and Ben joined in with enthusiasm.

Grace shut her eyes. This was outrageous—they were discussing her future as though she were not even present. She tuned them out and directed her thoughts inward. She had spent her entire life guiding, loving and nurturing others—first her children, then her elderly mother-in-law, and in the end her sick husband. She was an only child with an autocratic father whom she loved dearly but who was a strict disciplinarian. She got married soon after graduating from high school, moving directly from parents to husband. The old saying that girls marry men similar to their fathers must be true. Peter had been a wonderful husband but he made all of the major decisions in their marriage. She accepted that. Now her children were trying to call the shots. Grace pursed her lips. She would not let it happen.

She held up her hand to slow the flow of conversation. "I know you both mean well but I have been giving my future a lot of thought. This has to do with my spirit, with my desire for a life that has meaning." She took a deep breath. "What I must do, Ben, is move forward and not feel that the end of your father's life is the end of mine. I have just been treading water since his death. Filling my days with mundane tasks."

Ben removed his hand from her arm, and it felt like rejection. "Mom, you mentioned a job. Dad left you well provided for didn't he?"

"Yes."

"But you've never worked. You have no experience."

"When your father's company was on strike for a year, I drove a school bus."

"No offense, Mom but that doesn't count for much." Ben's brow wrinkled in vexation. "Traipsing off to Alaska is a darn fool idea. I can't believe you are serious. The next thing you'll tell me is you're planning to race sled dogs in the Iditarod."

"Hmm. I hadn't thought of that."

A small smile began to creep across Susan's face. Grace turned to her. "And you, honey? What do you think of your crazy old mother's idea?"

A thousand expressions had crossed her daughter's face as Grace unveiled her plans. Disbelief, dismay, and finally, just now, admiration. At least it seemed like admiration. Did she dare to hope it was?

"I think I am meeting a mother I never knew," Susan said softly.

Grace's face brightened. "Kids, I know this has come as a surprise but it's just an idea I have been turning over in my mind. We'll talk more later. I appreciate your concern for my future. Now both of you go home. Your mom needs some time to think."

Ben and Susan picked up their jackets and Grace walked them to the door. It began to rain, the cold bite of winter already in the air. She watched them sprint to their cars. Ben looked downcast, but Susan turned and gave her mother a thumbs-up with a big grin. "Go for it, Mom," she called.

After her children departed Grace went to the kitchen, brewed herself a cup of hot tea, and carried it back to the den. In the hall the grandfather clock bonged the hour. Grace closed her eyes and pressed herself deeply into the pliant contours of Peter's worn recliner. *I should replace it*, she thought. *But, oh, it is so familiar and comfortable.* But wasn't that just the point? She didn't want to settle into an existence that was soft and predictable.

The corduroy recliner was restful and the nubby texture brought her husband back into the room. She saw him napping, his glasses halfway down his nose, the *New York Times* open on his lap and she smelled his aftershave that still lingered in the fabric. Dared she think of selling the house they had built and raised their children in—setting off alone to a place like Alaska? She sat up straight, raised her chin and smiled bravely as a sudden spurt of adrenaline coursed through her veins. Why not? Too many people put off doing something that could bring them joy just because they hadn't thought about it, didn't have it in their schedule or were just too rigid to depart from their daily routine. She jumped up, crossed to the bookcase, and pulled out the latest edition of *National Geographic*, its cover a gorgeous photo of the Aurora Borealis—the Northern Lights.

Darn it all—it was not too late to pursue a dream.

After voicing her idea it began taking on a life of its own. She had stacks of literature advertising the various campgrounds, wilderness lodges, and Inside Passage cruises in Alaska. She brought Peter's laptop computer down to the kitchen and set it up on the table. For the next few days she spent hours researching places to stay and job opportunities in Alaska. She didn't have to work but she was eager to meet new people and taste new experiences. Articles about the Denali Wilderness where Lois had her lodge, drew her attention and she happily reread Farley Mowan's novel 'Never Cry Wolf.' The family structure of a wolf pack had always intrigued her and she had numerous books about wolves. As a teenager she had dreamed of becoming a guide in one of the national parks. She was probably too old for that now, but Alaska would be a fun place to live and she could always come back to Pittsburgh if she didn't like it.

According to the Internet the tourist season in Alaska started in mid-May, a good time to move. She wrote Lois that she would come just for a visit next year. That way she could share the coming holidays with her children, Alaska's long winter months of darkness would be over, and it would give her plenty of time to sell her home. *I must sell it*, she thought sadly, *it's way too big for me now, it is fifty years old and needs a lot of repairs, and the neighborhood is changing. Just last week there was a drug raid only a block away.* But, it would be so hard to leave. She and Peter built a life together here. Every room and piece of furniture brought back a swarm of memories: grandma's china closet, the hand-carved Irish blanket chest, the cradle that had held both of her babies, and later, her two grandchildren. How could she possibly decide what to keep and what to sell. After several nights of fretting she arose one morning with a decision. She would keep nothing. The children could take what they wanted—the rest would go to auction. She needed to enter this new life unencumbered. If she was going out on a limb, it was better not to let *things* bend the bough.

There was one exception. Resolutely, she marched downstairs and into the living room where Peter's cello still rested in its stand beside the bay window. She had spent many winter evenings sitting quietly by the fireplace, book in hand, listening to him play. It was part of the fabric of their life together—the one thing she had refused to let Ben cart away, the only possession with which she would not part.

She sank down on the sofa and closed her eyes, empty and very much alone. Was she doing the right thing? What lay ahead for her? Shirley Cramer, her best friend, thought her plan wildly exciting, although she admitted to some uneasiness. For that matter so did Grace. One moment she was filled with uncertainty, the next giddy with excitement. She wasn't dumb or naive, but her desire to escape the routine, predictable existence her children planned for her was overpowering. She couldn't let them take over her life. She was hungry for life and adventure and all the things she had missed out on by marrying young and raising a family. Grace felt her lips twitch and her mouth curved in a grin. This was not at all like her. Gone was the careful planning, second thoughts and reappraisals, fence sitting and self-doubt. Calm belief in herself and a feeling of strength and competence rose from somewhere deep in her subconscious. With God's help, she could and would pursue a dream. She was going to Alaska!

CHAPTER TWO
New York City
October, 2003

In lower Manhattan, a few blocks from NYU, John Hathaway set out for his usual early morning walk with Bandit, his three-year-old yellow Lab. It was a beautiful fall day: bright sunshine, a slight breeze, temperatures in the high 60s.

Bandit enthusiastically lifted a leg at each shrub, tree, and hydrant he passed, sniffing around for the perfect place to leave his most serious deposit.

"Come on boy," John urged. "You're being too darn finicky this morning. We're almost there."

As though he understood the importance of the matter at hand the Lab began to search more diligently. At last he found a spot that suited him, circled and squatted.

John scooped and placed the deposit into the plastic bag he carried in his pocket for this predictable part of their morning routine.

He and the dog rounded the corner, heading for the familiar Golden Arches in the middle of the block. Bandit was familiar with the route and strained at his leash, eager for the treat that lay ahead.

John led him to a weathered silver-gray picnic table that sat behind the restaurant, well removed from traffic. Bandit looked up and gave him a doggy grin, tail wagging furiously, while he lavished his tongue on John's hand. The dog knew what to expect. His master would disappear into the building for a while, then return with the treat—a large hamburger, minus the bun, wrapped in greasy white paper.

Although Bandit was well trained to "stay," John secured his leash to the table before proceeding into the fast-food restaurant.

The clerk, her black hair braided into cornrows so tight John almost winced in sympathy, greeted him with a wide smile.

"Mornin' Mr. Hathaway."

"Good morning, Gladys."

"The same, sir?"

"Yes . . . and no. I feel like pancakes this morning."

"Sausage?"

"Yeah. Oh, and a senior coffee, too."

"Hash browns?"

"Better not," he said, patting the bulge above his belt.

"Got that nice dawg with you?"

"Yep. I wouldn't come without him. Go ahead and ring up his hamburger. I'll get it on my way out."

With his order complete, John carried his tray to a far corner where the usual gathering of men occupied adjacent tables. Several acknowledged his arrival with a nod but most were busy discussing the latest war news.

They were an interesting bunch, all seniors, most retired. Joe, never without his Yankee baseball cap, worn backwards, was once the CEO of a major corporation; Bert, an obese eighty-five-year-old with myopic eyes behind thick glasses, had been a shoe salesman; Sam a retired veterinarian constantly chewed on a toothpick since he gave up smoking; Arnold, a retired New York city fireman, wore a gray sweatshirt with a large fish emblazoned across the front.

"I listened to the president's speech last night," Bert said. "Bet he's going to win reelection."

"Well, you're a Republican . . . guess that's one sure vote," Arnold said.

"I'm not too sure about a second term, though," Bert replied in a quavering voice."

A man from a nearby table spoke up. "I think the president is doing a damn good job."

From there the conversation drifted to the sorry state of the U.S. Government. John thought it best to change the subject. "Remember, fellas, we have a pact. No politics and no religion."

Sam, who had been scanning the morning newspaper, tore out the latest grocery ad from Shop and Save and stuck it in his pocket. "There's a good special on pork loins today—only a dollar ninety-nine pound," he said from around his toothpick. "Think I'll run over and pick some up. Stick them in the freezer till New Years when the wife cooks sauerkraut."

Joe poked his baseball cap. "Shop and Save is all right for staples but I don't trust it for meat."

Sam removed his toothpick from his mouth and pointed it at Joe. "I never got any bad meat . . . an' you sure can't beat their prices."

"I shop at Saul's Market," Bert said. "They give seniors a five percent discount on Tuesdays."

John poured extra syrup on his pancakes and listened with amusement to the conversational tidbits being bounced back and forth. Everything came under discussion—the price of gasoline, the latest action by the zoning board, people they knew listed in today's obituaries."

Sam tossed the newspaper aside and looked at Bert. "I hear you're going to have a prostate operation."

Bert rocked back in his seat and nodded. "Next week."

"Don't let them remove the prostate. It can ruin your sex life."

"What sex life?" Bert guffawed. "I'm eighty-five years old, for God's sake."

Everyone laughed.

Arnold, seated beside John, took a gulp of coffee. "I had a date the other night—took her for the Early Bird Special at Denny's. She still ordered the most expensive thing on the menu."

John smiled.

Arnold turned to look at him. "Ever think of remarrying, John?" Mary's been gone . . . what, three years now?"

"Never. I could never replace Mary."

"I don't think of another wife as a 'replacement'. I'm just looking for companionship. I get damn lonely since Edith died. Just maybe someone to cook and clean, and whatever."

John shook his head and laughed. Knowing Arnold as he did it was probably the "whatever" that was most appealing.

"She told me I needed to get a haircut," Arnold added. "I don't like a woman telling me what to do."

John ran his hand through his own hair, pausing for a second as he smoothed the back of his head. It was considerably thinner there. Maybe he should let it grow longer, although he still had a full hair line. He had to admit though, he was vain about his hair. Once coal black it had only recently aged to an attractive silver.

His gaze brushed the group of seniors around the tables. He looked forward to the rhetoric of the men who gathered here each morning. Some were widowers like him, several had wives who simply wanted to sleep longer in the morning, and several just enjoyed the male companionship. For him, since Mary died, it broke the terrible isolation of facing each morning alone. Establishing the routine of walking Bandit to McDonald's every day helped to ease the loneliness.

Their coffee finished, the conversation dwindled. Several men rose to take their leave.

"Behave yourself," someone quipped to Bert.

"At my age, what more is left to me?" He chuckled. "I gotta behave."

John wiped syrup from his mouth and drained his coffee. The waitress, seeing that he was preparing to leave, brought Bandit's hamburger over to his table.

"Here's your burger, Mr. Hathaway," she said. "I'd say that there is one lucky dawg."

"I'm the lucky one. I couldn't ask for a better pet."

"Have a nice day, then"

"Thanks, Gladys. You too."

Bandit jumped up, tongue lolling, tail swinging wildly when John emerged from the door. He unwrapped the burger and handed it to the dog who gulped it down, clearly enjoying every morsel. John reached down to scratch the silky ears. Bandit closed his eyes in delight.

When John was looking for a pet, Sam, his vet friend, had recommended a Labrador. A Lab, he'd said, was like a big teddy bear—loveable, friendly, ready to lick you to death. Bandit was that and more. He was big as a bear and gentle as a puppy, intelligent, ready to play at a moment's notice but also willing to lie quietly at John's feet if companionship was all that was required.

As they strolled home John reflected on the pattern he seemed to have established for himself. A sense of unease nagged him. A feeling that he was settling for something less than what life offered. He reflected that life has a way of accelerating as we get older. The days were getting shorter—his list of youthful promises unfulfilled. Was he to spend the rest of his life eating breakfast at McDonald's with a group of old men—accepting only the companionship of a dog to fill the days and nights ahead of him?

He climbed the brick steps leading to the brownstone's ornately carved front door, where a brass knocker gleamed in the early morning sunlight. He unlocked the door and stepped into the warmth of the entry hall. Bandit trotted ahead of him, heading straight for John's office where a bed awaited him. John smiled. He knew the dog well. First Bandit would meticulously attend to his personal grooming, then he would circle in his basket three times, fling himself down and hang his head over the edge with a look of total self-satisfaction.

John unzipped his worn leather bomber jacket and carefully hung it in the hall closet. He was fastidious by nature. As he walked down the hall he glanced into the formal living room, conscious of its beauty and elegance. Mary had done well, haunting antique shops and auction galleries for just the right piece to reflect the period of the brownstone.

John had lived in this house his entire life. When discharged from the navy he returned to his family home with his bride, then a month later, when his parents were killed in a tragic automobile accident he inherited the brownstone. His children had all been raised here, had attended the same schools and church he had. But the brownstone fit him like an old shoe, worn and comfortable with age. A few tears had been shed within its walls but mostly he remembered love and laughter. He remembered the sound of shoes clattering up and down the curving wooden staircase and squeals of excitement on Christmas morning. He remembered birthday parties and one-on-one basketball games in the back yard. The house still held the smell of Mary's cooking, the cupboards still overflowed with her collection of exotic spices. It was here he planned to live out his remaining years. He vowed he would never sell the house, if neither of his two boys wanted it maybe one of his grandchildren would. It should stay in the family.

He joined Bandit in the small room under the staircase he had outfitted as an office. Like the rest of the house it was tidy and well organized. A new Apple computer rested on a table beside a massive oak desk. The desk was his pride and joy—so large they had to remove the hall door to get it into the room. The slatted roll-top stood open to reveal dozens of cubby holes stuffed with papers and notes.

His answering machine was beeping and he hit the play button. The first message was a solicitation from a credit card company and he impatiently flicked it again. Then again. And again. After two hang-ups he almost pushed the delete key but the last message was from his former boss at the *New York Times* and with wrinkled brow he replayed the tape.

"This is Sheila," a familiar voice said. "Mr. Doyle has an investigative piece he would like to propose to you. Please call him . . . today if possible."

John pulled out the swivel chair at his desk and sat down. He ran a hand through his hair. Did he really want to get involved in what that might entail? He had been retired from the *Times* for almost fifteen years but on several occasions had accepted out of town assignments. He didn't really need the income. Still, the work might provide a welcome break from the humdrum tedium of his life.

He glanced at his watch, then returned Sheila's call and made an appointment for two P.M.

John took the subway uptown. Maybe after speaking to Ed Doyle he would have dinner at PJ Clarks, his favorite restaurant on the east side . . . an easy walk from the *Times*. He had a car, a ten-year-old BMW, freshly waxed, newly outfitted with four brand new Michelin tires, a Bose sound system, and the latest G.P.S. gadget sitting on its dash. No car today, though. He had a firm appointment and would hit traffic going and coming. The subway was more reliable. He wasn't due at the *Times* until two but he made good connections and walked into the old familiar building at one-thirty. After exchanging greetings with the door man John rode the elevator to the fourth floor. He spent a few minutes chatting with Sylvia before being summoned inside by Ed Doyle. The office was small, every flat surface in the room overflowed with papers, a single window held a yellowed plant and Ed's Armani cologne lingered in the air.

John's former boss was short and stocky with sandy hair that needed a cut and blue eyes that smiled warmly behind gold-rimmed glasses. His white shirt was open at the neck, his tie askew, his shoes sloppy, suggesting that he slipped them on and off without bothering to tighten the laces. He was not the neatest person in the world.

He slid back his chair, extending his hand. "Glad to see you, John."

"And you, Mr. Doyle."

"Ed, please."

"Of course . . . Ed."

"Take a seat. I have an interesting proposition for you."

They talked about generalities for a few minutes before Ed got down to the business at hand. "It's been brought to our attention that industrial logging is set to resume in the Tongass. The U.S. Forest Service is moving forward with plans for two controversial timber sales in road-free areas of the Tongass National Forest. These decisions were made despite a recent court ruling that found this procedure to be in violation of the law. So far the public has been told nothing about how the agency is proposes to set about doing this legally." His voice rose. "Still, they have no problem barreling ahead with what is in reality a taxpayer-subsidized logging project."

John's mind began to race. "And I imagine that would involve massive road building in wilderness areas."

"Right. This sale would impact three large areas and require thirty-five miles of new road to be built. Over two thousand acres of pristine old-growth forest would be clear-cut."

John's face hardened. "Last fall I attended an activist's lecture at Columbia on this very subject. The gentleman spoke with passion about the squandering of taxpayer money building roads that serve only a few logging companies and the destruction of old-growth trees in supposedly protected areas."

"More importantly, it's illegal as hell," Ed said. "The courts have ruled that a 1997 plan adopted by the U.S. Forest Service exaggerated the demand for Tongass timber. As I understand it they can't even sell what the logging companies cut. There is no demand in the global market. Piles of logs have been left to rot and roads to deteriorate." He pushed his glasses forward on his nose. "They . . . the forest service . . . didn't even consider options that called for timber cutting in other already accessible areas. Since 1982 the Forest Service admits it has lost over eight hundred fifty million dollars subsidizing logging companies in the Tongass. That's a lot of taxpayer money, John, and that's why we feel a *need* to address this issue."

Ed went on to explain the numerous problems that had arisen in the industry and John listened intently, fascinated. But did he really want to take on an outside assignment and the travel it would involve?

Ed leaned back in his chair and studied him. "Are you interested?"

John's mind flashed back to his muses of the morning—of letting life and new adventures pass him by. This research sounded intriguing. In spite of himself, he was interested. He shifted in his chair and felt his face flush. "I must admit, I'm not familiar with the Tongass."

"Oh, sorry. I should have been more specific. The Tongass National Forest is the last great expanse of old growth temperate rain forest in the United States. It covers a thousand-mile arc along the Pacific coast between the communities of Ketchikan and Kodiak."

John felt a hearty surge of excitement. That could only mean the one state he had never visited.

"Ah, of course." He grinned. "Alaska!"

CHAPTER THREE
Pittsburgh, Pennsylvania
March, 2004

March roared in like the proverbial lion. High winds stripped the last brown leaves from the oak in the backyard, lenten roses and white-petaled snowdrops bloomed on the south side of the house, days of sleet and snow followed days of balmy warmth. Grace got the bird feeder ready and listened for the cheery notes of the song sparrow.

The house still had not sold and she began to worry that she might not make her self-imposed deadline. Dispirited, she carried the morning mail into the den and sorted through it. An electric bill, more advertisements from Alaskan tour companies, department store shiny sheets, and a familiar purple envelope. She opened that envelope first.

The next meeting of the Sunshine Chapter of the Red Hat Society was being held at Carolyn Quine's house on Monday, March 9th at 2 P.M. Grace almost tossed the note aside, then thought better of it. She had not informed her friends of her plans because she felt they were premature until her house sold. She felt the sympathy card had been played enough, but, maybe it would do her good to just go in her purple dress and fancy red hat and be herself, not Peter's widow.

The Red Hatters were a social organization, proud of their lack of rules and bylaws, whose main function was to drink tea, have fun and enjoy themselves. It was founded by Sue Ellen Cooper after she bought a dashing red hat and then read a poem which depicts an older woman in purple clothing and a red hat. She and a group of friends formed the society to provide simple friendship for women over fifty. There was no planned agenda, they were free to talk about any subject they chose. The only stipulation was that they wear a purple dress and a red hat.

On the day of the meeting Grace woke to stinging sleet striking the windowpanes. She debated going to the get-together that afternoon. It was a good day to clean out the cupboards in Susan's old bedroom, but it would also be good to say goodbye to arduous responsibilities and obligations for a little while.

The Red Hats won out. She needed to put some joy in her life.

"Alaska!" a chorus of eight voices cried out.

Grace wore a silly grin. "That's what I said. Society today tells us to greet middle age with enthusiastic vigor, liveliness and humor. And girls, that's just what I plan to do."

"And I told her I hope she can keep her sense of humor when the temperature drops to twenty degrees below zero and the wolves howl all night," her friend, Shirley, said.

"I understand Anchorage is quite a cosmopolitan city," one of the ladies said. "No wolves there."

Grace frowned. "I don't expect to settle in the city, though. I'm hoping to find a quiet, scenic village, away from everything."

"Wolves and mosquitoes, then."

"Don't forget grizzly bears."

One by one the women joined in with jokes, advice and genuine enthusiasm for what she planned to do. Remarks like: "go for it with gusto," "you've got guts," and "welcome to life after fifty" abounded. The real bond of affection expressed by the Red Hatters comforted Grace.

As tea was being poured Grace admitted, "I go from being delirious with excitement to sick with terror by what I'm doing."

Carolyn placed a silver tray laden with pastry cups filled with crab salad, miniature poppy-seed muffins, and tea sandwiches on the coffee table. "You will conquer your fears, dear . . . I know you . . . and emerge as your true self," she said.

The ladies loaded their plates and chatted with each other. "These are delicious," Grace said as she bit into one of the muffins. "Wherever did you get the recipe?"

Carolyn held a small book aloft. "I found this on the Internet. The ad read, "Why delay gratification? Eat Dessert First." It's a cookbook full of delectable desserts, compiled by Red Hatters from all over the country."

The afternoon ended all too soon. Grace left buoyed by a shower of good wishes. She was so glad she'd come.

Grace's house sold in May, but did not settle until late June, giving her a much later start than she had anticipated. Ben and Susan took what furnishings they wanted, the balance went to the local auction house. It seemed strange to be so unencumbered—like beginning life as a new bride. A sudden stab of anxiety shot through her stomach and her fingers trembled as she turned over the keys to her home to the new owners. "God help me" she prayed silently, "I hope I am not making a terrible mistake."

The day after the closing Grace was packed and ready to depart on her great adventure. She was stepping out in faith, with no firm plan, but excited and confident. Ben, Emily, Teddy, Kelly, and Susan were all gathered around her at the airport to say goodbye.

Grace looked at them with pride. They were a striking family. Emily, was dressed in an elegant egg-shell linen suit with matching cream-colored heels. Though almost a head taller than Ben, she stood with shoulders erect, her slim frame straight as an arrow. Her hair, once red, had darkened to a deep auburn that framed clear olive green eyes and flawless skin.

Both grandchildren looked more like their mother than their father. Teddy, at seventeen, was built like an athlete with long arms and big hands. His hair was rusty and a sprinkling of freckles covered his nose and arms. Kelly was also tall with shoulder-length fair hair, parted down the middle and pulled back behind her ears. She had Ben's brown eyes, wide straight brows, and a full mouth, but she had her mother's pale, creamy complexion and elegant posture.

Kelly began to cry. "I don't want you to go, Grandma. You won't see me graduate from college."

"Of course, I will, dear. I'm not going to be gone forever. Alaska isn't the end of the world." Her mouth curved into a smile. "I've already signed up for a frequent-flyer pass."

Teddy shifted his feet. "I'll send you a picture of me in my new basketball uniform," he mumbled.

They began to call her flight over the loudspeaker.

Ben crushed her to him in a bear hug, his broad face stricken. "Call me right away if anything goes wrong, Mom. I can get the next plane."

"Everything will be fine."

She turned to Susan, who was dabbing at her eyes with a tissue. Grace kissed her wet cheek and whispered, "I love you."

"I love you, Mom."

"Good luck," Emily said with a squeeze of her hand.

Grace took a last look at her tearful family, squared her shoulders, grabbed the handle of her carry-on and marched through the gate.

She had been lucky to book a flight from Pittsburgh to Anchorage with only one short layover, and arrived in the early evening. Despite the fact that this was the first time she had ever flown, she was amazingly calm, interested in everything going on around her. She had specifically asked for a window seat and after saying a quick prayer as the plane revved its engines for take off, she pressed her forehead against the glass to watch the disappearing Pennsylvania landscape.

After a brief acknowledgment and exchange of names the female passenger beside her buried her head in a book, emerging only long enough to eat lunch, then promptly went to sleep. *So much for making a new friend with your fellow passenger*, Grace thought with chagrin. People seemed more private, more self-centered, nowadays. That's why when she found a place to settle down she would like to get a job. It would be easier to make friends.

It was dusk when they began their descent over Anchorage, the city aflame against a gorgeous sunset. Heart soaring, Grace gathered her belongings and unbuckled her seat belt. Her adventure was about to begin.

Nervously, Grace fell into line behind the crowd of deplaning passengers heading for baggage claim. She had no idea how this was done. She would just watch and copy what everyone else did.

She recognized a tall man with silver hair as a fellow passenger. He should be easy to follow. She took a firm grip on her carry-on, set her lips in determination, and hurried to keep him in sight.

Because she was still uncertain where she was going to settle, she had only one large suitcase to claim. She planned to take a comprehensive tour of Alaska, studying the pros and cons of each city, before deciding where to make her home. Susan would then ship her the rest of her clothing. And Peter's cello.

Large overhead signs pointed to the baggage claim area, and she hurried toward it before stopping in amazement. The room was huge, stretching as far as she could see, with dozens of moving belts carrying luggage past crowds of noisy, jostling people. She had lost sight of the silver-haired man and had no idea which belt might provide her with her suitcase.

She listened intently as loud speakers boomed instructions. Then she heard a garbled message. Her flight was unloading at platform number nine. She peered up at the large signs. Number nine was at the far end of the cavernous room. "Oh, mercy," she muttered under her breath. "I'll never get there in time."

Full of apprehension she pushed her way through the mass of people and arrived at the carousel just as it rumbled into action. Luggage began to drop out of a chute onto the moving belt. Passengers pressed close, reaching out to grab bags as they went by. With a sinking heart Grace realized that two out of three of the suitcases seemed to be of the same green fabric as hers. Then she noticed that most were identifiable by brightly colored ribbons. Unseasoned traveler that she was, she had not thought of such a ploy.

She watched the moving conveyor delivering bag after bag, until a large green bag resembling hers rumbled into sight. With a surge of relief she reached out and gave it a mighty yank. It tumbled to the floor beside her.

As she pulled it upright she noticed a wide strip of duct tape attached to the front of the case with the name "John Hathaway" printed in large black letters.

"Oh dear," she gasped with dismay.

Behind her a man said, "I'm afraid that is my bag."

She tilted her head to look at him. It was the gentleman with the silver hair she had tried to follow.

"I—I'm sorry. They all look the same. I didn't think to attach anything larger than a small identification tag, which you can't possibly see as your bag goes by."

"Is your bag as large as mine?"

"I'm afraid it is."

"Then, I'll give you a hand to get it off when it comes by," he said. "They are hard to handle."

"Thank you." Grace noticed with a sinking heart that new luggage had ceased to emerge from the chute. Only a few un-claimed bags continued to circle and none of them were hers.

The belt made a few more revolutions, then ground to a stop.

"It isn't there," Grace stammered. "It's missing. What do I do?"

"Unfortunately, the same thing has happened to me several times. I'm afraid this is what is known as the 'lost luggage' syndrome."

"But . . ."

"Come with me. I'll help you find the claim office."

"Thank you. I hate to impose on you this way."

"Glad to help." He grabbed the handle of his own bag and set off across the crowded terminal.

He walked easily and confidently ahead. As she followed close behind him, she got a sense of his self-assured stride and broad back. The black turtleneck he wore was a startling contrast to his thick, white hair. Despite her predicament she was very much aware of his masculinity.

He did not attempt to make small talk, but Grace felt compelled to explain her ineptitude. "My husband died recently and I have never traveled alone."

"I'm sorry . . . for your loss that is." He gave her a half smile. "Somehow, I suspected that you were not an experienced traveler."

"I've never even flown before."

"Here it is." He stopped so abruptly she almost banged into him. He pointed to a small glass-enclosed office with a Baggage Claim sign dangling in the window. "I'd stay and help you but I have to pick up my dog in another part of the terminal."

As Grace reached out her hand to squeeze his in thanks she looked directly into his eyes. They were amber-brown, soft and dark, like melted chocolate, framed by heavy, uncivilized eye-brows. His strong fingers gripped hers and he smiled. The cells in her body reacted alarmingly. Had it been that long since a man touched her? *Get a handle on it, girl,* she mentally chided herself.

"Thank you, again," she managed and turned away.

It was two days before the airline found Grace's luggage and delivered it to her room at the hotel. She used the time to shop and take a bus tour of Anchorage. She could almost feel the city vibrating with spirited energy. Home to nearly half the state's population, it was beautiful, framed by mountains, full of parks breaking open with wildflower and budding trees. But it quickly became evident to her that this was not to be her home, not where she wanted to spend the rest of her life. Once off the prosperous main avenues, the suburbs were a repetition of urban sprawl everywhere—monotonous dwellings, small stores, garages and filling stations, restaurants and dark brick schools. Grace had lived her entire life in metropolitan Pittsburgh and she wanted no more of the hustle-bustle of a large city. It was the unknown Alaskan wilderness that beaconed her.

She had a plan. She would make the grand tour of Alaska's most promising cities—Fairbanks, Skagway, Juneau, and Ketchikan. Then she would visit Lois at Eagles Nest Lodge, now open for the season. Only then would she pick a place to settle down and find a job.

Eager to start her new adventure she picked up a handful of brochures in the hotel lobby. One in particular captured her attention, a folder for Denali National Park. She had planned to visit Lois last but Eagles Nest was close to Denali. She would go there first.

Grace hurried back to her room to make a reservation.

CHAPTER FOUR

John nursed a Crown Royal on-the-rocks in the Anchorage Tower Hotel.

He was keenly aware of an attractive woman, several bar stools away, casting looks in his direction. She wore a vivid red dress, was slender, with shoulder length blond hair, and was obviously alone. Should he or shouldn't he buy her a drink? His loneliness was like a deep ache in his gut. An advance on his part would give him someone to talk to and possibly a companion for dinner.

He glanced at her again.

The din of conversation reverberated in the lounge while couples paused for a drink as they waited for their table to be called. Enviously he watched laughing, chattering couples filling the dining room. As usual he was a single. Once more he would have to order a table for one. But he suspected the blond was not the answer to his loneliness. For a brief moment he remembered the lovely widow with the lost luggage he had helped at the airport. He thought he had seen her tonight at the brochure rack in the hotel lobby but by the time he walked over to speak to her she had disappeared.

Darn it—what was wrong with him this evening? What was he thinking? Any alliance with a woman was doomed for failure. Always, in his subconscious, he was aware of his physical short-coming. Or was it only Mary's illness and his concern for her comfort that had caused his impotence?

As he aimlessly pondered his problem a man claimed the empty stool next to him. He was middle-aged, pudgy, and smelled of tobacco. John wrinkled his nose in annoyance. Since he quit smoking the smell of cigarettes made him slightly nauseous.

The stranger was on his second drink before he turned his head and spoke. "Here on business or pleasure?" he asked.

"Business. You?"

"Same." He extended his hand. "Name's Russ Sinclair. I'm with Hoffman-LaRoche Pharmaceutical."

"John Hathaway."

They shook hands, then John added, "I'm actually a retired journalist, here on a special project."

"You writing a book, or something?"

John laughed. "Nothing quite that ambitious, I'm afraid. I'm doing a piece for the *New York Times* on the Tongass Wilderness."

"Where the hell is that?"

"The Alaskan panhandle . . . southeast of Ketchikan."

"Wish I was retired . . . got ten more years to go. I do plan to slip off and get in a little salmon fishing while I'm here, though."

John nodded in agreement. "Can't beat the wild Alaskan Sockeye for excitement. And it is delightful . . . especially smoked. I order it every chance I get. At least it's free of mercury."

"I thought all fish had some mercury. I usually don't keep what I catch."

"True, but you can eat Alaskan salmon . . . they rank among the healthiest in the world. I did a piece for the *Times* before I retired. A lot of contamination comes from fish farming. The Alaskan government was smart enough to see the problem and they outlawed fish farms a number of years ago."

Russ looked skeptical. "What possible effect do fish farms have?"

"Well, for one thing fish farms usually float huge nets or pens a few hundred yards off shore. Typically, close to fifty thousand fish share a single pen and their untreated effluent flows directly into the sea. It can infect the wild species. That's why farming was outlawed."

Russ raised his glass in a salute. "I guess bureaucrats occasionally do something worthwhile. If I get a good catch maybe I'll have them shipped home. The wife would like that."

"I plan to do some fishing myself. I'll be working on my article in Ketchikan while the King Salmon are running. Unfortunately, just like the logging industry, there's growing political pressure to resume fish farming for economic reasons."

"That figures. It's always about the bottom line."

Russ held out his glass and caught the eye of the bartender. "I'll have another and one for this gentleman . . . whatever he is drinking." He gave John a quizzical look. "You didn't say the fish raised on farms in the states are dangerous though, did you?"

"No. Antibiotics can keep most of the farm salmon alive long enough to reach market size. It's their effluent that sheds bacteria and fungus into marine currents."

"What about the government? Isn't the industry regulated?"

"Yeah, but farm raised fish require little oversight. Another problem is the use of the drugs." John grinned. "You should know about that. LaRoche has a product named astaxanthin. Are you familiar with it?"

"I believe it's used to change the natural color of a salmon's flesh from gray to pink."

John nodded. "When the fish reach market size, the farmers add the astaxanthin, a pigment similar to beta-carotene, to their feed. It's kinda like a paint store swatch . . . just another alteration to the natural species."

"Makes them look damn pretty though." He turned back to John with a wry grin. "Sounds like you're not much in favor of pharmaceuticals."

"Well . . ."

A waiter approached the bar. "I have a table for you, Mr. Hathaway," the young man announced.

John looked at Russ. "Would you care to join me? You seem to be alone."

"I'm not ready to eat, yet. Besides," he added, looking over his shoulder, "there's a lady down there been casting looks our way. I don't know if she's interested in you or me, but I think I'll buy her a drink and find out. Unless, of course, you have the same idea."

John winked. "She's all yours." He slid off his stool and followed the waiter to a table set for one.

John studied the menu and decided on Kachemak Bay Halibut. After all he was in Alaska and seafood, either halibut or smoked salmon, was the name of the game. Fortunately his table was by a window and he relaxed, mesmerized by a spectacular view of mountains so close it felt like you could reach out and touch them.

The waiter appeared and placed a whiskey sour on the table. He noticed John's gaze out the window. "See that outline on the top of the ridge? Folks have named it the Sleeping Lady."

"It does resemble a body," John said with a smile. What mountain range is that?"

"The Chugah."

The waiter departed and John nursed his drink. From the air Anchorage had presented a beautiful sight. It sat on a high bluff at the base of the towering mountains along the coast of Cook Inlet. He had purposely given himself a week to explore a bit of Alaska as a tourist before getting down to work. Anchorage was a good place to begin.

After finishing every morsel of the succulent halibut John headed for the gift shop off the lobby to pick up a copy of the *New York Times*. A woman emerged from the shop and he recognized her immediately. It was the lady he had helped at the airport.

She was attractive, tall and trim, wearing a black cardigan with a white blouse and gray wool slacks. An antique gold locket rested on her chest. He guessed her to be in her sixties, with thick gray hair ending above her shoulders. Her eyes were green, clear and happy as she tilted her head back to look up. Lovely really. They made her beautiful.

"Well, hello," she said.

"Hello. I thought it was you I saw earlier in the lobby."

"She raised a bag. "I came down to pick up a paperback for some bedtime reading."

"And I'm looking for a newspaper." They stood awkwardly for a minute before she chuckled. "Like passing ships in the night, I guess."

He studied her. Did her face always look so warm and flushed?

"I'd ask you to dinner but I just finished."

"Oh, I ate early. Thanks for asking, though."

"Will you be in Anchorage long?" he asked. He would really like to get to know this lovely lady a little better.

"No, I leave early tomorrow for Denali National Park"

Disappointed, he gave her a half-smile. "Have a good trip, then."

"You too."

He watched her walking across the lobby, hips swaying grace-fully. He slapped his forehead in dismay. Some Casanova he had turned into tonight. Why hadn't he asked her to have a drink with him?

He could hardly run across the lobby after her and he couldn't call out. He didn't even know her name.

The next morning Bandit whined softly and pawed John's sheet. He opened one eye and Bandit ran to the door wagging his tail, then back to the bed to make certain his need was recognized.

"Okay boy," John mumbled. "Give me time to get my pants on."

He retrieved a pair of running pants from his suitcase and pulled them on, then grabbed his bomber jacket from the closet. Morning temperatures were still cool even for July.

All business was taken care of within two blocks of the hotel so John elected to take Bandit for a quick run. He had been told by the desk clerk that they were only a mile from the Tony Knowles Coastal Trail, a beautiful eleven mile bike path that runs along the shore of the Knik Arm of Cook Inlet. The trail would be a great place to get rid of his jet lag.

With Bandit on a leash John ran the mile to the trail, then entered what could only be described as a paved slice of Alaskan heaven.

The trail went from level to a mild incline, It was lined with lush vegetation dotted with daisies, fireweed and wildflower of every color. He sauntered along taking his time. The last incline was very steep but the reward was breathtaking. He could see snowcapped Mount McKinley across the gray water, and smell the salty breeze off the mud flats. They were descending the trail when Bandit skidded to a stop, his hackles rose and a deep growl rumbled from his throat. A bull moose was just three feet off the trail munching on vegetation. John held tightly to the leash as Bandit fell back on his haunches vibrating slightly.

The moose ignored them.

He was a full-grown bull, with huge antlers, standing at least seven feet tall and probably weighing close to two thousand pounds. "My God, he's big," John muttered in astonishment—then he began to laugh. The moose was really a ridiculous-looking creature, with jackass ears, a punching-bag nose, an overhanging muzzle, a dewlap that dangled from its throat, rough brown fur, rounded shoulders, a short body, a tiny rump and long skinny legs.

Bandit whined and John reached down to pat the dog's head and reassure him that all was well. "I guess God had a purpose in outfitting the poor creature that way in order to survive in the wilderness, but he sure looks funny, doesn't he? Nowhere but in Alaska will you find a full grown moose grazing beside a bike path."

He glanced at his watch. If he wanted breakfast he had better get back to the hotel. He would return to his room, shower and have breakfast at the Waffle Bar.

Grace saw him the moment he entered the restaurant.

John picked up a tray and walked directly to the food counter, studying the morning's offerings. With a slight nod of approval he stopped in front of the waffle iron and began to pour batter onto the grill.

Grace's insides gave a funny lurch. His silvery hair shone in the reflected overhead light, his rugged handsome face thrown into half-shadow.

She left her seat and walked over to the coffee urn. "Well, I see we meet again," she said, turning to smile at him.

He raised his brows. "It must be fate . . . Good Morning."

A prickle ran down her side, as he reached around her to retrieve a packet of syrup. Silly goose. She had no business being attracted to this trim, handsome, white-haired, brown-eyed man. As she had commented last evening they were "like passing ships in the night."

"May I join you?" He gave her a charming smile as he removed his steaming waffle from the grill.

"Of course." She added a packet of creamer to her coffee. "I'm afraid I'm just having a second cup of coffee while I wait for a cab. My train leaves in an hour."

"Denali, you said?"

"Yes. And you?" She led him to a small table where she had stacked her luggage.

John placed his plate on the table and sat down. "I'll be in Anchorage for a few days, then I head north to Fairbanks. I'm on a business trip." He sipped his coffee and glanced at her. "I plan to play tourist for a few days before I start to work."

His brown eyes have flecks of gold in them, she thought foolishly.

"I'm visiting a friend at Denali then I plan to play tourist too." She glanced out the window and saw a yellow taxi pull up to the entrance. "Darn," she muttered. "There's my cab." She jumped up, grabbed her purse and overnighter, and reached for the handle of her large suitcase.

"Let me help you," he said.

"Thank you."

Together they hurried out to the cab where John hefted her bags into the trunk. He helped her into the taxi, his hand warm and strong. Her nerves were humming a little. She supposed it was due to the way he looked at her, his frank appraisal uncomfortably intimate.

"Goodbye . . . again." She was about to ask his name when the taxi driver revved his motor, anxious to be off.

"Goodbye," John said. "Next time we meet my treat." He grinned and closed the door.

CHAPTER FIVE

That night John wrote a few postcards to his friends back home, then called his son, Adam, to report his whereabouts. He missed both of his boys and especially his grandchildren. They were a close-knit family and when he was home he saw most of them at least once a week. Adam had a good job in the mortgage department of Chase Bank while George, his youngest, had followed in John's footsteps and worked at the *Times*.

After his call he sat deep in thought. He was lucky. His sons had never given him an ounce of trouble. Both boys did well in school and college; neither smoked or drank to excess. George was still single but Adam was married with three delightful daughters whom John adored and who, as far as he could tell, adored him.

He and Mary had wanted more children but she miscarried her third pregnancy and a year later required a hysterectomy. His love for her had never faltered—he loved her as much the day she died as he did the day he married her. And he had a successful career doing a job he loved. A journalism major at NYU, he had secured a job at the *New York Times* where he worked for forty years until he retired.

A good life—a happy life.

Why then, did he feel this vague sense of disquiet?

Eagerly, Grace hurried from the Denali train terminal, her wheeled suitcase bouncing on the rough cobblestones. Lois had been unable to meet her due to weekend commitments at the lodge so Grace had reservations at a local resort.

She approached a baggage handler that was busily piling luggage onto a cart. "Excuse me, which way to the Princess Wilderness Lodge?"

"See that fellow over there holdin' up a sign says Princess

Tours? He's a tour guide. Follow him an' that bunch of people around him."

The group he indicated began to walk up a hill toward a large cluster of log buildings. Grace fell in behind them acting like she belonged.

The lodge itself was storybook Alaska—long, low, rustic wooden buildings nestled against snowy mountain slopes. Flower beds abounded with geraniums and arctic poppies, the air sharp with the tang of firs and cedars. The subtle sweet scent of blackberries warming in the sun mingled with alder smoke from sleeping woodstove fires.

After registering she was directed to her room. Inside, she flipped on the lights, tossed her shoulder bag on the table and hefted her suitcase onto the luggage rack. Eager to investigate, she quickly changed into jeans and a sweatshirt.

Saturday's balm and glorious blue skies energized her and, smiling jauntily, she set out to explore the park-like grounds. The Princess featured an extensive viewing deck with hot tubs she vowed to visit later in the evening. After a full day of travel a good soak would be delightful. She noticed a small beauty shop tucked into the corner of the deck and walked over to check its hours. Her hair had gotten longer than she liked and was hard to care for while traveling. She would call tomorrow and make an appointment to get it cut short.

Taking note of what looked like a lovely restaurant and nearby theater she walked down the hill to the terminal where she made bus reservations for the morning Wilderness Tour. A cluster of small shops sat in a prim row directly across from the terminal and she made a cursory examination of them before returning to her room to dress for dinner. The restaurant had looked rather elegant so she changed into a pair of black silk pants, black tee, and red embossed jacket with a mandarin collar.

The Princess dining room sat on a bluff above the Nenana River, looking out towards Denali National Park. That evening she indulged in a glass of wine and feasted on a combination platter of prime rib and snow crab legs. She ate alone and for the first time in days felt once more the sharp pang of loss. *How Peter would have loved this.*

After eating she walked over to the theater and took in the

hilarious western show then availed herself of a soak in the hot tub before placing a call to Lois.

"I'm sorry I couldn't meet you at the train," Lois said, "but we have more guided trips on the weekends than Marvin can handle on his own."

"Oh, I understand. Actually, I've arranged for a wilderness tour from the park tomorrow morning."

"I hope you see some wildlife. Sometimes you do and sometimes you don't. Anyhow, I've arranged for my daughter to cover the desk Monday. I can meet you for dinner at the lodge around six. Will that work for you?"

Grace hesitated. It would delay her departure for Fairbanks but she had resolved not to fall into the planned itinerary trap. "That will be fine. I can't wait to see you. It's been at least twenty years since you and Sam left Pittsburgh."

Lois laughed. "Don't be surprised . . . I'm now what you call pleasantly plump, wear glasses, and my hair is quite gray."

"I've changed, too. Maybe we should wear a carnation in our lapels."

"Or a ribbon in our hair. See you tomorrow, then."

"Right, goodnight Lois."

"Goodnight."

As she climbed beneath the luxurious comforter Grace smiled with satisfaction. She was doing quite well for herself. This was fun.

When Grace woke the next morning it was overcast and cloudy. She swung her legs over the side of the bed and padded into the bathroom. Her bare feet on the tile floor made her shiver and shocked her awake. After a quick shower she pulled wool slacks and a hand-knit green sweater from her suitcase. Temperatures were not expected to rise above sixty degrees.

Grace stood in front of the mirror and assessed her appearance. She was still trim and the well-tailored slacks hugged her narrow hips. She patted her belly. There was a roundness there she didn't like. Next time she'd forgo the prime rib. The sweater intensified the green of her eyes and emphasized the ample swell of her breasts. She smiled coyly. She hadn't missed the sweeping appraisal of the *airport man*, as she now thought of him.

Grace ate a sensible breakfast, then walked down the hill to the welcome center and boarded a yellow school bus for the tour. She had been surprised to find that school buses were used—the only road into the Denali wilderness was restricted—closed to regular vehicular traffic.

Most of the passengers appeared to be couples from the tour group she had followed the day before. Grace stopped in the aisle beside a gray haired lady who seemed to be alone.

"Is this seat taken?" she asked.

"No, please join me. My friend had a touch of dysentery this morning and felt she should stay at the lodge."

After names were exchanged—her seat companion was Lucille Good—Grace settled back for the trip ahead. Their driver, a husky young man she guessed must be in his late twenties, turned on a microphone.

"Folks, my name is Victor and I will be your guide for today's tour of Denali Wilderness Park. If we're lucky you'll see many forms of native wildlife, but unfortunately we cannot guarantee what, or how many, you might see. This is a wilderness area that covers over six million acres so we are at the mercy of the animal's movements on any given day."

"I feel lucky today," an elderly gentleman called out from the back of the bus.

"Good, keep that positive attitude. And if we really get lucky we might get a break in the clouds and see North America's highest mountain, Mt. McKinley. Now, I must keep my eye on the road and if I see anything I will stop. But if anyone sees wildlife please call out its location for all to hear. For example, 'moose on right at one o'clock or moose on left at ten o'clock.' Got it?"

Several men practiced their calls and Victor laughed. "Fine, now let's get going and keep your eyes alert for any movement outside your window."

For the next fifteen minutes the driver described the efforts of the government to keep the rugged tundra a wilderness area, free of man's pollution. Suddenly the woman behind Grace screeched, "Moose . . . Moose . . . ah . . . right side . . . ah, ah . . . oh my . . . three o'clock."

Victor braked and everyone scrambled to the windows. Sure

enough the bobbing antlers of a moose poked from the willows in a marshy thicket. In fact there were two moose among the willows, a cow and her calf. They were obviously feeding and paid no attention to the idling bus.

Victor picked up his microphone. "On the right, along the berm you can see several little brown birds. Those are ptarmigan, and they change their coloration from the brown tundra of summer to snow white in the winter. The ptarmigan is the state bird of Alaska.

"Not the mosquito?" someone in the bus quipped.

Everyone laughed.

"I'll admit our mosquitoes are large and annoying," Victor said with a grin. "A good trick before coming up here is to take regular doses of vitamin B-1 for a few weeks. Once you build the concentration up, mosquitoes seem to think you stink and they leave you alone."

Grace scratched a fresh bite on her arm. "It's rather late for that."

"You might want to try some of Avon's Skin-So-Soft as a repellent. It works pretty good and it's non-toxic," Victor advised.

Slowly, the bus resumed its journey.

High on the mountainside, and hard to see, they spotted several curly-horned Dall sheep and someone saw a red fox but Grace was unable to pick it out. Darn, she should have saved Peter's good binoculars. She'd have to buy herself a pair as soon as she got back to Denali.

Victor stepped on the brakes and stopped. "Folks . . . look off to the left. You are lucky today. Mt. McKinley is visible in the distance."

Grace whipped out her camera. The sun had come out and the clouds rolled by. They could see it clearly, looming against the pale sky, a 20,000-foot mass of jagged granite, its peak swathed in snowy whiteness. *Spectacular!*

Another tour bus approached from the opposite direction and stopped beside them. The two drivers leaned out of their windows and conversed for several minutes, then the second bus pulled away. Victor turned to face his passengers.

"I've just been told that a mature grizzly is sleeping on the left side of the roadway about a quarter of a mile ahead. I'll approach slowly and stop for you to take photos but you must remain absolutely quiet. We do not want wild animals to get accustomed to hearing human voices." Victor paused and stared at his passengers intently. "The minute I hear a sound from any of you I will pull away" he said, his voice soft and subdued yet firm.

The bus inched forward, then came to a quiet stop. Grace leaned across Lucille to peer out the window and sucked in her breath. Unbelievably, a huge brown bear lay stretched out on its side, eyes closed, only inches from the road.

The only sound in the bus came from camera shutters and the idling vehicle. If ever there was a Kodak moment this was it. Grace snapped pictures from every angle, hoping the window glass wouldn't distort the image.

"I can't wait to tell my roommate about this," Lucille whispered.

"Shhh," the woman behind them hissed.

The driver gave them a good five minutes before moving away.

They traveled several miles without seeing anything other than a few scampering ground squirrels. Victor pulled into a clearing and picked up his microphone. "This is as far as we go," he announced. "You can get out to stretch your legs and get water from a container strapped to the back of the bus. It is important that you do not leave any trash behind. No cigarette butts, candy wrappers, paper cups, or food. The animals must not learn to identify our human scent with something good to eat."

After fifteen minutes at the rest stop they started back to Denali. Victor unexpectedly slowed down and Grace stiffened to attention. Victor applied his brakes and pulled off the road. He put a pair of binoculars to his eyes and scanned the tundra off to his right.

Excited murmurs broke out among the passengers as they, too, spotted movement in the distance. Grace and Lucille had traded seats for the trip home and Grace pressed her nose against the bus window.

Victor opened his microphone and told them where to look. "One o'clock, on your right, on the hillside under that large orange-beige rock outcrop. A family of wolves."

Even without binoculars Grace could see them clearly.

Victor spoke softly. "I count seven adults and six pups. The males are tall and light in color, the females shorter and darker gray. Notice that the pups are romping close to their mother. Now, look out to the very edge of the group by the stream. See the wolf standing guard away from the pack? He is undoubtedly the 'alpha' male and the pappa. His tail and ears are up, he's standing stiff-legged and alert, very much in control."

A man several seats behind Grace, using a camera with a telephoto lens, spoke up. "Off to the left, about nine o'clock, a large wolf is trotting back towards the cubs carrying something in its mouth."

Victor nodded. "All members of the pack—male and female— act as nursemaids feeding, and rearing the pups. It's truly a communal effort. In fact the pups are the center of the pack's universe. The pack structure is much like that of a human family. It is only the alpha male and female that mate in January or February and produce offspring. Wolves are not promiscuous. No other pack members breed and there is only one litter born per year per pack."

Grace felt a tug at her heart as she watched the frolicking pups. They were like adorable puppy dogs under the watchful eye of the entire pack. All of the wolves seemed to be keeping an eye on the family, the father confidently standing guard on the far edge of the clearing.

"What is their prey?" someone asked.

"This close to the den they are taking ptarmigan, arctic hares and birds. At times the adults will go far afield for larger animals like deer, elk, moose, caribou, mountain goats, or sheep. Feeding six growing pups is a strenuous job. The wolves spend seven to nine hours a day hunting. Remember, in the wild animals kill only for food. Unlike humans they do not wage wars or kill for pleasure."

"I notice one of the wolves keeps ducking her head and looking up at the sky," Grace commented. "Why is that?"

"Perhaps from constantly being dive-bombed by predatory birds attempting to protect their tundra nests." Victor answered.

Conversation died as the group sat in fascination watching the magnificent tableau before them. Grace was enchanted with the antics of the pups scrambling back and forth, chasing one another, tackling, play fighting, rolling, wagging the entire rear halves of their bodies with great gusto. Grace smiled when one pup wandered away and an adult wolf immediately rounded it up, bumping it along with its nose until the juvenile was safely back with the others. Grace felt a constriction in her chest and tears sprang to her eyes. How human they seemed—a devoted family group, totally unlike one's stereotype of a wolf. *We humans judge these creatures by our own standards,* she thought. *If they kill, they are bad. If they take only the old, the sick, and the weak, they are good. If they mate for life, that makes them better. If on the western plains they cannot distinguish between a rancher's calf and a deer to feed their family they are bad.*

When Victor pulled away, returning them from this beautifully preserved wilderness back to the reality of automobiles and TV antennas, Grace felt a profound sense of loss.

"You are welcome to join Betty and me for dinner tonight," Lucille said as they alighted from the bus.

Grace readily agreed. She had found that restaurant tables are always set for even numbers—two, four, six or more. She did not like dining alone—constantly reminded of Peter's absence.

That evening she located the two women at their table next to a window overlooking the river. Lucille was a large woman with broad shoulders, an earnest face with a round chin and inquisitive blue eyes, while her friend, Betty, was thin as a rail with short, snow white hair. Betty greeted her with a warm smile and a fragile handshake. Grace immediately liked her. She was jovial and easy to talk to.

Throughout the dinner they chatted about the wilderness tour. Betty was especially intrigued by Grace's fascination with the wolf pack. When Lucille related the tale of the grizzly, with a few embellishments, they all had a good laugh.

"Grace, Lucille tells me you were recently widowed," Betty commented.

"Yes, it will soon be two years."

"You're up here alone? Not on a tour?"

"It's a long story. I would like to relocate. To live in Alaska."

Betty nodded. "Too many memories back home, I suppose." Her mouth twisted in a half-smile. "I hear Alaska is a good place to look for a husband. The men outnumber the women two to one." She glanced down at Grace's hand. "You'd better take that wedding ring off, though."

"Oh, I'm not looking for a husband," Grace said.

"You just haven't been alone long enough," Betty answered.

"After a few years of declining invitations from your married friends, with nothing but female companionship for all of your social engagements, you'll likely change your tune."

Lucille watched Betty with raised brows but said nothing.

Grace worried the ring on her finger. She wasn't ready to remove the symbol of her marriage, couldn't imagine any man other than Peter sharing the intimate moments of her life. Why did everyone think happiness depended on having a spouse? Weren't friends just as important? Of course, one couldn't isolate oneself and live a solitary life, but surely a simple friendship with a man could be satisfying without requiring a marriage license. "I might consider a relationship with a man," she offered, "but I certainly don't want to marry again. I'm savoring my independence."

Lucille spoke up and directed a level look at Betty. "My experience with men, especially widowers, is that they don't like the new role they've been placed in . . . cooking and cleaning . . . caring for themselves. They're looking for someone to take over the house and do everything for them. They've had their great love and made their babies."

Betty dabbed her mouth with her napkin and chuckled. "Well, I've had one memorable date since my husband died and it wasn't a housekeeper he was interested in. He took me out to dinner and a show, and when we returned to my apartment I invited him in for a nightcap. I thought I was being very modern and sophisticated. Before I even got settled beside him with glasses of very expensive wine he flew into action. I almost jumped off the couch. *Whoa*, I said. He paid no attention. I was so surprised I spilled wine all over my new dress. It turned into a real wrestling match."

"And?" Lucille prompted.

"He was determined, I'll give him that. But I was just as determined that an expensive dinner did not entitle him to free dessert. His groping nauseated me. I requested that he leave." She threw back her head and laughed. "Requested? Hell, I ordered him to leave."

"I dated a nice gentleman last summer," Lucille offered. "Remember, I told you about him."

Betty grinned. "The one who couldn't keep his dentures in?"

"For heavens sake, he was in his eighties." Her face grew pensive. "I could easily have gotten married."

"What happened?' Grace asked.

"He died."

"Oh."

The waiter approached their table. "Dessert anyone?"

They all chuckled and the poor fellow looked bewildered.

Betty and Lucille each ordered crème brûlée but Grace settled for hot tea. She remembered her resolution to cut down on her eating. Especially desserts. Too many restaurant meals, like this one, were loaded with calories.

"You mentioned that your plans are to relocate in Alaska, dear," Betty said. "Where, specifically?"

While they leisurely ate their dessert Grace told them of her plans to make a mini tour of the entire state before choosing a home.

"And Lucille tells me that you plan to find a job."

"Yes. Right now I am intrigued with Denali." She smiled. "I think I fell in love with a wolf pack today."

Betty gasped. "Tell me you don't plan to work with wolves."

"Hardly. But I think being a guide on the Wilderness Tour might be exciting. I plan to explore the employment opportunities."

"The park isn't open all year though, is it?" Lucille asked.

The question surprised Grace. She hadn't thought of that. What did tour guides do in the winter? But then again it wasn't really important. She didn't need a full-time job. "I haven't inquired about the season, but I'm nowhere ready to make a decision. I have a lot of Alaska left to explore. I also want to visit Seward and the Kenai Peninsula and they say that Juneau is a lovely city."

Betty frowned "There are no roads to Juneau, you know. You can only get there by boat or plane. Why in the world a place as inaccessible as that is the state capitol I'll never know."

"Where do you go from here?" Lucille asked.

"I have a friend living here that I plan to see before I leave for Fairbanks. Then I fly back to Anchorage where I have booked passage on Princess Lines for the Inside Passage cruise. We visit Skagway, Juneau, and Ketchikan. By then I should have a fair idea of where I want to expand my search for employment and housing."

"Lord, girl, I admire you," Betty said pensively. "I wish I had the courage to do something like that. But I have two small grandchildren at home . . . my daughter depends on me to baby-sit. Maybe someday."

Ah, and isn't that the problem with most people, Grace thought ruefully. Always putting off tomorrow. Always thinking—when we get Mitchell toilet-trained we'll go back and visit the grandparents—after we get the new family-room carpet we'll entertain—after we get the kids through college we'll go to Alaska. Then, one morning we wake up and all we have to show for our lives are the promises of: *I'm going to, I plan on,* or *Someday when we have more money.* And all too often that someday comes too late.

The waiter brought checks and they said their goodbyes. Grace sauntered along the moonlit path to her room. It had been a delightful day What a fortunate decision she had made to stand up to her children and look for more in life—to choose what was right for her.

The brochure said that weather in Denali could be extremely variable and it was certainly true on Monday morning—with temperatures more like fall than summer. However, the day was sunny and bright and it would have been perfect except for the inevitable mosquitoes which seemed to have no respect for Grace's heavy application of Skin-So-Soft.

She spent the day visiting the park museum and strolling the lovely grounds around the lodge. With bird book in hand she delighted at the variety of birds she encountered: yellow-rumped warblers, white crowned sparrows, ruby-crowned kinglets, and rusty blackbirds, their song rippling through the deep canopy of trees.

She wasn't due to meet Lois until six, so late in the afternoon she ambled down to the strip of shops facing the rail terminal. The lone sidewalk serving the strip shopping area was jammed with tourists. She dawdled her way along the street. Grace wasn't a dawdler by nature but the soft air was filled with birdsong and the hum of nature. She passed a bookstore, a pizza shop and a camera store where she stopped to buy a pair of binoculars and loaded up on film. All of the specialty shops seemed to be doing well; she could probably get a job in any one of them. One of the busiest seemed to be a tiny ice-cream parlor with customers forming a line that snaked through its doorway onto the sidewalk. Her mouth watered at the sight of a couple sitting in front of the shop licking their dripping cones of chocolate and she went inside to purchase a dish of 'moose tracks.'

Grace had just carried her ice cream to an outside table when she heard someone call her name. Surprised, she looked up to see a stout, gray-haired woman coming toward her. After a moment she realized who it was.

"Lois? Lois Yost?

"Grace!"

They smiled at one another. Lois's eyes sparkled with delight as she sat down beside her old friend from high school. She married Sam Yost shortly after graduation and Grace had served as bridesmaid. In fact it was at the wedding that Sam introduced Grace to Peter. The Yosts moved to Alaska after their children were grown and although Lois and Grace exchanged Christmas cards and letters they hadn't seen each other for years.

"I had some shopping to do, so I came in early," Lois said.

"And I was just killing time until six."

"Do you mind eating early? My daughter is tending the desk at the lodge, but I must get back this evening to close up. How long can you stay?"

Grace shrugged, unsure herself. "I more or less have an open schedule. I'll explain over dinner."

"Great. . . . Let's go."

Dinner finished, they moved to the lounge and sat across from each other in front of the fireplace sharing a bottle of wine. In high school they had been such good friends. Grace regretted that they'd lost track of one another in the years that followed.

During the meal she had learned that her friend's oldest daughter, Jill, was recently divorced and working at the lodge until, as Lois said, "she could recover from the trauma." Grace brought her up to date on her own children, the lives of mutual acquaintances, and the renaissance of downtown Pittsburgh. "Now, tell me about this lodge of yours," she said.

"It's really a rather rustic compound about thirty miles into the park. We have one main building and seventeen cabins. It's quite charming, Grace. The cabins are log, lighted by gaslight, and all have a magnificent view of Mt. McKinley. I employ one guide, a native Alaskan. Together we give scheduled wilderness tours."

"It sounds like something I would love."

Lois frowned. "You know, honey, when you wrote that you were coming just for a visit I assumed you were not interested in a job at Eagles Nest. I asked Jill to stay on and work full time and I'm afraid that is all my budget will allow."

"You needn't apologize. My plans are too uncertain and I'm not even sure where I want to settle. I wanted to be free to travel and didn't want to make a commitment. You seem very content here."

"We've been lucky. The lodge has become quite popular and we are full most of the season. I serve home cooking in the dining room and have an excellent staff." Lois poured each of them another glass of wine. "Have you any idea where you want to live?"

"Not yet. I've a lot of Alaska to see. The Princess has an opening for a cook. I thought of applying, it would be low-pressure, but . . ." Her voice trailed off.

"But?"

"I just don't know. It doesn't answer a need in me. Alaska is such a beautiful place. I want to be outdoors and . . . I know it sounds corny . . . but I want to do something with the rest of my life that has some meaning."

Lois smiled gently. "In other words—you're not just looking for a job but spiritual fulfillment."

"Oh, I'm not religious," Grace hurried to answer.

"Spirituality and religion are not the same thing, dear. By spiritual I mean developing a personal peace with who and what you are . . . establishing a meaningful purpose for your life. It's your soul, a form of wellness, much more than just physical wellbeing."

"That sounds rather complex to me. I'm not sure I understand what you're saying."

"It is complex and often misunderstood. Many people pursue better health through exercising, eating right, watching their cholesterol and blood pressure, wearing seat belts, and so on. That's the physical part. And, you may be already doing things that nourish your spirituality without even realizing it is a part of your overall health." Lois directed her sweet smile at Grace and her eyes twinkled. "Like telling your kids to have a life, then coming off to Alaska to live your own." Lois started to refill their glasses but Grace waved her hand away.

"I believe I've had enough," she said.

"And I need to get home. Why don't you come out to Eagles Nest tomorrow? See how the life I have chosen nourishes my spirit. Are you free?"

"As a matter of fact I am."

"I'll have Marvin pick you up. He's the guide I mentioned and he drives our shuttle van. A great guy. I think you'll enjoy him. Would nine o'clock work for you?"

"Perfect. It will give me plenty of time for breakfast. I'll be waiting out front."

"Fine. Now I must get back. It's later than I planned on staying. See you tomorrow."

The next morning Grace arose full of anticipation. She had an uncanny sense that today would be important for her. She was a little put off by Lois's spirituality talk but looked forward to a trip off the beaten track in the wilderness park.

Grace immediately liked Marvin, Lois's guide. In keeping with the geography he was part Russian, part Tlingit Indian, a product of the Aleutians. A big bear of a man, he dwarfed any other person around him. His skin was the color of strong tea, he was smooth shaven with straight black hair and extremely round-headed with a large lower jaw. He drove the lodge van with one hand on the wheel, the other hanging out the window gesticulating wildly at every species of wildlife they passed. An August sun glittered on the rolling Alaskan tundra stretching into infinity. The narrow Denali Park road twisted and turned as it followed the Savage River past Riley Creek and park headquarters. The road made a final curve and Marvin swung off the park road onto a narrow gravel road. Within minutes Eagles Nest Lodge stood revealed nestled against a forest of heady spruce and alder.

The rustic main building was built of log with a shingled roof. Long windows fronted a wide porch lined with rocking chairs. A trailing ivy hung near an American flag, both moving gently in the breeze. Green lawns stretched to vistas of shrub and woodland, ornamental flowerbeds, and a carpet of white anemones and red dwarf alpine rhododendron.

A dozen or more guest cabins, also built of logs, were clustered around the main building like chicks around a mother hen. Each had a porch angled to catch a glimpse of Mt. McKinley in the distance.

Lois greeted her at the door with a big hug and took her into the lodge's lobby.

Grace gasped with delight. Framed charcoal prints of native wildlife flanked a massive stone fireplace; plump couches upholstered in warm green gingham rested on a braided rug of browns and golds; soft lamps glowed on primitive twig end tables of willow and birch.

"It's lovely," Grace said.

Lois smiled warmly. "The lobby serves a dual purpose. It is also my living room. That door at the far end leads to my private bedroom, bath and kitchenette. She swept her hand to the right. "And over there is the public dining room and main kitchen."

Through French doors opening off the lobby Grace could see a room with exposed log walls and gaslights. Round tables covered with green gingham tablecloths and small baskets of wildflower, were grouped in front of yet another stone fireplace.

Lois walked her over to the reception desk and introduced her to her daughter, Jill.

Grace gave her a hug. "I certainly wouldn't have recognized you," she said. "You were only a child, when I last saw you."

"I'd have recognized you, though. You haven't changed a bit, Mrs. Maguire," Jill said.

A customer approached the desk asking about a tour and Lois pulled Grace aside. "We offer two excursions a day to our guests . . . one in the morning and one in the afternoon. You've met Marvin, he takes the afternoon trips. I was going to offer one to you but since you already took the Denali tour we'll hold that until another time. Now, I want to show you the rentals."

They exited the rear door of the lodge and headed across the lawn to the cluster of cabins.

"I have one empty that I can show you," Lois said. "The guests had a death in the family and had to vacate sooner than expected."

The cabin had a fairly large central room with a small kitch-enette at one end. A rugged couch with denim cushions and a plump recliner fronted a stone fireplace. A small bedroom with a double bed and tiny bath opened off the living area.

"All of our units have a private bath and ample closets for a month stay," Lois explained. "However, to keep them rustic they are lit only by gaslight." At Grace's look of surprise, Lois added: "Sam insisted on it."

After taking a brief tour of the immediate grounds they returned to the lodge for a late lunch featuring grilled caribou salad. They were on their second cup of tea, chattering away, when they heard the van horn.

"Oh dear, Marvin must be back from his afternoon trip and ready to take you back to Denali. Where in the world did the time go? You're more than welcome to stay longer if you want. The cabin I showed you is empty."

"Thanks, Lois, but I'll take a rain check. I promise to come back after I've finished the grand tour. Tomorrow I'm scheduled to catch the excursion train to Fairbanks." With a kiss on Lois' cheek Grace hurried out to the waiting van and the ride back to the Princess Lodge.

CHAPTER SIX

The Denali Star, a double-decker domed observation car, was fitted with tables for four. John approached a table where a middle aged couple and a young girl sat.

"Is this seat taken?" he asked.

"No . . . please do join us." The man rose and extended his hand. "Matt Grigsby, my wife Deborah, and my daughter Loren."

"John Hathaway," John said, returning the handshake.

He pulled out the empty chair and sat down. He had barely settled himself when a waitress appeared at his side. He noticed the Grigsbys had drinks in front of them so he ordered a whiskey sour. "Please ask them not to make it too sweet," he requested.

The waitress smiled and he smiled back.

"I don't recall seeing you before," Mrs. Grigsby commented. "Are you a member of our tour group?"

"No, as a matter of fact I'm not. They overbooked the passenger cars and asked if I would take a seat in a private car with a tour group. Of course, I didn't mind. I understand you have a guide aboard and I'm interested in learning all I can about Alaska."

"Is this your first visit?" Loren asked.

"Yes. I'm here on business." His drink arrived and he smiled in appreciation as he took a tentative sip. "Sour, just the way I ordered it. Unusual for train service."

Loren grinned, her open smile revealing beautiful white teeth. Large brown eyes were accented by elegantly arched eyebrows. Her skin was flawless and she wore her brown hair pulled tightly back in a ponytail. John placed her age to be somewhere in her late teens.

She noticed his scrutiny and blushed. "I just finished high school. This trip is my graduation gift."

"Pretty nice present, I'd say."

All heads turned to the front of the coach as a woman in a

brown uniform tapped the microphone and gave everyone a welcoming smile.

"Good afternoon, ladies and gentlemen. I'll be your tour guide during this segment of your trip to Fairbanks. We should arrive around four." She smiled. "Now sit back and enjoy a fully narrated tour as you journey along the base of the spectacular Alaska and Talkeetna Ranges. The views are stunning; I'm sorry to say our beautiful Mt. McKinley is still hiding in clouds this morning but if you're fortunate, and the clouds part, you'll catch sight of its snowcapped majesty through the glass dome of our railcar.

"First, a little background on the Land of the Midnight Sun. Our beautiful state stretches through four time zones, has three million lakes, more national parks than all the other states combined, thirty-three thousand miles of coastline, and fourteen of the highest peaks in the United States."

She leaned forward slightly. "I don't want to bore you with a canned speech. Please feel free to ask questions as we go along."

"How cold does it get here?" someone called out.

"Ferociously cold. From November through March in the city of Fairbanks, the thermometer often dips to minus fifty degrees. Don't worry though . . . I'm told that today you can expect sunny skies and a temperature of sixty degrees."

The guide continued her commentary. "Along this route you are almost certain to see moose. Watch for bobbing antlers. Animals are herbivorous and you'll see them standing among birches and aspens eating leaves and berries or feeding on aquatic plants in ponds or marshy areas. Unfortunately, as many as five hundred moose a year have been struck by our locomotives and our train has been given the name 'Moose Gobbler'."

The guide continued to briefly describe the Alaskan wildlife they might pass, then said, "I'll be back with you before we reach Fairbanks," and clicked off her microphone. As she put her microphone aside John noticed a woman making her way down the aisle. She stopped beside the guide and they were soon engaged in animated conversation.

John stared in surprise. Despite much shorter hair it was undoubtedly the woman he had helped at the Anchorage airport and talked with later in the hotel.

The guide handed the woman several pamphlets and they shook

hands. John watched intently. The woman turned and began to walk back to her seat, peering lazily over the passengers. She faltered when her gaze encountered John.

She recognized him—that was evident—and looked quickly away, then stopped and turned back to give him a big smile.

He quickly rose from his chair and extended his hand. "It's good to see you again."

John noticed the Grigbsys watching their exchange with interest. "I'd introduce you," he said, "but I'm embarrassed to say I don't know your name."

"Grace Maguire. I'm afraid I don't know yours either."

"John Hathaway."

After introductions to the Grigsbys were made he hastened to explain. "When Grace's plane landed in Anchorage she had the misfortune to discover her luggage missing. I was able to help her find the airport claim office."

"I've had that happen to me," Mr. Grigbsy said. "They always manage to locate your bags but it's very disconcerting when it happens."

Grace smiled in agreement. John noticed deep laugh lines around her eyes and mouth. He liked that.

"Are you alone?" he asked her.

"Yes, I am."

"Then, we'll get another chair for you if you'd care to join us."

"Oh, I wouldn't want to impose on your friends."

"I'm alone too. I just met these good folks. They were kind enough to let me share their table."

"Please join us," Mrs. Grigbsy said.

Grace looked uncertain but John had already motioned to the attendant to bring another chair.

"I'm surprised to see you again," John said.

"I boarded at Denali after visiting a friend and sightseeing for a few days. And you?"

"I decided to take a side trip to Fairbanks before beginning my assignment in Juneau. I only stopped in Denali long enough to pick up this excursion train."

Soon they were all engaged in lively conversation. Grace was animated and laughed easily, telling them of the sleeping grizzly bear on her wilderness tour. John smiled thinking how much he enjoyed her company.

"Are you sure it wasn't dead or just a decoy?" Loren asked.

"Nope. He was still sleeping when we returned but he raised a paw to brush away a mosquito and I saw a pile of poop beside him."

How cheerful and natural she is, John thought.

The guide picked up her microphone to resume her narrative. "We are entering a portion of the Athabascan Indian territory, originally settled as a Russian trading post. If you remember your history, Siberians first inhabited Alaska, entering on a land bridge that no longer exists. In the last century, before being sold to the United States, the country was owned by Russia. When gold was discovered in Fairbanks the population in this area swelled to over twelve thousand. Today it's home to only four hundred Athabascan."

The guide faltered and a deep frown creased her brow. John noticed her looking with annoyance at a group of four boisterous women sitting in the middle of the railcar. They had undoubtedly had too much to drink and were not paying attention to her monologue. It was evident their laughter was disturbing the people near them.

John wondered how she would handle it.

She clicked off her microphone and walked up the aisle toward the group. John watched her place her hand on the shoulder of one of the women and give her a big smile. Instead of reprimanding them she seemed to be gently joking with them. Then her face turned more serious and she proceeded to talk softly. Whatever she said seemed to work. They quieted down immediately.

Grace had been watching the guide intently. "She is good," she commented. "Very professional. Apparently being a guide involves much more than just knowing history and geography. She handled those women with ease . . . never lost her winning smile and uplifting attitude."

"I noticed you speaking to her earlier," John said. "Do you know her?"

"No, I was merely interested in her job. I think it is something I'd like to do." She smiled. "I plan to stay in Alaska and I'm looking for some interesting work. A new challenge . . . something different from anything I've ever done."

"Cool," Loren commented. "I like that." She glanced coyly at her father. "Dad thinks I need eight more years of schooling. He wants me to be a doctor."

"College is important, honey," Grace said. "I saw to it that both of my children were educated. This Alaskan adventure is just the whim of an old lady."

John was beginning to like Grace Maguire more and more.

The guide had returned to her post and resumed her narration. John ordered another round of drinks but Grace declined. Good. He didn't like to see a woman drink to excess. He wondered if she smoked. He didn't like that either.

Raucous laughter once more exploded from the table of four women and with a sigh the guide concluded her talk. "We will be arriving in Fairbanks soon," she said. "Enjoy your stay and thank you for traveling Alaska Railways."

Grace rose from the table. "I must return to my seat and collect my belongings. It's been a pleasure talking with all of you." She smiled at him, eyes a dash of dazzling green. "And it was so nice to see you again, John, and have another opportunity to thank you for helping a helpless traveler at the airport."

John jumped to his feet. "I think you are anything but a helpless lady." Immediately he realized that he did not want to see her go. He cleared his throat and looked at her nervously.

"Would you care to join me for dinner in Fairbanks?" he said. "Unless that is, you have other plans."

"Only to investigate the city. I'd love to dine with you."

"Then, let's have an early dinner and investigate together." John laughed. "You know it doesn't get dark this time of year until close to midnight. Where are you staying?"

"The Goldrush Inn."

He raised his eyebrows. "How interesting . . . so am I. That makes it easy. I understand the hotel has an excellent restaurant. Why don't I meet you in the lounge . . . say six o'clock? We can have a drink together, then dinner." He noticed a slight flush on her face. "Is that all right with you?"

"It's fine."

"I'd accompany you to the inn but I have my dog in baggage. I need to claim him, then place him in the motel kennel. Pets are not permitted in the rooms."

A warm smile lit up her face. "Then, I'll see you at six."

John felt an unexpected lurch in his chest. There was something about Grace Maguire that was different from other women-friends he occasionally asked out for dinner. He was looking forward to this evening. And just a little bit afraid of his interest.

Grace's heart sang. She had a date. An honest to Gawd date.

One moment she was buoyant with excitement—the next cold with terror. How long had it been since she'd had a date? It had to be over fifty years. *Oh good heavens, what does one do on a date? I'll be so nervous I'll never be able to make sensible conversation.*

She hurried to her room and lifted her suitcase to the bed with a grunt. What should she wear? Something dressy and feminine or casual and comfortable? She had one hour to shower, shave her legs, and dress. Thank heavens her hair was short and would dry quickly. She rooted through her cosmetic case and extracted a special bottle of perfumed body wash. She almost giggled as she carried it into the shower. She was acting like she was having a delayed adolescence.

After finishing her shower Grace pulled a fluffy white towel from the rack and patted herself dry. Tentatively she looked at her naked body in the full length mirror attached to the back of the bathroom door. Her breasts, once firm and upright had begun to droop slightly. She frowned as she ran her fingers along the scar of an old surgery. This was clearly not the body of her youth. Still, she liked the way she looked. Grace sucked in her breath, overcome with overwhelming guilt as she realized where her thoughts were leading her. Was she wondering how she would look to a man other than Peter? She was of the old school when a girl was expected to be a virgin when she married and she still adhered to the moral code that had sustained her then. Her emotions were a jumble of contradictions. She didn't know how to cope with such feelings. Grace threw the towel aside and shook her head in chagrin. It was only a date for heavens sake, she was only going out to dinner with John, she wasn't going to bed with him.

She deliberately pulled on plain cotton panties and a well worn bra, then stood staring into the closet. Casual or dressy? What kind of a restaurant would they go to? She decided against slacks and pulled out a skirt. Peter always said she had sexy legs. She flushed.

What in the hell was she thinking? Was she trying to be sexy for this man? Yes. No. She didn't know.

Grace changed her outfit three times before she was satisfied with her appearance: a gray wool skirt, a pale blue cashmere sweater that she thought hid her slight tummy, and a navy blue blazer. She agonized over her shoes. If they were going walking after dinner she should wear something flat. She settled on a pair of red sandals. Not as elegant as heels but certainly more practical.

With a final glance in the mirror, full of trepidation and a racing heart she headed out the door.

CHAPTER SEVEN

John was waiting for Grace in the lobby. He regretted telling her to meet him in the bar—she appeared to be very much a lady and should be treated like one. As she walked toward him he could not help but admire, once again, how attractive she was. She moved with an air of poised, self-assurance.

He swept her with an appreciative glance. "I love women in skirts and sweaters, especially when they wear them to such advantage. You look great."

"Thank you. So do you," she said, and he did: khakis, blue oxford shirt, leather bomber jacket filled out by very broad shoulders.

He put his hand on her arm and steered her toward the cocktail lounge.

After ordering a whiskey sour for himself and a glass of Chardonnay for Grace he said, "I guess we should start at the beginning and get to know one another. What brings you to Alaska?"

"It's a long story but basically after my husband's death I decided to make a major change in my life. I've spent the last fifty years as a wife and homemaker. I know it's a cliché, but now I need time out to find myself . . . to examine what I want to do with my golden years."

"I think everyone reaches a point like that in their lives." He grinned. "Though not everyone would be inspired to come to Alaska to find the answer."

Her animated eyes sparkled. "I saw a poster recently that read, 'Do Seniors need to Retire or Refire?' I'm planning to refire. You indicated you were here on business. Where are you from?"

"I live in New York City. I'm a retired journalist on a special assignment."

The waiter brought their drinks. As Grace sipped her wine John continued, "I retired from the *New York Times* but I occasionally write special pieces on subjects that interest me. I've been asked by the paper to write an article on the logging industry in Alaska and its impact on the ecology of the area. When I learned that the United States government is spending millions to subsidize several large lumber companies, and building roads that serve only their interests, I was intrigued enough to take the assignment and leave my cozy nest in New York."

Grace fingered her glass. "I know something about that. Peter and I subscribed to the American Arts Lecture series at Carnegie Mellon. We heard an activist speak about that very subject and how the lumber companies were recklessly denuding thousands of acres of old-growth timber. The poor man almost cried when he spoke about the devastation."

"That's true. It might be the same gentleman I heard lecture at Columbia. He stated that Alaska has one of the greatest tracts of rain forest outside the tropics. He also claimed that subsidized logging is tearing it apart." John noticed that her glass was about empty. "Another wine?" he asked.

"Not really. Maybe with dinner."

"Of course. Why don't we go to the dining room now. It's not crowded and hopefully we can get a table by the window."

They both ordered clam chowder, then smoked salmon for Grace and swordfish of John. Candlelight reflected by the dark varnished wood of the intimate room, danced in Grace's eyes. As they ate she filled him in on her personal history. He learned that she had lived in Pennsylvania all of her life, first in Scranton, then in Pittsburgh where her husband worked in management for Allegheny Steel. She had two children, a boy and a girl, and two grandchildren.

"Do you have brothers and sisters?" John asked.

"No, I was an only child. You?"

"I had a sister, older than me, who died two years ago. Both of my parents are dead. I was only in my twenties when my mother and father were killed in an automobile accident."

"How sad. Was that before you were married or after?" Grace asked.

"Shortly after. We lived with Mom and Dad for a month so Mary did get to know them. Of course, none of my children knew their grandparents." He went on to speak of his wife and two sons, of Mary's inability to have more children, of his years in the military, and life in New York. Then he spoke of Mary's battle with cancer. He cared for her for two years and she died at home.

Grace's soft gaze rested on him, filled with warmth and compassion. She reached across the table for his hand and squeezed it gently. He studied her face and swallowed, feeling a sudden jolt.

"In the lounge you mentioned that you plan to relocate in Alaska. Where?" he asked.

"I don't know yet."

His eyebrows rose.

Grace laughed. "I guess that does sound odd." She explained her plan to take the grand tour and then decide. "Where are you headed?"

"The Tongass."

She looked puzzled. "Tongass?"

"Otherwise known as The Alexander Archipelago or Alaska's panhandle." Grace still looked confused. "It's really a string of fjord-footed islands separating British Columbia from the Pacific Ocean. Cruise ships advertise the area as the Inside Passage and Glacier National Park."

Grace's face brightened. "That's where I'm going next. I'm going to take a seven day cruise with Princess Lines. I want to consider Skagway, Juneau, and Ketchikan as possible home sites."

John noticed that everything Grace said, she said with vitality. He enjoyed this woman. "I will be working out of Juneau next week," he said. "I'm picking up a photographer and joining a guide from the Sitka Conservation Society. Maybe I can wave as you go sailing by."

Grace laughed. "I'll be the one hanging over the bow of the ship wearing a red scarf."

"I certainly couldn't miss that."

"Seriously though, your project sounds awfully exciting. Do you have a title for your story yet?"

"Roads to Nowhere."

"I remember the activist talking about that. He said the government built miles of roads solely to accommodate the lumber companies, then, after the timber was harvested, the roads were abandoned."

The dining room was full, glasses clinked, chinaware rattled. He smelled her faint perfume and it was enticing. The way she'd taken his hand across the table had been electric—pure shock and power surging through his body—and he couldn't wait for dinner to end so he could hold her hand again.

An obese, flashily dressed man, immediately behind Grace had his chair pushed tight against hers and appeared to be listening to their conversation.

The man turned his head and flashed her a gold-toothed grin. "The way to get rich in Alaska today is to get into the big-company logging business. Once the fortunes made up here were in gold, then oil, but the dough now is in lumber. What Alaska needs is progress. I'm a contractor. Why, we're cutting in roads everywhere."

John's mouth tightened. "But the roads don't go anywhere."

"So, what if they don't go anywhere? If we push the forests all the way to the ocean someone will come along and build houses on the empty land."

John's bushy eyebrows drew together in a straight line. "Alaska isn't that populated. Where would all the people come from?"

"If we build the roads they will come." he said, paraphrasing a line from the movie *Field of Dreams*. He laughed hugely at what he considered his own wit.

"What a blowhard," Grace whispered. John, his face stony, signaled for the waiter in an effort to halt the conversation. He and Grace ordered coffee and New York Cheesecake. They lingered over their coffee, talking quietly, pointedly ignoring the windbag at the next table.

"Are you up to a walking tour of the riverfront?" John asked as he signaled for his check.

"I can't wait. I keep stealing glances out the window. Do you see that huge sternwheeler in the harbor?"

Following her gaze, John fumbled in his jacket pocket. "I picked up a brochure in the lobby. It's the river boat *Discovery*. It takes you on a four hour narrated cruise on the Cheka and Tanana river. Sounds interesting . . . they stop for over an hour at a reconstructed Athabascan Indian village." As he handed the brochure to Grace he noticed the hopeful expression on her face. He felt slightly off balance—surprised at his own feeling of disappointment. "I'm flying to Juneau, tomorrow or I'd suggest taking the trip together," he said.

"Well, I have another day here in Fairbanks before I fly back to Anchorage to catch the cruise ship. I think I'll take the river boat trip. It does sound worth exploring." Her lips curved in a smile. "I'm sorry you can't go along."

"So am I."

After settling for the check with his credit card he escorted her from the restaurant, placing his hand on the small of her back. Her cashmere sweater was feminine. Underneath he felt her tremor at his touch. There was definitely a chemistry building between them.

When they stepped outside, the air had a chilly bite, although it was still daylight. They spent the next hour strolling the sidewalks, taking in the sights and sounds of the busy harbor. Fairbanks with its goldrush history was only eighty-nine miles from the Arctic Circle. Every summer, this area was filled with people—tours from nearby cruise ships, tourists staying in hotels, couples strolling after supper. There was a striking beauty to the evening. The flavor of salt mingled with the heady scent of pine and fir. The black water shimmered. Boats rocked at anchor.

When Grace turned to look up at him a slight breeze ruffled her hair. A chill wind blew off the harbor. She shivered slightly and fastened the button on her blazer.

"It is getting cool," he said. "Why don't we head back to the hotel?"

She nodded in agreement.

They walked in companionable silence for a few minutes. John couldn't remember when he had felt so completely at ease. He felt peaceful with this woman he was slowly beginning to know. She didn't need to fill every moment of silence with a stream of constant chatter as some females in the fast world of today did. He clasped her hand in his as they slowly circled back to the inn, retracing their steps, pausing occasionally on the busy street to examine window displays in what seemed to be an inordinate amount of jewelry shops.

"Tell me about your dog," she said. "You've mentioned him several times."

"Bandit goes everywhere I go. He's a yellow Lab, large, affec-tionate and intelligent. A perfect pet." John chuckled. "I must admit to his one weakness, though. He's terrified of loud noises.

Gunfire and thunder undo him completely."

"We had a dog like that. You could always tell a storm was coming when you found Duke with his rump sticking out from under the bed. I wonder why that is?"

"Native instinct—a fear of fire. In nature thunderstorms bring fire and all animals panic. Dogs have been known to crash through glass windows and tear furniture apart when alone in a house during a storm."

"Bandit! I love the name. Where is he now?"

"In the motel kennel. I left him home, once, in one of New York's finest kennels and he nearly died of starvation. He simply wouldn't eat until I returned. He apparently recognizes the difference when we travel. I'll admit it presents a problem securing a motel that is pet friendly. But he is my buddy and he goes where I go."

They walked on, past the Palace Theater where tourists lined up for the evening performance, past Pioneer Park where people sat almost motionless with their newspapers and glowing cigarettes, then turned toward the waterfront and walked out on the dock to admire the sail boats at anchor. John had an odd feeling in his gut. Watching Grace lean against the rail, face to the wind, was doing something to him. He felt a tightening in his groin that wasn't entirely unpleasant. Maybe all wasn't lost after all. He slipped his arm casually around her waist and she leaned against him.

"Lovely, isn't it," she murmured

Ah, yes, he thought, and he didn't mean just the evening. They stood there for a few more minutes, listening to the sounds of boat rigging slapping against masts, breathing in the salty tang in the air. He noticed she kept tilting her head back to look up in the sky.

"I was hoping to see the northern lights," she confessed. "It's one of the reasons I came to Fairbanks."

"This is the place to see them, but I believe it's more of a fall and winter phenomenon."

"Oh," she said sounding disappointed.

"Keep looking, though. You might be lucky." He tightened his arm around her waist and felt her shiver. She turned to look into his eyes and then said, "I think we had better move on. It's been a long day." He pulled away and reluctantly said, "I believe the hotel is but a short distance."

Grace fell into step beside him and all too soon they entered the lobby of the Goldrush Inn.

John felt uncertain how to end the evening. Should he kiss her goodnight or shake her hand? "I'll see you to your room," he said, waiting for her reaction.

She pointed to a long hall to the left of the lobby. "Number 206."

At the door she paused and fumbled in her purse for her key card. She withdrew it and hesitated slightly before inserting it in the lock, then turned and raised her eyes to meet his. "Thank you. I had a good time this evening."

"So did I." He shifted from foot to foot, unsure what to do next. "Ah . . . I'd like to keep in touch. Do you have a cell phone?"

She nodded. "The kids gave me one before I left Pittsburgh. She dropped her gaze, looking sheepish. "I'll admit I seldom have it turned on. When it rings I still get confused over which button to push."

"It has voice mail, doesn't it?

"Yes."

John reached in his wallet and fished out two name cards. He handed one to her. "Take this, it has my cell. Give me your number and I'll write it on this other card."

Again she gave him with a sheepish smile. "I don't remember the number. Wait here and I'll get it from my room."

He waited in the hall for her return, disappointed that she hadn't invited him in, then wondering why it mattered so much.

Grace quickly returned and handed him a piece of paper with her cell phone number. "Thank you again, John, for a lovely evening."

He took her hand and squeezed it. It was soft and warm, comfortable in his. She smiled and he felt his heart thump. Then he surprised himself. He cupped her face in both hands. Her eyes searched his. He bent down and touched his lips to hers.

She leaned into his body as if she belonged there and kissed him back.

John's heart was racing; could she feel it? Her mouth was so warm. Grace made him feel more alive than he'd felt in a long, long time. He'd never believed he could feel this way again. Was this real?

Without warning all of his inhibitions were gone, it was just him and Grace, and so much pent up desire. He pulled her into a tight embrace. Was that his heartbeat or hers? When he felt her tremble he realized that she was also stimulated. This was new territory for both of them. She looked so beautiful and soft. And vulnerable. He touched his lips to hers again.

"Thank you," he said, caressing her cheek.

"For what?" she whispered.

"I was afraid I'd forgotten how to kiss a woman, feel awkward, like a teenager," he whispered back.

"So did I."

With considerable effort he resisted the temptation to ask her if he could come into her room. But he couldn't say the words. Instead he said, "I wouldn't be a bit surprised if we don't run into each other again for a repeat engagement."

And then Grace took his hand and grinned. "Remember I'll be the woman with a red scarf hanging from the bow of the Princess Star."

"How could I forget?"

Alone in her room, Grace wondered why she hadn't invited John in. There was no doubt in her mind that she was drawn to him and he to her. She sensed that he wanted to do more than give her a soft kiss. He wanted sex, and darn it so did she. But developing a relationship with him, or any man for that matter, could only complicate her plans to build an independent life in Alaska. Better she forget him and simply be grateful for the pleasure of a lovely evening with a handsome, interesting companion.

She donned a nightgown, switched off the light, and climbed into bed. Yet, sleep would not come. She tossed and turned. Their conversation during the meal and their walk through town played endlessly in her mind. Frustrated and angry, her hormones racing, she punched her pillow. She did not want this. She did not want to be tied to a man. It could destroy all her glorious dreams for adventure. In the morning she would tear up his card.

After a restless night John rose early. The weather forecast was for a high in the seventies so after a quick workout in the hotel exercise room he showered and donned running shorts. He had time to take Bandit for a run before departing for Juneau.

He headed for Pioneer Park, Bandit trotting happily beside him, tail swinging. The park was teeming with activity, not what he was looking for, so they left and found a deserted stretch of beach along the riverfront, open to the water. John withdrew a beat-up tennis ball from his pocket. Bandit had been waiting for just that moment. His tail wagged wildly. "All right, go get it," John said, and the ball went sailing into the air. He watched the dog bound through the grass and into the water with a huge splash.

They played for a time before Bandit flopped on the edge of the grass, panting, tongue lolling. He lay there for a few minutes then slowly picked up the ball and trotted back. He peered up at John with questioning eyes.

"Okay, once more," John told him and the slimy ball went sailing into the air. Bandit ran full speed in hot pursuit, only this time when it was returned, John pocketed the ball and walked over to a fallen spruce tree. He brushed loose bark and bird droppings from the dead trunk and sat down. Bandit hunkered down beside him and rested his big head on John's thigh. John stroked his head. Bandit closed his eyes and thumped his tail.

As John watched the busy river traffic a loud horn announced the approach of the sternwheeler he and Grace had seen last evening. "I wonder if she is on it?" he murmured softly to the dog. Bandit pricked up his ears and cocked his head to listen. He always seemed to know when John was sad or lonely.

"She was a really nice lady, Bandit. And pretty too. You'd like her. Only trouble is she wants to live in the wilderness and I can't wait to get back to the city. You and I will be going home soon. Not much point in getting better acquainted."

CHAPTER EIGHT

John decided to begin his investigation of the Tongass National Forest with a trek designed to examine the natural plants and wildlife of the rain forest. After flying to Juneau he rented a Jeep and with Bandit at his side, went to pick up Richard Skaggs, a bush pilot and freelance photographer recommended by the *Times*.

Richard, in his late fifties, tall and lanky, wore a long-sleeved plaid work shirt and baggy camouflage pants. The outline of a hard-pack of cigarettes bulged in his shirt pocket. He pushed his camera equipment into John's jeep. A lock of thinning, sun-streaked hair flopped onto his forehead and he brushed it off with a sun-browned hand. He frowned. "Better leave that dog behind," he said. The area we are going into is full of hungry grizzly. Wouldn't want your pet to get downwind of a bear."

"What will I do with him?"

"Leave him here. I have three Malamutes and they love company. He'll be okay."

After turning Bandit over to Richard's wife they drove back to town to pick up Larry Myers, a wildlife biologist working with the Sitka Conservation Society who would accompany them and provide detailed ecological information.

Larry was the exact opposite of Richard. The biologist was younger, short and stocky with a bushy black beard and flattop haircut. Khaki safari trousers were stuffed into high leather boots. He reeked of insect repellant and tobacco smoke.

Larry looked at John and blinked with surprise. "I hope you have a jacket or something with long sleeves with you. The mosquitoes will eat you alive."

"I'm covered with insect repellent and I have a parka in my backpack," John said.

"You'll need that and more. I have an extra safari hat with mosquito netting I'll lend you." He jumped into the Jeep and the three of them took off for the river where Richard kept an aluminum skiff moored.

"Where are we going?" John asked Larry as he helped to transfer the rifles, camping gear and photo equipment into the boat.

"A section of old-growth forest lying along the Switzer Creek Trail, just outside Juneau. There's a stand of landmark spruce two miles inland I want you to see."

In less than an hour they pulled the boat up on the bear-tracked shore of a winding creek. At first, the beach looked relatively clean. A strand of weathered rope looped over a piece of driftwood, a red buoy nestled among river rocks. The stuff looked like the decorations in a seafood restaurant. Picturesque. It almost belonged. But then other items popped into focus: a plastic water bottle, a pulverized lump of Styrofoam, a quart container that once held motor oil. On a remote beach in the Tongass these things clearly should not have been here. They were enough to dissolve anyone's illusion that this place was pristine. Trash was every-where. Shards from a discarded Cup-of-Noodles, pieces of fishing net, a plastic bottle cap, an empty beer bottle.

John frowned. "I don't understand this litter," he said.

Richard shook a cigarette from his pack and lit it. "What is it they call us—the Ugly Americans? Fishermen, surveyors, loggers looking to mark stands of lumber for cutting . . . they all leave their imprint on the land. There is a volunteer cleanup program—a nonprofit arm of the fishing trade association—however it's a daunting project." As Richard talked he began to unload their camping gear on the beach. "We'll have to hike in. You up to it John?"

"Sure . . . just don't go too fast. Remember I'm not as spry as I used to be."

True to the nature of a rain forest, it was raining. Their boots made loud sucking sounds as they slogged through squishy, boggy ground created by the gravelly soil left by ancient glaciers. The going was tough and John began to tire but Larry and Richard were younger and had experience on their side. They chatted easily as they explained the ecology of an old-growth temperate rain forest.

After several miles, soaked and leg-weary, they stopped to catch their breath at the edge of a stream quivering with salmon.

"What you see are living canyons of spruce, hemlock and

cedar—some more than six hundred years old," Larry said running his hands over his beard. "I never get over their beauty."

John gasped. "My God, that one tree must be at least two hundred feet high."

Larry smiled. "They're called 'Landmark' trees—the last giants of the American rain forest. Conservation volunteers hike into the forest to map and measure them . . . that's where they got the name 'landmark' . . . and to show anyone who'll come along what the Tongass once looked like."

"This is your bird and moose habitat, just before it's turned into catalogs and toilet paper," Richard said.

John could only stare in wonder. Isolated rays of sunlight pierced the clouds hanging thick over the shrouded trees. It was magnificent. "I wish Grace could see this," he murmured.

"Who's Grace?" Larry asked.

"Just a friend."

Larry winked and smiled.

John compressed his lips. *Now why in the world had he thought of her when he was deep in the Tongass. He was letting this woman creep into his thoughts way too often.*

He stood in silence, awed by the overwhelming beauty of the misty, cloud-shrouded Sitka spruce and hemlock. Rain fell gently on the leaves, a peaceful sound. There was very little vegetation on the ground, just a wonderfully soft bed of pine needles. Although he had read extensively about the Tongass in preparation for his article, nothing prepared him for the sheer beauty of the forest. It was like standing in a cathedral.

John issued a deep sigh and Richard looked at him knowingly.

They walked on but soon saplings began to close in on them and they had to move out into the shallow stream bed. "Now, I see why you insisted on high boots," John said with a chuckle.

"This is where the old-growth was cut. These new, second-growth trees all grew in at the same time. They're so dense there is little for animals to eat, and notice that you no longer see salmon. The water is too cold and murky."

Larry's face was glum. "You know, John, we conservationists aren't just talking about saving old trees. An entire ecological cycle is affected in the wake of logging. During the summer protein-rich insects are needed to feed young birds whose population has fallen dramatically in the past few years.

"I know," John said, "but while this pristine forest is beautiful we can't forget the economic impact of the logging industry on this area."

Larry raised his brows. "True. When the pulp mill closed in Ketchikan over five hundred jobs were lost." He pulled at his beard. "I think you should talk to my brother-in-law, Steve Miller. He operates a saw mill, a short boat ride across the channel from Ketchikan. What say we take a ride over there when we get back tomorrow?"

"I'd like that. I'm sure there are two sides to this debate."

Toward dusk they started to retrace their steps to the campsite. Larry and Richard strung up a tarp against the pouring rain with silent efficiency while John looked for a place to pitch his one-man dome tent. He had it half up when Larry walked over to him. "Look down, John . . . that pile of brown stuff at your feet is bear scat. You are erecting your tent in the middle of a bear path."

The small hairs at the back of John's neck stirred. Paw prints fully seven inches wide were visible in the soft soil. Without hesitation he moved the small tent quickly, placing it smack up against the one Larry and Richard were erecting.

"No food in the tent tonight," Richard warned. "And keep your rifle handy."

John nestled into his sleeping bag and was on the cusp of sleep when the night sounds began—loud thumping noises, screeches, scurrying feet, whining mosquitoes, howling wolves. He practically jumped out of his skin when outside his tent rocks clattered as something heavy trundled about. Probably the bear whose tracks he had avoided. Or maybe a moose. Then the mighty *hot-hobo* call of a great horned owl rang out. Whirs of wings and beaver-slaps resonated in the pattering rain. Damn it all, he was cold and miserable. It never stopped raining. How could anyone elect to live in this wilderness? His thoughts drifted to Grace Maguire and her choice. Confusing thoughts. He squirmed, unable to get comfortable, unable to dismiss his reflections and vague longings. Eventually he slid into a groggy dream where he and Grace were making wild, uncontrolled love in a rubber boat in the middle of the ocean.

He awoke the next morning, an hour before dawn, to the humming sound of mosquitoes swarming against the thin fabric of the tent and the music of wolves. The singing began with a baritone howl that drifted on the wind. It was answered by a chorus of tenors, their voices uneven and charged with what John detected as pure enjoyment. The wolves sang on as dawn's crimson sky, reflected against a charcoal cloud bank, illuminated the sky.

John staggered his sleep-deprived way toward the smell of coffee. Larry was already turning a large salmon filet on a make-shift spit of hot coals. "Hey, sleepy head," he yelled, "I've already been down to the river and caught us our breakfast. Dig in. Time we get packed up and move out."

They broke camp and headed straight into the drooping, tangled murk beneath giant Sitka spruce and western hemlock. It had begun to rain once more but Richard and Larry were in their element, escorting a novice on a voyage of discovery through an American frontier. They spent the morning photographing the colossal conifers, leading John to spruces they judged to be about 700 years old, explaining that western red cedars can live at least a thousand years.

Rain pelted John's face and ran down his back, his feet were cold and wet, and he itched from a hundred mosquito bites. At the same time his misery was overshadowed by a sense of mission. They had come, after all, to study the ecology of the rain forest. Toward dusk they began to trek back to their boat. With rapid, silent teamwork in the downpour they covered their gear with a tarp and started across the gray, choppy water. John was silent on the trip back to Juneau, his mind obsessing about a hot shower, dry clothes, and a decent meal. He retrieved Bandit who, while glad to see him, seemed a little reluctant to leave his new friends.

The next morning at nine John picked up Larry and they boarded the biologist's boat for the trip to talk to Steve Miller.

"Cutting down old-growth provides a living for many of the people who live in the Tongass," Larry shouted above the roar of his motor boat. "People like Steve. He was raised in a logging camp, his Pap and Grandpap were both loggers. Now, he operates the family sawmill, but he barely makes a decent living. The closure of the pulp mill affected everyone."

They found Steve carefully sawing thin slabs from blocks of eight-foot diameter spruce. He was a large, broad-chested man, middle-aged, with graying hair and a full beard. He finished cutting the log in the cradle, then, while brushing saw chips from dirty dungarees held up by broad red suspenders walked over to greet them. He stuck out his hand.

After introductions were made, and John's mission explained, Steve seemed eager to talk. "Timberin' here ain't what it used to be," he stated in a deep, raspy voice. "The damn government has cut our allotments on federal land almost in half. The only part of my business that's left operating today is a victim of some right-wing industry folks who push back the harvest levels for independent loggers. Them an' the damn tree-huggers that say 'don't cut any of it'."

Larry interrupted. "Steve says he'd like to be able to cut only the newer trees . . . save more of the old-growth . . . to make the forest truly renewable. But he can't do that."

"Second growth trees just haven't had a chance to grow big enough yet," Steve agreed. "Takes a long time for a tree to mature."

John pursed his lips. "So, as I understand it, to be a viable industry and satisfy the demand, some old-growth must be cut. The debate continues. How much of it can be cut without strangling Alaska's wildlife? And as the timber jobs evaporate, what will replace them? That pretty much describes the dilemma doesn't it?"

"Yep," Steve said bitterly. "And somebody damn well better figure it out before I lose my business. In five more years my wife and I planned to throw in the towel and retire here. Instead conservationists decided they had to save all the trees, the pulp mill closed and everyone in Ketchikan started to starve."

John studied him critically. "It's my understanding that a sharp recession in Asia and a slumping world market for pulp were the reasons for the closure of the mill, not the conservationists."

Steve's face grew red. "This is a damn rain forest. It was put here to be logged."

"It's only logging the landmark trees that get folks bent out of shape," Larry interjected.

"But them's the ones the Japanese want. The tight, evenly

spaced grain of the old trees is what they prize."

John knew this was true, part of the dilemma faced by the Forest Service in trying to satisfy both the industry and the conservationists. "Ketchikan seems to be thriving, though," he said. "The harbor is crowded with huge cruise ships. Vacationers throng the streets and restaurants are jammed."

"Don't help me none. I ain't about to operate no damn souvenir shop. I don't know nothin' but logging." Steve ground out the words between clenched teeth. He hitched up his pants and held out his hand. "Gotta get back to work. You write your piece you be sure to tell my side of the story."

"I'll do that."

"And good to see you again, Larry. Give my love to the wife." With that he walked back to his saw.

As Larry guided their boat back to town John gazed at the cruise ships anchored in the harbor. One bore the colors of the Princess Lines. *I wonder if Grace might be aboard,* he mused. *She said she'd be hanging over the bow of the ship wearing a red scarf.*

Larry snugged his boat up to the busy dock. "I'd buy you a drink but I'm sorry to say souvenir shops have replaced the good old logger's saloons." He pointed to the luxury ships anchored offshore. "Those babies disgorge over eight hundred thousand passengers a year. The tour companies only advertise salmon fishing, our totem pole park, whale sighting trips and visits to inlet glaciers. Frankly I think the people of Ketchikan are missing a bet. Instead of fighting over the loss of the logging industry they should capitalize on promoting visits to see the rain forest and landmark trees. The best way to preserve old-growth is to get the tourists back into the woods to see the really big stuff. We must accept that some old-growth will be logged, but more will be saved if people actually see these trees."

John agreed. It seemed to him that walking into a misty, fern covered forest of incredible cathedral-like stands of century-old trees was a transforming type of experience. An experience few would ever forget. He never would.

Now he had to pursue the other side of the picture. He would spend the afternoon talking to the owners of several nearby logging camps and tomorrow Richard would fly him over Prince of Wales Island. He wanted to see first hand the impact of clear-cut logging.

The next morning John parked his Jeep in Richard's driveway beside a modest one-story home of cedar logs. A neatly mowed lawn stretched to the edge of the river where Richard's floatplane, a Piper Super Cub, was docked. Half a dozen grebes floated in the water and three ducks loitered at the edge of the grass. Since Juneau cannot be reached by highway it is as common for residents of the capitol to have a plane parked beside their home as it is for people elsewhere to have a car in their driveway.

Richard came out the side door zipping his leather jacket. A long silk scarf fluttered around his neck and he wore a warm grin.

"Ready for another adventure?" he called.

"Ready. Can Bandit stay here? He tends to get a little air sick."

"Sure. Besides, I think he has something going for Mandy. She's the silver malamute. Gonna make a good sled dog, someday. I don't know about the other two."

John opened the door of the Jeep and Bandit bounded to the ground with an excited yelp. He went flying across the driveway to join his dog friends of several days past.

Richard hopped onto the front seat of the Jeep. "Pull down to the river and we'll load your things directly into the plane."

When all of the equipment and lunch supplies were aboard the little two-seat plane Richard gave John a boost onto the wing and into the cockpit. John had never taken off from water in a small aircraft and his heart raced as Richard taxied to the downwind end of the river. He turned the aircraft into the wind for takeoff, gradually adding power until he had full throttle, then roared ahead.

The forest floor ahead of them took an abrupt rise and John let out a strangled cry. "You're going to hit those trees."

Richard just grinned. The river was L shaped and he banked to the right. They sailed into the air.

"You scared the hell out of me," John sputtered.

"Relax buddy. I've been a bush pilot for years. I know these airways like the back of my hand."

"What exactly does a bush pilot do?"

"Aerial mapping of timberland, patrolling for forest fires, and when needed, acting as an ambulance to fly injured workers out of remote logging camps."

They gained altitude and John gradually relaxed. "Precisely where are we going?"

"Prince of Wales Island. It is the most heavily logged area of the Tongass. We carry enough fuel to make a quick fly over. Look below. That's the famous Mendenhall Glacier. Before we head south I thought you'd like to catch a glimpse of a moving river of ice." He pointed to his right, shouting to make himself heard over the roar of the plane's engines. "Now, we're passing over Admiralty Island. Notice how lush it is. It's a protected, roadless wilderness. Quite a difference from what you'll see when we reach Prince of Wales."

John held his breath. The tiny plane seemed to drop vertically, barely skimming the tops of the trees.

"I can see just fine," he shouted. "You can fly a little higher."

Richard chuckled.

Within the hour they reached the island. From the air the logged areas were clearly visible. Richard nosed the plane as close to the inhospitable stretch of lakes and brush, shorn of trees, as he could go. Logging roads etched the denuded mountain in all directions. John issued a deep groan. "It's like a moonscape."

Richard nodded. "Originally this island had the largest and most productive big-tree forests in the Tongass. Clear-cuts are only the most visible of the ills of logging in the Tongass. The damn loggers leveled the land. Miles of subsidized roads were built, serving only the lumber mills. Every logging area has its own road network. In addition to the main lines large enough for logging trucks, secondary roads snake for miles into the forest. What makes it even harder to swallow is that the raw logs went to Asia, not the American market." He pointed to a towering wall of crumbling logs extending for hundreds of yards along a trickling streambed. "And when the market for them went belly-up they were left here to rot."

"Subsidies were given to the lumber mills, weren't they?"

"Yep. Tens of millions of dollars annually, coming out of the pockets of U.S. taxpayers and padding company profits. Give-aways of public resources don't get more blatant than that." Richard dipped low over the barren terrain. "And notice that you don't see anything moving down there . . . no deer, no bears, not even eagles. You know, John, the greatest worry we Alaskans have is not over the trees themselves, but over wildlife lost in the wake of logging. A rain forest in its natural state is ripe with vegetation necessary for their subsistence . . . the result of clear-cutting is a barricade of shrub-stems, spruce sapling needles and sharper thorns."

They continued to circle until John shouted that he had seen enough. He had a bitter taste in his mouth. It would be hard to write about clear-cutting and not reflect the dismay he felt.

John woke the next morning to one of those rare, hot, blue-sky mornings. He had found lodgings at an inn that welcomed dogs—after all this was Iditarod country. He took Bandit out for a run then devoted the rest of the day to investigating in a kayak, paddling out to Chichagof Island where he and his guides had camped a few days ago. He hiked ashore and sank down beneath a towering hemlock on a mat of moss and pine needles, closing his eyes, letting his mind wander. Mentally he began constructing the article he had come here to write, but try as he might his mind kept drifting. To thoughts of Grace. He had taken several women out to dinner after Mary died, mostly women from the church where he was a deacon, but no one he had been moved to kiss. He never thought he would love again—did not want to. But Grace stirred passions of his youth.

He groaned in frustration. There was still much work to do. He did not want his article to be biased. Tomorrow he would go into the Capitol and interview anyone who might give him political insight. He also needed to talk to officials at the Tongass National Forest agency. Perhaps, more importantly, he wanted to talk to shop keepers and average townspeople.

That night, however, his schedule took on a completely different priority. When he went to the kennel to retrieve Bandit for his evening walk he found the dog pen empty.

John whistled, certain his pet was nearby, playing a prank on his master, enjoying some unexpected freedom. When the dog did not come bounding across the lawn John looked more closely at the enclosure. An obvious tunnel had been burrowed under the wire.

Bandit had never done that before. Whatever had gotten into him? John began to walk over the grounds, calling his name. Nothing. He went into the lodge and talked to the desk clerk, then several of the maids. No one had seen a loose dog. They called the manager who seemed more concerned over the damage to the kennel than the loss of one of its inhabitants.

There was only one road leading into Juneau and John walked slowly whistling and calling. No one had seen Bandit. Yellow Labs were uncommon in this area, most residents owned Huskies or Malamutes, and he would have been noticed.

John returned to the lodge. Surely he would find an exhausted dog lying at the door waiting for him.

But Bandit was not there.

Did Bandit think he had been deserted? John stood before his door in a quandary until the sudden ringing of a telephone jolted him. It was coming from his room. He raced inside and gabbed the receiver. It was Richard.

"You missing something?" Richard asked.

"Yeah, my dog."

"He's over here. He's taken up with Mandy, my silver malamute." Richard chuckled. "Guess he likes blonds."

"I'll be right over."

"Aw, let him stay tonight. I think the damage is already done. They are both sleeping behind the shed."

The next morning John picked up Bandit. The dog, though happy to see him, appeared exhausted. Richard walked John to his Jeep. "If Mandy has pups I'll give you a call," he said, grinning.

CHAPTER NINE

Three days later Grace was indeed hanging from the rail of the Princess Star as it plowed the icy waters of the Inside Passage.

A noise from deep inside her purse startled her. It took her a moment to realize it was her cell phone. *Could it be John?* She raised the phone to her ear, the pulse in her throat beating rapidly.

"Hello," she trilled.

"Hi, Mom."

"Oh, it's you Ben," she said.

"You sound disappointed. Were you expecting someone else to call?"

"No, of course not, dear. When my cell phone rang it threw me off balance. I'm still not used to the darn thing."

"How is everything? Are you enjoying the trip?"

Trip? Ben still has not accepted my true intent, to make Alaska my home, she thought with dismay.

"Honey, everything is fine and the cruise ship is fabulous. It's like a grand hotel. And I can't begin to describe the scenery. Just this morning we had the most amazing experience. The ship was in Glacier Bay and we actually saw a glacier calving."

"Calving? What's that?"

"When glaciers reach the sea their ragged front floats until pieces break off and form icebergs. The sound is ear-splitting and the impact shoots water hundreds of feet into the air."

"That sounds exciting."

"It was. I wish I could share it with you and the grandchildren. I miss them."

"They miss you, too. Especially Teddy. He says he is going to write you a long letter."

"I'd love that. I'll admit I'm a little homesick. We've always been such a close family. Maybe all of you could come to Alaska for the holidays. Wouldn't that be fun?"

"Not under the present circumstances." Grace noticed the slight hitch in his voice

"What circumstances? Ben . . . is everything all right between you and Emily?"

Ben hesitated before he replied. "We're having a few problems. She says she needs to go back to work and I don't think that is fair to Ted. Kelly is in college but he is still at home. You know how she spends money. Both of my credit cards are maxed out. We'll work things out, though." He cleared his throat. "I wish you were here to talk to her."

"Even if I were home I wouldn't want to get involved in your private affairs. Emily wouldn't be open to that."

"Still, I wish I could talk to you."

Grace could not miss the accusatory tone in his voice. She felt a flush of guilt. By running off to Alaska was she abdicating her role as parent? Did she have the right to upset the pattern, not only of her life, but of those dear to her? Her children were confused—she didn't even have an address—they could reach her only by cell phone. And then only if she remembered to turn it on. Her grand-children would grow up without her presence in their lives. Peter had taken great pains to leave her a home and an income that would provide for her future. He would be aghast at her decision to leave the security he had provided and strike out for the unknown.

Someday she would have to settle down and resume a normal life.

Someday . . . but not this day.

"Ben . . . I . . ."

The ship's loudspeaker abruptly boomed a message. "Whales have been spotted off the right starboard."

"I heard that, Mom. Don't miss seeing a whale. I'm sure you have a lot to do during the day. I'll call you tonight, when we can talk better."

After a few words of farewell Grace dropped the phone back into her purse and scurried off towards the group of people huddling at the rail with cameras pointed out to sea. Shutters clicked and the tourists exclaimed as whales breached amid vast sprays of water.

Over the next week she sailed the Inside Passage, stopping at

Juneau and Ketchikan before landing in Vancouver and flying back to Anchorage. Short stays in most places—just enough time to look around, talk to people in the shops, get a feel for how it would be to live there. She still hadn't seen Seward where Lois spent her winters so she took the train south and spent two days in that lovely little seaport town, then returned to Anchorage to make her decision.

At times guilt assailed her. Ben called frequently. He was very possessive and clearly did not understand what she had chosen to do. Grace worried about his marriage. Susan also called and although she was supportive she talked about a man she was dating who was still married.

Family. It just didn't get more complicated than that.

Grace spent two more days in Anchorage pondering her next move. Although she had seen many spectacular towns on her tour of Alaska, only two places spoke to her heart—the picturesque coastal town of Seward, which she had seen only briefly, and Denali's wild charm.

I'll go back to Denali first, she mused. *It's getting late in the season and Lois will be getting ready to close the lodge. At least I can scout out employment opportunities in that area for next year. Then I will head south to Seward, have Susan ship the rest of my belongings, and spend the winter.*

She was getting ready for bed when her cell phone rang. She grabbed the phone from her purse on the third ring.

The voice that answered her "hello" sent a chill up her spine. She recognized it at once. His voice was deep and warm reaching across the distance.

"Grace, it's me, John Hathaway."

Just the way he said her name unsettled her.

"Well, hi. Where are you?"

"Sitka. I finished my research last week. Now I'm taking a little R & R and looking for a nice quiet place to put the article together. And you? Where are you?"

"Anchorage. I've done the tour and am about ready to go back to Denali. I'm taking a second look. My choice has been narrowed down to Seward and Denali. I guess it will depend on the job opportunities. My travels didn't take me to Sitka. Where exactly is it?"

"It's an island in the Bay of Alaska midway between Juneau and Ketchikan. A quaint fishing town . . . you'd like it. Too bad you didn't get to see it. Ah . . . will you be in Denali long? I'd like to see you again and it just might be a good place to write."

The oddest sensation invaded Grace's stomach. He wanted to see her again. Her hand trembled as she grasped the phone. The last time she'd felt anything like this was the time, back in high school, when Peter called her for a date. There had always been a powerful physical attraction between her and her husband and she felt the same pull now.

"I have no specific time frame." She paused, and laughed. "Isn't it wonderful to be able to say that? To have no pressure of time."

"Why don't I come to Denali, then? Where will you stay?"

"The Princess Lodge for now. I'm afraid it's very busy, though—a hubbub of tours. Another more isolated place might suit you better."

"Why don't I book into the Princess for one night and then decide. This is Sunday. It will probably be Tuesday or Wednesday before I can get there."

"Wonderful. I'm . . . uh . . . eager to hear all about your travels in the Tongass."

What she dared not say was that it was him she was eager to see.

"I'll call this evening and let you know my travel plans. Bye, Grace."

"Bye, John."

The next morning after a quick shower she called the Princes Lodge and made reservations for a week, then called Lois to say she would arrive in Denali around three that afternoon. Lois was full of questions but said she would have Marvin pick her up at the Princess around four and bring her out to the lodge for dinner. Her questions could wait till then.

Over a scrumptious meal of stewed venison Grace recounted her travels and her conclusions. "For now I'll secure lodging in Seward and spend the winter. I'm in no hurry to get a job, in fact I want to be free to go east and spend the holidays with my family. I might just settle for volunteer work at the local senior facility. What do you do to keep yourself occupied during the winter?"

"I normally volunteer at the library but I'm afraid I won't be there this winter. I'm going to get a two-bedroom in Anchorage so Jill can stay with me. She needs the financial support and she will have better job opportunities in the city. However, you might be interested in my room at Mrs. Benoit's Arctic Paradise B & B. She is a lovely lady, a wildlife biologist, and offers wildlife tours and adventure packages. I think you would love her and the room is clean and homey."

"Great . . . I'll look into it . . . but I'm sorry you won't be there."

"Jill needs me," Lois said simply.

After dinner Grace and Lois carried tall glasses of iced tea onto the lodge's wrap-around porch. Guests sat on Adirondack chairs, murmuring among themselves, busily snapping pictures of Mt. McKinley—its overall whiteness tinted a hazy blue, lavender and gold by the evening light. After claiming two empty chairs they sat in silence absorbing the peace of the park. The broad expanse of flat tundra stretched before them before it disappeared into neighboring spruce forests. A golden eagle wheeled high in the sky, haymice chirped in the grass.

Grace couldn't remember the last time she had felt so utterly content. It flowed through her like molten gold and she closed her eyes feeling a closeness with God she had never experienced. No wonder Lois called this place her spiritual home.

After a prolonged silence Lois spoke. "How long do you plan to stay in Denali?"

Grace remembered with a jolt that John would be arriving in a few days and that all of her plans were completely up in the air. She took a gulp of tea and did not meet Lois's inquisitive eyes. "I really don't know. I had a call from a friend yesterday who plans to stop by Denali to see me. He may be here for a few days."

"He?" Lois smiled.

Grace felt the heat rise in her face. "Yes, I met him at the Anchorage airport." She chuckled. "My luggage was lost and he took me to the claim office. Then I ran into him again on the excursion train from Denali to Fairbanks. We had dinner together in Fairbanks."

"Hmm"

"Silly as it sounds, when he called I got all flustered." Grace leaned back in her chair with a rueful grin. "I'm too old for this sort of thing."

"Nonsense. As long as you are breathing you are not too old. I think it's wonderful that you've met someone who brings some excitement into your life."

"I feel like a giddy youngster. Look at me, I'm blushing." She sighed deeply. "It's not a good idea to get involved with him."

"Why not?" Lois said, then rushed to add, "if it's none of my business say so. But if you want to talk, I'm a good listener."

"Lois, I'm free for the first time in my life. And, as I told you earlier, Peter was ill for a number of years before he died and I cared for his mother for a long time before that. John and I are both seniors and who knows what lies ahead. I know it sounds callous but I don't want to be a care giver again."

Lois reached over to pat her hand. "I understand. You need to grow into your own person . . . develop your spiritual health. Aren't you jumping the gun a little, though. Being good friends with a man doesn't have to entail marriage."

"Oh, I know that. It's just that I am so attracted to John it scares me."

"Tell me more about him."

Slowly Grace recounted all she knew.

When she finished Lois nodded her head sagely. "From what you have told me he sounds like he has all of the qualities important in a man . . . intelligence, character, an interest in ecology. It certainly sounds like a friendship worth cultivating."

"He needs a quiet place to finish his article for the newspaper. You showed me an empty cottage the last time I was here. If it's still empty and he is interested would you be willing to rent it to him?"

Lois thought for a moment. "It's only available for a short time. You know we are closing for the season on the fifteenth. I planned to get an early start on winterizing, that's why I didn't offer it to you, but if he needs a place to write bring him out and let him have a look." She flashed her sweet smile. "Besides I'm a nosey old devil. I'd like to meet him."

CHAPTER TEN

John called the next day to say he would arrive Tuesday afternoon by train.

That night sleep would not come. Grace tossed and turned, her emotions in chaos. She knew she did not want to marry again. But what eluded her was what she did want to do with her future. Common sense told her she was tempting fate. She should meet John tomorrow, maybe have dinner with him, then move on. She had plans and they did not include a romance.

And then, there he was, striding down the steps towards her, with his shock of silver-gray hair glinting in the sunlight, a large dog trotting by his side.

Grace's knees felt like rubber. She hesitated for a second, then ran forward to give John a quick hug. The dog pushed between them and whacked her with his tail.

John chuckled. "Grace, may I introduce you to Bandit. Bandit this is Grace."

Bandit cocked his head, first to the left, then to the right, evaluating her. His liquid eyes locked on hers and he gave her a doggy grin.

She held out her hand. A wet, black nose poked into it and a friendly tongue lapped her palm. Grace's lips curved with laughter. "He's delightful, John."

"I think so too." He reached down to scratch Bandit's ears. "He's also my best friend." Bandit wiggled his rear end with pleasure.

John looked around as he pulled out the handle of his wheeled suitcase. "How far is the hotel? Do we need a cab?"

Grace pointed. "Just up the hill. We can walk easily." Chattering nervously, she led him and the dog up a winding brick walk to the

Princess Lodge. "I hope you checked about the hotel's policy regarding dogs," she said.

"I did. They are pet friendly. Surprisingly I haven't had a bit of trouble in Alaska."

They entered the lobby and she stood quietly by John's side as he registered for a single room with a king size bed. The desk clerk threw her a knowing grin.

John picked up his key. "Give me an hour to get settled and freshen up. Then we can have dinner together and catch up on our mutual travels."

"Great. I've so much to tell you."

"What room are you in?

"401."

"I'll pick you up around five."

Afterward, Grace could not have said what she had to eat. She was enthralled with his stories about his journey into the rain forest. He was serious one moment, then had her laughing the next. The tale of Bandit and his romance had her in stitches.

For his part John listened intently to an accounting of her voyage through the Inland Passage. He seemed puzzled by her return to Denali and her fascination with the wilderness area. "Denali does not strike me as a hospitable place to make one's home," he said.

"It seems to answer a deep need in me I can't quite explain. I just want to spend more time here before I make a major decision." Her eyes danced. "Besides I appear to be impossibly drawn to a pack of wolves that den nearby."

John chuckled and signaled for the waiter. "What is so intriguing about wolves? Sounds like fodder for an article by yours truly."

"They have a strong family structure, similar to humans. The dominate male and female mate for life and the care and feeding of their offspring are the prime concern of all the aunts and uncles in the pack. Wolves are seriously maligned by people. We make them out to be wanton killers when in truth they hunt only to eat and feed their young."

"I guess it's what they eat that scares the hell out of us."

"Come on John. They don't kill people. They hunt deer and elk. And those herds are kept strong because it's only the old and weak that are their natural prey not the strong and swift. Wolves used to hunt buffalo but man ended that. The buffalo were viciously slaughtered for their hides until they became extinct." Grace's eyes shone with intensity.

John nodded. "The biggest threat to man on this planet is mankind itself. We know that, yet we keep blundering on, refusing to learn from history."

The waiter brought their check. "I hear music coming from the lounge," John said. Would you care to have a drink?"

She was playing with fire. She should say no.

"Yes," she said. "I'd love to."

Grace ordered Chardonnay, John a whiskey sour. The lighting was subdued, a combo played music from the forties and a small fire crackled in a fireplace.

John led her to the tiny dance floor. The last time she had danced was at her fiftieth wedding anniversary. She smiled at the irony of the music. The combo was playing "The Second Time Around." A momentary flash of betrayal pricked her consciousness, then she relaxed as the music thumbed through her. John slipped his hand behind her back then tucked her fingers into his other hand. He held her gaze as he pulled her close. Her head nestled against his shoulder as slowly they began to move to the music. She could smell the starch in his white shirt. A shiver ran down her spine and she felt a heady rush. She raised her head and looked into his eyes. They were warm and brown. And knowing.

Grace was barely conscious of the other couples on the dance floor. As the music played she leaned in so close she could feel the beat of his heart. His eyes were closed and his hand tightened on hers. In that instant nothing else mattered. Not the problems this might present, not the fact she might never see him again. Only this, only this night, only the feel of his masculine body pressed against hers. They moved in languid circles on the tiny dance floor, oblivious to the other couples, in a world of their own.

The music stopped and reluctantly she let herself be taken back to the table. What would happen now? She didn't know if she knew how to do this anymore. Still, some romance would be nice—it had been a long time since a man made love to her.

They had another drink, then another dance. The lounge was beginning to fill with noisy tourists and cigarette smoke hung heavily in the air.

"It's a mild evening and still light for another hour or so. Let's leave and go for a walk," John suggested.

They strolled in the fading light, past the small shops with their doors open. At the end of the short street they settled on a bench away from the lights. John gently took her hand, raised it to his mouth and brushed her knuckles to his lips.

She couldn't breathe. Oh, my. This would never do. She had to think of something inane to say to defuse the moment before she dissolved in a puddle at his side.

"I talked to Lois Yost yesterday," she said. "Remember I told you about visiting her at Eagle's Nest. It's a lodge deep in the Denali wilderness. She happens to have an unexpected vacancy in one of her cabins. It might be an ideal place for you to write your article." *And put a little distance between us*, she thought.

John shot her a puzzled grin. "Deep in the wilderness? Not trying to get rid of me are you?"

"Oh . . . I . . . it's really not that far. *Deep* is probably misleading, but it is isolated and accessible only by a gravel road."

"I'll admit this place is swarming with tourists. I would like a quieter place to work."

"Then, let me show you Eagles Nest. The park road is closed to private vehicles past mile post fourteen but Lois will have someone pick us up. She provides a shuttle for all of her guests."

John stopped and turned to face her. His soft brown eyes seemed to engulf her. "Would we be able to see each other from time to time?" he asked quietly.

"If you want to," she answered struggling to keep her voice from shaking.

"I do."

Slowly they wandered back to the lodge and down the open passageway to her door. She withdrew the plastic entry card from her purse. "Thank you, John. I had a lovely evening."

They were standing close together, almost touching. As he looked at her, heat flooded her cheeks and she heard his breath catch.

"I'll see you in the morning for breakfast?" he asked.

She nodded. He leaned down and gave her a lingering kiss, then stepped back and she walked into her room.

As he walked away John's system was in a turmoil. *I wonder what she would have done if I had pushed the door open, entered the room, and threw her on the bed*. The thought shot straight to his groin. Maybe he didn't have a problem. Maybe with her it would be different. He didn't know why he had hesitated. Perhaps it was fear of failure that made him step back from that sweet kiss. He was physically attracted to Grace Maguire—no doubt about that. It left him alarmed and shaken. At this stage of life he didn't want to be interested in romance. Yet there was something about her—a vitality, a joy of life—that kept him off balance. Maybe it was a good idea that there would be some distance between them. He would be leaving in a week and almost certainly would never see her again.

Lois sent the lodge van in the morning and when John saw the cabin he knew it was the perfect place to write. He booked it till the fifteenth; the week should give him plenty of time to polish his article before he headed back to New York.

The cabin was small but had a sizeable porch and an un-obstructed view of Mt. McKinley. His unit was on the outer fringe of the cluster of rentals—perfect for the undisturbed peace he needed. With Grace's help he set up a small table and chair on the porch where he could work, weather permitting. Although the cabins were lit only by gaslight the main lodge had an electric generator where he could recharge the battery on his laptop computer.

Bandit loved the lodge. He had acres of tundra on which to run, strange burrowing animals to sniff out and snowshoe hares to chase. It was doggie paradise. Jill also had a pet, a Jack Russell terrier named Bruce, and the two dogs spent hours running and playing together.

John was writing, Bandit lolling at his feet—deep in a dream twitching sleep—the first time the distant howl of wolves cut through the darkness. Lured by the sound, Bandit bounded to his feet and took a step forward, head cocked and hackles up, beside himself with anxiety. He listened intently, then pointed his nose to the sky and issued an answering call long and wolf like, eerily wild and native, causing John to shiver.

"No, Bandit," John commanded.

Bandit froze, then with a whine, came back to press against John's side. John reached down to comfort him. "I understand, fella. Your reaction is pure wild instinct. It's a call to you're ancestors, long gone, howling down through the centuries. In fact, all you dogs, big and little, are the direct descendants of those wild wolves." He stroked Bandit's silky ears and chuckled softly. "Hard to imagine when you see a strung out dachshund with stubby legs, isn't it? That's genetic engineering, fella: man fooling around with Mother Nature."

Bandit looked at him quizzically, turning his head from side to side.

Another mournful call cut through the darkness and Bandit answered. John reached down and grabbed the scruff of his neck to restrain him. *The instinctive urge to join these wild animals must be tremendous*, he thought. *For Bandit's own protection I must keep him on a leash when we go outside.*

Marvin stopped by the cabin the next afternoon and over a cup of coffee they talked about the wolves. "Three wolf packs live in Mt. McKinley park," he said, "each within a clearly established domain. The dividing line between these territories are set off by scent posts—clumps of grass, an exposed root, even a rock—on which the wolves urinate. Each pack patrols the borders of its territory leaving a scent signal to warn other packs to stay out. It takes one hell of a lot of pee but all members of the pack pitch in."

John laughed. "And what about the howling? What is it used for?"

"Either to advertise the pack's territory, or to keep another pack from trespassing, or just for fun. Wolves love a good howl," Marvin assured John. "Before a howling party starts, the pack members wag their tails and whine. Then one starts to howl, pointing its muzzle skyward. The howl may last from one to fifteen seconds. Then another wolf joins in, and another, until the whole pack is howling. I'm told it's their way of communicating—they are really talking to one another."

"I worry about Bandit's response," John said.

Marvin shook his head as he got up to leave. "I've seen you leave the dog run loose on the tundra. That could be dangerous."

"He loves to run free. I guess you're right, though. I'll keep him on a leash."

"How'd you like to take our wilderness tour. I might be able to show you some wild wolves."

"I'd love that. Grace seems intrigued by them."

"This afternoon? I have a small group going out."

"I can do that. What time?"

"One o'clock. I'll pick you up here."

The van horn sounded and John hurried out to the shuttle. Two other couples, Joe and Rhoda Silverstein from Maryland and Jim and Angela Redcay from Minnesota, were already aboard. Marvin shot a smile at John and patted the seat next to him.

They hadn't gone a mile on the park road when they had to brake to let a lumbering elk cross the road. Marvin drove at an unhurried pace, arm hanging out the window, and in his gruff, heavily accented voice explained the wildlife that inhabit McKinley Park.

"You'll see the moose, the caribou and the Dall sheep. They each have their own place in the park and rarely compete for food. The moose browse mostly on aquatic greens in marshy areas where they live. The caribou summer on the tundra and up in the alpine pastures where they feed on lichens and assorted plants and shrubs. The sheep live high in the mountains among the rocks and eat grasses and other plants.

"The biggest herds are the caribou. Both males and females carry antlers; though no two pair are alike." He grinned. "The boy's are bigger. They're handsome to watch in large herds but up close caribou look odd. They have big, big feet. From a distance you'll think they're wearing overshoes." He laughed at his own joke.

"What about reindeer?" Mrs. Silverstein asked.

"They were brought over from Siberia in the 1890s and for a while they did well. But instead of being herded back and forth from winter to summer ranges they were allowed to stay on the same range year around. That was dumb. They soon over grazed the slow growing lichen. It takes lichen from fifty to one hundred years to regenerate and there was no chance for the range to recover. Reindeer died by the thousands and today there are few left in Alaska."

John suddenly asked Marvin to stop. He pointed off to his left where high on the mountainside they could see numerous white spots. While they watched the spots began to move.

"Dall sheep," Marvin said. "They're the only white wild sheep in North America . . . about the handsomest animals anywhere."

"Could we get closer?" Joe asked.

"Further ahead the road curves and hugs the mountain cliffs. We may see a few there and if we're lucky we might get to see another species of Alaskan wildlife. This area is used heavily by denning Toklat wolves. Igloo Creek Campground was recently closed to protect the packs."

"To protect the wolves," Mrs. Silverstein retorted. "What about the people?"

Marvin's face grew hard and angry. "Never, in the reported history of our people, has a wolf killed a human. The poor animals have been persecuted and harassed for so long they've developed a fear of humans. Wild wolves tend to run away, but here in the reserve they have become used to seeing people and seem to have lost their fear. So, rather than run the other way when they see a human, they just stand and watch you. As curious as you are."

"Well, I for one don't want to get close enough to find out if they are curious or hungry," Mr. Redcay said with a loud guffaw.

John listened intently as Marvin proceeded to talk about pack behavior. Slowly Marvin pulled the van to the side of the road and continued to speak in hushed tones. "There, halfway up the slope, you can see the wolves. They probably have taken over an abandoned fox den in those rocks."

"I count at least four," Mrs. Smith cried in excitement. "Oh, and over there several are lying down."

Marvin nodded. "They nap during the day and hunt at night."

They watched the pack for several minutes but Mr. Redcay was anxious to move on. He wanted to see a bear so he could brag to his friends back home. They did see a lopping herd of caribou and several more curly-horned Dall sheep but, unfortunately for the Redcays, no bear.

Whatever the reason for the wolves "howling parties" John did not immediately enjoy the chorus although eventually he came to appreciate the full-throated, low pitched, melodious communication between the wolves. The deep, mournful moan that poured forth from a wolf's throat was one of the most stirring and beautiful of all wilderness sounds. He remembered a line from Jack London's 'Cry of the Wild' that said "it was invested with the woe of unnumbered generations."

On Saturday morning John was at his desk, hard at work, classical music on his battery radio playing softly in the background when he looked up to find Grace coming around the corner of his cabin, a Thermos in her hand. He was jolted by the amount of joy he felt at seeing her. Not that she hadn't invaded his thoughts at the oddest times—especially at night when he lay alone and cold. Only last night, for the first time in his life, he had allowed Bandit to sleep beside him on the bed.

As she drew closer he began to laugh. She was covered with red blotches. Her face, arms, and legs were smeared with some type of chalky lotion. It was not a pretty sight.

Grace's green eyes, crinkled at the corners from years of laughing, looked sad. "The travel brochures never mentioned mosquitoes."

"Try Skin-So-Soft. It's a good repellant."

"So I've been told," she said reaching up to scratch her ear. "It's chilly. I thought maybe a cup of hot coffee would taste good."

John jumped to his feet. "Wonderful. The weather is turning cold." He took the Thermos from her hands and looked at her with raised brow. "How did you get here?"

"The park service shuttle to Savage River, then I rented a bike." She reached down to massage her thighs. "I may not be able to walk for several days." She smiled brightly. The expression lit her eyes with a warmth he could almost feel.

"I'm glad you came. I've been looking for an excuse to take a break."

Bandit brushed against Grace's leg and looked up at her with adoring eyes. The old boy was completely smitten. Grace idly scratched his ears and Bandit closed his eyes in bliss.

John took two mugs from the cupboard. He carried them out to the table on the porch and poured the steaming coffee. *Ah, hazelnut*, he thought with delight, inhaling the tantalizing scent. *This lady knows the way to a man's heart.*

Grace took a seat at the small table and Bandit flopped down beside her, his big head on her foot. "Tell me more about your trip," she said. "You were pretty general when we talked the other evening."

"It was awesome, honey. Someday you must see a rain forest for yourself. It's unique and beautiful, teeming with unbelievable wildlife. Midsummer is a prime season for grizzly bears, that's when the salmon come upstream to spawn. They furnish the bears with unlimited dinner. The entire Tongass is crisscrossed with tens of thousands of salmon streams. At one stream near Juneau you could actually walk across the backs of fish to the other side. And, of course, the bears know that. And the eagles. The branches of huge landmark trees were filled with beautiful bald eagles waiting to swoop down and feed on the fish."

"Why do they call them landmark trees?"

"I don't really know. I'm told the Eskimos used to call them temple trees, because that reflected the way the natives viewed those forests. The trees are massive and numerous, there is a sense of being . . . well . . . of being in a place of worship."

"I wonder why they changed it. I like that name. Temple trees."

John frowned. "I think because it smacked of environmental zealotry. You know—people laugh at naturalists, calling them tree-huggers, interested only in preserving the habitat of the horned owl and other exotic species. Then they gasp with surprise when they see photos of landscape that was once teeming with wildlife now barren as a moonscape."

John went on to explain the two sides of the problem; on the one side the acres of clear-cut logging and miles of abandoned roads, and on the other side the economic effect of mill closings. Slowly they drained their cups of the fragrant brew and John rose to refill their mugs. "I've finished a draft of the article. Now, I need to polish it . . . what we authors call a "rewrite."

"Are you happy with it?" Grace asked.

"Very. I tried hard to present both sides of the picture . . . not to let my personal feelings influence the piece. I'll admit that was hard because, as you know, I feel very strongly that government greed is responsible for over cutting."

"But you mentioned the economy of the area. Didn't the closure of logging camps affect a lot of people?"

"It did. I talked to a number of Native Americans. They say logging made many of them wealthy, but it wiped out fish and game too. They admit that tourism is easier on the land. To the untrained eye the Tongass looks as pristine as it might have two hundred years ago. However, when you go in with experts, as I did with Richard and Larry, you learn that human hands have changed it significantly." He smiled at Grace. "I have a copy of the article if you would like to read it."

"I certainly would." Her eyes twinkled. "Any rules about what I should say?

"I guess the truth would be fine."

"Are you open to criticism if I disagree with you?"

"Of course."

John went into the cabin and came out carrying his briefcase. He sat down, swung it onto his lap, took out a sheaf of papers and handed it to her.

"Now don't be too hard on an old fellow," he teased.

"I won't." Grace dropped her gaze. She looked down at her coffee cup, picked it up, held it, replaced it in the saucer. "I guess this means you'll be leaving soon?" she asked with a hitch in her voice.

John averted his eyes. There was a thoughtful silence. "My rental here expires next Sunday and I understand Mrs. Yost will be closing the lodge for the winter. I've made my reservation to fly home next week. Friday, in fact."

"I see. I . . . I'll miss you."

"And I'll miss you." John noticed Grace's lip tremble. "We'll keep in touch though," he added hurriedly. "Now, enough about me. What have you been up to?"

"Well, first of all Lois's daughter secured a job at a Great Western in Anchorage and will be leaving tomorrow. Lois asked me to stay and help her close up."

"Will you stay in one of the cabins?"

"No, I'll stay in the main lodge with Lois. I can use Jill's room. As the cabins empty she wants to get them winterized. Marvin will take me back to the Princess tomorrow and wait for me to pack and move out."

"Great."

"And there's more news. I checked the Internet for job opportunities at Denali. The area near Kantishna has several lodges with a number of openings for next season. The one that particularly appeals to me is for a beginning naturalist and guide at Big Bear Lodge. I called them and have an interview Tuesday."

John smiled. The job fit her. "Naturalist, huh. Think of all the PR you could do for those wolves you seem so attached to. Though, I'll admit I don't understand your fascination."

"I guess part of it is the comparison between the monogamous family structure of a wolf pack and our needs as humans."

He shook his head, his eyes dark with concern. "Will you stay in the park over the winter? I've been told the winters in Alaska are not for the faint of heart. One of the biggest problems, they say, is not the cold, it's the darkness. For many months you lose the sun all together. Can you cope with the endless hours of darkness?"

"Millions of Alaskans do. It can't be that bad."

"Well, I certainly wouldn't want to." With a negative shake of his head John picked up the empty cups. "It's a beautiful day and I've been promising Bandit a nice run. Would you like to go with us?"

At the sound of his name Bandit, lying with his head on Grace's feet, looked up and cocked his head.

"I'd love to," Grace said, "but I promised Lois I'd help to clean out the flower beds this afternoon and take down the hanging baskets."

"You'll have supper with me, though, won't you?"

She nodded. "I should be finished by four."

John removed Bandit's leash from a peg by the door and the dog leaped to his feet, tail swishing.

"I've taken to using a leash on him when we're out in the tundra," John explained. "There are wolves close by and I don't trust Bandit's self control."

"That's probably a good idea. I read the other day that the Park Service is considering a ban on all dogs and other pets inside the park. Unleashed dogs invade the wolf's territory and try to mate with their females, provoking incidents of aggression."

John grinned. "I'd get aggressive too, if someone tried to take my girl."

Grace actually blushed and started toward the door. John glanced toward the table. "Just a minute." He picked up the empty Thermos and handed it to her. "The coffee was great by the way. How did you know I was partial to hazelnut?"

"Lucky guess."

John fastened the leash to Bandit's collar and opened the door. "I'll meet you in the dining room around six."

Grace walked resolutely down the porch steps, then turned toward the lodge with a wave. He watched her go, his mind pondering her revelation that she had a job interview. It was upsetting that she appeared determined to make a new life in Alaska. What was more upsetting was the fact that he was upset. Why should he care? In another week he would be leaving for New York to resume his normal life.

Bandit gave an impatient bark and strained against his leash.

"Okay buddy, time to fertilize the tundra." John took off at a run determined not to think anymore about Grace Maguire.

Resolved not to show her despair Grace dressed carefully for dinner that night. She chose a silk skirt, navy with tiny white flowers, and a sheer white blouse over a white silk tee. With a secret smile she dabbed John's favorite cologne behind her ears and slipped into white sandals leaving her freshly shaved legs bare.

That night she and John sat for two hours, over repeated cups of coffee, talking and sharing memories of their respective childhoods. Something had triggered a memory of John's and he began to talk of his wife. At first he seemed hesitant, as though not sure of Grace's reaction, but after she told a funny story about a disastrous camping trip she and Peter had taken he seemed to relax and the words spilled forth. Grace sensed a great need in him to talk openly of his love for his wife. He told her of the hardship of his early married life, how Mary had worked to provide income while he attended college on the G.I. bill. They had two boys in rapid succession but her third pregnancy ended in a miscarriage. He and Mary wanted a large family but the doctor warned that she might not be able to carry another baby to term. John refused to let her take the risk.

He spoke proudly of his boys and his love for them. George, the youngest was not married but Adam had three girls. John admitted that the three grandchildren were the apple of his eye and he and Mary spoiled them unmercifully.

And then he spoke quietly of Mary's breast cancer and death. He had cared for her at home and she died in their bed. Tears swam in his eyes and Grace almost wept at his pain.

"You must have loved her very much," she said.

"I did. I loved her as much the day she died as I did when I married her. But life goes on . . . you know that as well as I." He swirled the liquid in his cup and stared into the fire. "I still feel a little guilty about the amount of time I spent away from home. I was always off on some assignment, sometimes gone for weeks. Mary was left to rear the boys and dole out the punishments. But she would just laugh and say she appreciated me more each time I came home. The only thing I can say in my defense is that she had my complete fidelity. I was never unfaithful to her."

Grace liked the fact that he had been happily married for over fifty years, that he adored his wife and had never wanted anyone else. She liked the fact that his children were grown, with happy lives and careers and that he was proud of them.

She sensed that he was confused and frightened at his growing attachment to her and she liked that too. He was gazing at her intently and she could see the anxiety in his dark brown eyes.

The last guest had left the dining room and it was apparent that the staff wanted to close for the evening. "Why don't we retire to the lobby," John said. "I see Lois has built an inviting fire and we can talk out there. I'm afraid I've dominated the conversation . . . I'd like to hear about your husband."

And so they settled, side by side, on the snug couch in front of the blazing fire and talked some more—of her marriage and family. Peter had been a child of the depression and his family could not afford to send him to college. He secured an unskilled laboring job at Allegheny Steel where he was working when he met Grace. Fresh out of high school, she was introduced to him at Lois Yost's wedding reception in August and they were married on Christmas Day. Ben was born a year later and Susan two years after that. Peter was intelligent and loyal and quickly worked his way up through the ranks where he held a management position when he retired.

It had been a good marriage—a close relationship. Peter loved classical music and was a self-taught cellist. They both loved to camp and fish and all of their vacations with the children were in the outdoors. She told John about buying the motor home and Peter's dream of a trip to Alaska. And with a quavering voice she spoke of his long, agonizing death after the unbelievable diagnosis of Lou Gehrig's disease.

It seemed to be catharsis for both of them, this freedom to speak freely of their love for their spouses—to compare notes about the bottomless depths of exhaustion and grief.

As they talked their shoulders touched and John held her hand in his. Logs hissed and fell into the grate as the fire died down to embers. Lois discretely turned off the lights except for a small lamp on the desk. Finally they fell silent and Grace tilted her head back to look into his eyes. She placed her hand on his leg and turned to face him.

"John, whatever is happening between us I think we need to go slowly. I believe we're both afraid of attachments in our lives right now."

"Yes, I am," he admitted. "I'm afraid of losing someone I love . . . again."

"I'm afraid of losing someone, too, John. And of being a care giver. More than that I'm terrified of the idea that someone like you, who has had more than their share of grief, would have to care for me. But there is something else." Grace let out a long deep, breath. "I like the feeling of freedom—of being in control of my own life."

"I understand that. May I write to you?"

"I'd love it."

"The question is where? Moving around like you do, how do you get your mail?"

Grace chuckled. "I keep in touch with Susan and she forwards it to whatever post office is closest to where I am staying. They hold it for me." She drained her drink. "It's getting late," she said quietly, "you'd better get home."

He looked at his watch. "Good Lord, it's past two. I do have to take Bandit out for a run before I turn in."

They rose, their eyes locked on one another. The glow of the dying fire flickered on his silver hair. He reached out and pulled her to him, crushing her against his broad chest. She could smell his woolen shirt and the faint odor of after shave. His kiss, gentle at first turned hard and warm. Her insides gave a lurch. She responded in a way that surprised and frightened her, allowing herself to sag in his arms, to press herself against him.

Then, she remembered. In two days he was leaving. For several long minutes she allowed herself to be held. God, she never wanted to let him go. Then she pulled away.

"Goodnight," she said.

"Goodnight, dear," he whispered. He walked away, turning once to look back at her, hesitating, then walking on.

Grace went in to bed alone, her thoughts turned to expectant dreams. But dreams were all they were. Real sleep would not come. She blamed it on the coffee but deep inside she knew that was not the only problem. Why had she pulled away? Was it a way of hiding from the truth? Hiding from the fact that this man stirred emotions and desires best left unexplored. She shook her head to rid her mind of the fantasy.

Monday John would return to New York and his old life. She would move on with her plans. Distance would solve her problem.

Grace was not the only one who could not sleep. John tossed and turned, in the end getting up to settle on the recliner with a stiff scotch on the rocks. Bandit was there, pushing his head onto John's thigh, trying to comfort him. Idly John stroked the dog's silken coat. The evening should not have ended like it did. Damn it all, he wanted to make love to this woman. Still, he could not dismiss the knowledge that when he pressed himself against her all the fire was in his mind and not in his groin. He groaned in frustration and Bandit cocked his head, looking at him with concern.

"It's an odd world, Bandit. Nature demands that we guys between the ages of, say, thirteen and sixteen, become walking hormonal erections. Yet, according to society, you are too young to do anything about it except suffer. Then when you reach seventy or eighty, with the maturity to handle anything that comes your way, nature often takes the ability away. God has a distorted sense of humor, don't you think?"

Bandit pressed a moist, black nose into the palm of his hand.

"I'm no better than a eunuch." John muttered. "Before I make a darn fool of myself with that lady I'd better get back to New York."

He downed his drink and returned to his bed, patting the mattress to invite Bandit to lie beside him.

CHAPTER ELEVEN

Monday, Grace moved to Eagles Nest and began to help close the lodge. That evening she and John shared dinner and talked about his article which Grace had given serious critique. Nothing more was said about his departure.

On Tuesday Lois drove her to Big Bear Lodge for her interview. The lodge was situated between Wonder Lake and Kantishna, a small mining community located at the terminus of ninety-five miles of restricted park road. Lois smiled serenely, her eyes shining with pleasure. "I love September when the Park closes the road leaving us without traffic and noise. Bears begin to disappear toward their dens, the motor homes migrate back into their rental lots, and the loons wing off toward warmer waters. You can feel the solitude of winter in the air. Ah, and the colors, Grace. The fall colors are unbelievable. Cranberries ripen turning the tundra bearberry red, the birches turn golden yellow, and the fireweed blossoms turn to cotton."

As they approached Wonder Lake Grace touched Lois's arm. "Pull off for a minute. There is a moose standing in the lake."

A bull moose, ankle deep in the shallow water, bobbed its antlered head up and down as it chomped aquatic vegetation. He paid no attention to the humans watching him. Lois drew in a deep breath of the brittle air. "Can you smell him? It's a catlike musk."

Grace wrinkled her nose. "I don't care much for it."

Lois laughed. "I'll admit it does leave something to be desired." She pointed across the road. "Reflection Pond, on the far side of the lake, is a favorite of photographers when the mountain is visible. Too bad it's clouded over today. The reflection of Mt. McKinley in the water has been immortalized by Ansel Adams. You've probably seen dozens of his photos."

Grace smiled. "I had a calendar of his, in fact I had several of the pictures framed."

They sat quietly for a few more minutes absorbing the inde-
scribable majesty of the mountain disappearing into the clouds,
then drove on. Within minutes Grace saw the lodge ahead of them.
Big Bear, like Eagles Nest, was built of cedar logs. It's rooms were
in a long, two story structure with no auxiliary cabins. A long deck
swept three sides of a screened porch, providing a panoramic view
of the towering snowcapped mountain. There were larger trees here
than on the tundra and the lodge nestled under the branches of
willow and birch already showing their fall colors of russet, gold
and red.

Grace's heart began to race. Everything about this place said
yes.

Mrs. Ross, owner of the lodge, greeted them on the porch. She
was a slender, middle-age woman with long brown hair pulled
back and plaited into a single braid that reached almost to her
waist. She had a warm smile and a strong handshake. Grace liked
her at once.

The interview went smoothly. The job, classified as a Guest
Services Beginner Naturalist/Guide, would run from June till mid-
September. Grace learned she would need a first-aid/CPR certification and a Class B commercial driver's license, but with her
experience driving a school bus she felt she would have no trouble
qualifying. She assured Mrs. Ross that she would spend the winter
studying every book available on the region.

"We close down completely for the winter," Mrs. Ross said.
"My husband and I have an apartment in Anchorage. Where would
you plan to live?"

"I'll admit I haven't given it much thought," Grace answered
with chagrin. "I might go back to Pennsylvania and spend the
holidays with my family. I don't need to work over the winter. A
summer job will be fine for me."

Mrs. Ross tapped her pencil on the desk and looked thoughtfully
into Grace's eyes. "I wish you had a degree in natural studies . . .
or more experience. However I like your maturity. I would like
someone who could return year after year. We get a lot of repeat
customers, especially fly fishermen, and they like to see familiar
faces. I normally hire college students wishing to pursue a career
with the National Park Service, but they come and go." She smiled.
"The job is yours if you want it."

It was all Grace could do to keep from jumping up and hugging the woman. "Oh, I do! I really do. It's a direction I want to take. Thank you."

For the next half-hour they discussed salary, uniforms, living accommodations and the job description. Grace left the office in a buoyant mood, her arms filled with books and manuals.

Lois was sitting on the porch waiting for her. The minute she saw Grace's grinning face she jumped up with a whoop. "You got the job," she sang, her eyes sparkling with joy.

Grace nodded. "Next summer . . . right here in this beautiful place." They enfolded each other in a tight hug.

She was loading her reading material into the back seat of the van when Lois cried out. "Look dear, the mountain is out."

They shaded their eyes and looked up to squint in awe at the jagged, snowcapped peak looming against the golden sky.

Grace's inner voice whispered: *Wow—this is why I wanted to come.*

"It's an omen," Lois murmured. She squeezed Grace's hand. "The beginning of your spiritual journey."

By Wednesday Grace realized John's time at the cabin was coming to a close. *Would he ever return? Would she ever see him again?* So far he had carefully skirted talking about his future after he left Alaska.

Just as she was returning from breakfast he called and asked her to have lunch with him. She dressed carefully, choosing a soft green lamb's wool sweater, bought in Skagway and never worn. She thought it deepened the green of her eyes. Would he notice? Her stomach contracted into a tight ball. Why did she care so much?

Lunch was almost over when he mentioned that he planned to catch the train from Denali early Friday morning. His flight from Anchorage to New York left at five P.M.

Was this it then? He was just going to leave—walk off into the sunset? She regarded him with cold speculation. "I have an idea," she said, her mouth tightened into a stubborn line. "We still have tomorrow and the weather is good. Why don't we take a long hike and see if we can get closer to that den of wolves I've seen several times from the park road. I've been wanting to do that ever since I arrived here. It will be our final outing together."

John looked a little doubtful. "It's supposed to turn cold. Do you have enough warm clothing?"

"Plenty. I have flannel lined jeans and an L.L. Bean parka rated for twenty degrees below zero. Come on, John. Let's do it."

He laughed. "You're just like one of my kids when they were little . . . always looking for a new adventure."

"I take that for a yes. I'll have the kitchen box us a lunch and we can make a day of it."

"Fine. I still have some packing to do. I'll see you in the morning . . . say around eight?" He walked her to the door and gave her a peck on the cheek.

As she walked away Grace shuddered with disappointment. Why hadn't he asked to see her tonight? If she hadn't suggested the hike tomorrow would this lunch have been his goodbye? She rushed back to her room, despair wrapped about her like a heavy cloak. She lay down on the bed and let the tears come.

Damn it all! She had let herself fall in love with this man.

Dawn came early the next morning, after only several hours of twilight, and the sun was full in a cobalt sky when she and John set out with backpacks loaded with cameras, binoculars, bug spray, bottled water, fat ham sandwiches, some cheese and several apples. John left a disappointed Bandit at the cabin, fearing his reaction if they got close to the wolf den.

A well marked trail ran from the lodge across the rolling wilderness. As Grace walked through the broad land of the tundra she could clearly see what set it apart from any other terrain. The few trees of willow or birch were small, almost hugging the ground. Tiny, delicate forget-me-nots peeked from rock crannies and arctic poppies swayed on slender stalks. Grace took a deep breath, inhaling the unusual spicy odor of the carpet of tundra vegetation crunching under their feet.

They had walked about a mile, following a streambed, when John held out a hand to stop her. "Do you hear that?" he asked in a strained voice.

The sounds, a mixture of whines, whimpers, and howls, were

coming from the far side of the stream.

"Wolves," Grace whispered. She trained her binoculars on the rolling tundra but could see no movement.

"There's a slight ridge running parallel to the stream," John observed. "Perhaps they are on the other side."

"Let's try to get closer, John. Head for that spot downstream by the clump of birches. The water is not as deep there."

Eagerly they hurried forward till they reached the spot she had spied. "It is shallower here. If we take off our shoes and socks and roll up our pants I think we can safely ford the stream," Grace said.

John's bushy eyebrows lifted to the middle of his forehead.

"Come on, I want to get closer," she said.

The water was icy and their feet grew numb in seconds as they picked their way across the stream. They lingered on the far shore massaging their toes until circulation returned. Thankful for their warmth Grace pulled on her dry socks and laced up her boots. Despite heavy applications of bug repellent they were tormented by clouds of mosquitoes.

Gingerly they picked their way across broken boulders and gravel ridges till they reached the far bank. The wolf yelps were much closer now and Grace assumed they must be coming from young pups at play. Grace began to inch her way up the steep ridge with John reluctantly following close behind. He started to say something and she put her finger to her lips. If there were pups on the other side she did not want to startle them.

As they neared the crest of the ridge John motioned for her to get down on her stomach. Silently they crept forward. Grace slowly raised her head to peer over the top and gasped. A sickening wave of terror swelled up from her belly. She was peering straight into the amber gaze of a full grown wolf.

The wolf, evidently supervising a half-grown pup stalking a field mouse in the near distance, was lying down—her nose not more than six feet from Grace's, her golden eyes shining like candles in the night. They stared at each in silence. For seconds neither moved, then with a spring the wolf sailed down the far side of the ridge and gave her pup a mighty shove forward.

John let out a strangled cry and grabbed Grace by the leg to pull her back from the ridge. They both jumped to their feet and flew back down the hill toward the stream. When they eventually stopped, gasping for breath, John pulled her into his arms. His face was ashen.

"My God, that was close," he said.

"But the wolf made no move to attack us. I think she was as frightened as we were."

"I doubt that. I was scared stiff."

"And my heart was doing flip-flops," Grace agreed, glad for the warmth of his arms still holding her. She shivered.

John looked up at the sky. The sun was fading fast, the air moist, an approaching storm telegraphed by billowing gray clouds. "We need to start back," he said, his face clouded with worry. "Alaskan weather can turn from sun to snow in the wink of an eye."

A cold breeze began to whip Grace's hair. She pulled the hood of her parka over her head and nodded, suffused with a growing uneasiness.

It began as a slanting rain driving into their faces, quickly turning into a stinging sleet. She could feel the sleet on her cheek, feel it working under the cuffs of her jacket. She bit her lip. *This could get very bad.*

John took her hand and pulled her to a clump of brush. "Hunker down and crawl under those branches," he commanded. "They'll give us some cover from the storm."

But the rain only intensified and soon turned into swirls of wet snow. The brush offered scant protection and Grace was trembling with cold, sheets of sleet punishing her face. "We have to make a run for it, John. It's getting worse."

He nodded and they crawled out from the thick brush. "I can't see a thing," he said, "but the stream is just ahead of us. I can hear it."

The creek they had easily forded earlier was now swollen— hissing and swirling around hostile rocks. John paused and watched it in numbed horror. "I don't know, Grace. It looks very treacherous."

"We must cross it though, to get home. And its getting darker by the minute."

John shielded his eyes to peer through the mist. "I can barely make out the copula on the roof of the lodge. We can't stay here, it is getting worse and the water is rising fast."

Grace waded into the pulsing stream and without hesitation John followed. She let out an involuntary oath as the icy water slammed against her legs and soaked her jeans. Damn, it was cold! Sloshing water quickly filled her boots as she struggled to keep her footing on the slippery river stone. She leapt for a flat rock protruding from the surging stream, gained a foothold, then with a scream began to slide. She tumbled forward. Her head hit the rock and she landed face down in the cold water.

Water filled her mouth and she began to choke. Barely conscious she turned her head sideways get air, had a sensation of drowning, then everything turned black.

"Grace," John yelled frantically. He was right behind her and grasped at the fabric of her jacket but the swirling motion of the flooding creek began to carry her downstream. She was getting away from him. He struggled through the raging creek, staggered once and almost fell before his legs took purchase in the current. Just then her now flailing body was slammed against a log partially submerged in the water. John thrashed his way toward her, reached out and grabbed a leg.

"Hold on," he gasped. "I've got you."

Fighting for a foothold he caught her in his arms and lifted her from the water. He struggled against the current, his balance and strength not what they used to be. Grace swung her head back and forth, coughing and spewing water, a strangle hold on his neck.

"Don't fight me," he yelled. Cradling her in his arms like a baby, he fought his way to the edge of the stream and stumbled up the bank. With a groan lowered her to the ground. Grace retched muddy water and lay gasping for breath. John sank down beside her and rested her head in his lap. He shook his head like a dog, throwing sprays of water in all directions.

"That was close," he moaned. "I thought you were going to drown. I never saw a stream come up so fast."

Grace issued a small smile and fingered the swelling lump on her forehead.

"Are you hurt?" John asked, his gaze raking her face.

"My head aches and I think I may have twisted my ankle." She shivered. "And I am cold."

John jumped to his feet. "We must get you home and into some dry clothes." He held out his hand. "Can you stand?"

With his help she struggled to her feet, then let out a yelp of pain. She sagged against him. "I think I've sprained my ankle."

"Put your arm around my neck . . . I'll carry you. It isn't that far." He swooped her off the ground and began to walk through the swirling snow toward the lodge. Her head rested heavily on his shoulder. "Keep talking," he said. "Your head hit that rock hard. You might have a concussion."

"What can I talk about?" she asked rolling her eyes. "The weather?"

He almost laughed. "That will do." He tried to pick up his pace. Damn she was heavy. It was all he could do to carry her. Thank heavens for his fitness regime at the Athletic Club.

"My cabin is closer than the lodge," he said. "We'll head for it. Keep talking."

John let out a deep sigh of relief as he reached the porch of his cabin. He pushed the door open with a bang and stumbled inside. Bandit, loping across the floor, tail swinging, slid to a stop when he saw Grace in his master's arms.

John carried Grace to the small bedroom, deposited her carefully on the bed, then ran to the closet for extra blankets.

Bandit jumped on the bed and with paws on her chest, swept her face with his tongue. Despite her misery Grace began to laugh. "It was almost worth today's terrifying events to receive all of this attention," she said.

John fought to control a grin. What a special person she was. She had been eyeball to eyeball with a wild wolf and later almost drowned in rampaging water and here she was laughing with that easy smile he had grown to love on her face.

"Down, boy," he commanded, pushing Bandit aside and draping a blanket around Grace's shoulders. She was soaking wet. "You must get out of those clothes and into something dry. I'll get you a pair of my pants and a shirt." He hurried to pull the warmest things he could find from the closet, then hunted in his dresser for heavy socks. Thank heavens he had not yet packed. With a smile curving his lips, he pulled out a pair of undershorts and added it to the pile. *What the heck—they're warm and dry,* he thought ruefully.

He dumped the clothes onto the bed, nudged Bandit out of the way and pulled Grace to her feet. "Lean on my shoulder. I'll help you into the bathroom. While you change into these dry clothes I'll build a fire and get ice for your ankle."

"You're wet, too," she protested.

"After I get you settled, I'll change. Now, be a good girl and listen to Daddy. Can you manage yourself?"

"Are you offering to help," she asked with a coy smile.

John felt heat rise to his face. Her wet blouse clung to her body, the nipples of her breasts clearly revealed. Christ, even soaking wet she was beautiful. He wanted to sweep her into his arms and devour her.

Instead he raised her to her feet and helped her hobble into the bathroom.

"When you're finished, just give a yell," he said gruffly.

In the living room John hunkered in front of the fireplace, his emotions whirling. He was well aware that the flash of desire he had just felt for this woman should have triggered a physical reaction. Yet it hadn't.

As he placed tinder on the grate and applied a match he wondered how to handle what was happening. Because something was definitely happening.

The fire caught and he added a few pieces of wood, fanning them into a blaze. Bandit pushed up against him and poked a cold nose against his cheek. John rubbed his big head. "It's a fine kettle of fish, boy," he said. "Here I am, in a cozy cabin in a snow storm, a beautiful lady in my bed and I can't do a damn thing about it." John sighed. "Bet you'd know what to do, wouldn't you?" Bandit pricked his ears and thumped his tail.

"Thought so."

After adding some larger logs to the fire John pulled off his wet clothes and donned dry jeans and a wool shirt. In the kitchen he pulled his last two steaks from the ice box. He had planned to ask Grace to stop for a goodbye dinner after their outing, but certainly not under these circumstances.

The snow had slackened, but about an inch covered the ground. John got Grace settled with the ice pack and a warm blanket. Before starting supper he phoned Lois, told her about the sprained ankle and that he was going to keep Grace in the cabin overnight.

"That's a good idea," Lois agreed with a note of laughter in her voice. He thought so too. As he hung up the phone he heard Grace call from the bedroom and hurried in to help her. She stood smiling in the bathroom doorway, dry in his oversize khakis and flannel shirt. He put his arm around her and helped her hobble to the bed. "Lie back and rest. I'll bring you something hot to eat in a minute." As he left the room he turned back to smile. Bandit was sitting tight against the bed, his big head resting on Grace's lap as she stroked his ears.

Despite the pain in her ankle Grace felt content and happy. Through the open doorway she could see John washing up the dishes from their steaks. Bandit was stretched out in front of the flickering fire, snoring softly. It was very domestic and peaceful.

John finished in the kitchen, tuned in some soft music on his portable radio, poured two glasses of Merlot from his last bottle of wine, and came into the bedroom to settle on a chair beside her. They made quiet conversation for a few minutes then lapsed into an easy silence as they listened to the music.

Bandit, lolled at their feet, lost in a dream-twitching sleep

John refilled their glasses but instead of reclaiming the chair he settled himself on the bed and leaned back against the pillow next to her.

"Do you mind?" he asked softly.

"No."

He put his arm across her shoulder and she leaned against him, detecting the mingled scent of after shave, wood smoke and wool. A masculine smell. She twined her fingers in his big hand and placed it on his knee. The muscle in his leg twitched.

He downed his wine and cleared his throat. "Grace, I don't want to push you, neither of us came to Alaska looking for love, but I think you know how deeply I feel about you. It's been a long, long time since I slept with a woman in my arms. I ache with the need to do that. Even if just for tonight."

With no hesitation Grace snuggled closer to him. She looked into his anxious eyes and smiled her answer. Their lips met in a long, satisfying kiss. Slowly she began to unbutton her shirt. He stood up beside the bed his gaze never leaving hers. Gently he pulled the sheet over her. Then he stripped and crawled in beside her. With no hesitation Grace snuggled close to him, thrilling as their skin touched and their lips met once more.

John put his arm under her head and she found a soft, warm spot on his shoulder. Somehow she sensed that no more was expected of her after this terrifying day. "Just hold me," she murmured. "It's enough just to lie in your arms."

They kissed. His lips were gentle, as gentle as anything she could ever remember. They held each other for a long time, talking in whispers. She was almost asleep when she heard the clip, clip, clip of toenails on the wooden floor. Bandit stopped at her side of the bed and looked at her, then trotted around to the other side.

He stood, tail wagging, head cocked, a quizzical look on his face.

John chuckled. "Not tonight Bandit. The most wonderful girl in the world has all my attention."

The next morning Grace woke to sunlight streaming through the window. She pulled the comforter up to her chin, cozy as a kitten in a basket. From the distant hills a wolf issued a long, mournful howl. John snored softly. She listened to the strong, steady beat of his heart. Sleeping beside him hadn't felt wrong to her. In a way a great burden had been lifted from her heart—as though she'd been given a second chance to carry on with a different phase of her life. She lay awake, thinking. Thinking of the path she had laid out for herself when she came to Alaska. Unencumbered. And here she was lying beside a man who had the power to change all that.

Or would their lives go on as though they had not shared this night?

She reached over and touched John's bare shoulder. She had to admit she was a little puzzled. She respected him for not being aggressive, for not pushing himself on her when he knew she had been injured and traumatized by the events of the day. Yet, it was evident they were falling in love, and they *were* in bed together. She had expected some physical advance on his part to take place.

She wondered why it hadn't.

CHAPTER TWELVE

John woke, disoriented at the presence of a form lying beside him. Then he remembered. He sighed and reached out to pull her closer. She turned over and he pressed himself against her back. They had spent the night curled in e ach others arms, her head pillowed on his shoulder. He inhaled deeply. The smell of her was intoxicating. *Pheromones,* he thought. *A woman smell.* It had been so long since he felt like this. Felt the heady rush of physical desire. For now it was enough. Enough to have someone to hold in arms that had been empty too long.

Yet disturbing thoughts crowded in to spoil the peace he had found moments earlier. John was frightened. Frightened by his growing feelings for this woman beside him, amazed that his feelings for her ran so deep, that he wanted to hold her forever. He had no problem with the idea of a simple relationship with a woman, a companion to take to dinner and a show, to accompany him to parties or outings with another couple. But something was happening here that he was unprepared for. His feelings for Grace had changed from someone he was very fond of, to someone he was falling in love with. He wasn't ready for that—it threatened to disrupt the very structure of the life he had established for himself. He had a life back east that he had no desire to change. She had apparently chosen a life in the frozen north that he had no desire to experience.

Weak sunlight filtered through the small window in the bedroom and he realized with a start that he was due to leave for New York today. Marvin would soon be picking him up to take him to the rail terminal in Denali. But Grace was injured and needed help. After last night he couldn't just leave her like this. He would simply have to change his flight plans.

Grace stirred and he kissed the back of her neck. "Sorry to disturb you, dear, but I must get up. I have to call Delta and change my reservation."

She raised herself on her elbows and smiled at him. "You don't have to do that. I'll be all right."

"I know I don't have to. I want to."

Her eyes glinted with pleasure. She swung her legs off the bed and tentatively tried to place weight on her injured ankle. John saw her wince in pain. He squatted beside her and tenderly ran his hands over the bruised flesh.

"You need an ace bandage and a crutch," he said. "Let me look in the closets. Maybe I can find something."

The only thing he could find was a sponge mop with a removable handle. He unscrewed it and tested the handle for strength. "I'm afraid this will have to do," he said, handing it to Grace with an apologetic smile. "I'll call Lois. She may have a pair of crutches at the lodge. Do you have your cell phone? The battery on mine needs charging."

Grace nodded. "Bring me my purse; it's in the living room." Grace eyed the mop handle. "This will get me to the bathroom. I'd really like to take a shower."

"Good. While you're doing that I'll call the lodge." After retrieving her phone he handed her the makeshift crutch and watched her hobble to the door. He watched her gaze sweep the tiny bathroom, glad it was tidy, his towels clean and his toiletries put away in his ditty bag.

"I noticed you have a stall shower," she said. "I think I can manage that."

While Grace was taking her shower he placed a call to the lodge. Jill answered and he asked her to contact Marvin and tell him that he would not need to be picked up as planned. Then, he told her about Grace's injury and asked about crutches.

"I don't know much about our medical supplies," Jill said. Lois is busy in the dining room but I'll ask her to call you when she gets a break."

John was getting dressed when he heard a beeping noise from the cell phone on the night stand. Then, thinking it was probably Lois returning his call, picked it up.

"Hello," he said.

Dead silence.

"Hello," he repeated.

"Is Grace there?" a man's voice asked.

"She's taking a shower. Is this Marvin?"

"No. This is Ben. Her son." The voice was loud and strident.

Oh damn, John thought.

Just then the bathroom door opened and Grace appeared in his bathrobe, leaning on the mop handle.

"Just a minute," John stammered into the phone. "She's right here."

He covered the mouthpiece and handed it to her. "Honey, I'm so sorry. It's your son. I never should have answered your phone. I thought it was the lodge calling about the crutches."

Grace's face turned white. She took the phone with trembling fingers.

"Hi, Ben," she said with forced gaiety.

John could hear the angry response. "Who the hell was that?"

"Just a friend who made his cabin available to me when I got caught in a winter storm and sprained my ankle."

The conversation continued, Grace reassuring her son that she was all right, that the man who answered the phone was just a good Samaritan.

Swiftly the tone of her voice changed.

"No, Ben. That is not necessary."

The reply seemed to make her more agitated.

"No," she insisted. "It is not necessary for you to come. It's a simple sprain. You have a job and a family. I am perfectly capable of taking care of myself. In fact I may be coming back to Pittsburgh for Christmas. I have a job but it doesn't start until next summer. I planned to write you a long letter telling you all about it."

Grace was able to shorten the conversation by saying that they were coming from the lodge to pick her up and she must be ready to go. She promised Ben she would call him later in the day.

When she hung up she looked at John with embarrassment. "I hated lying to him. I'm not sure he believed me. He wanted to catch the next plane to Alaska. He's very protective . . . he would go ballistic if he thought I had a boyfriend."

For some reason the word "boyfriend" shook John. He was not an adolescent.

They both jumped at a sharp rap on the front door. Grace pulled his bathrobe tightly around her and John strode across the room to open the door.

Lois greeted him with arms laden. A pair of crutches were grasped in one hand and a large bag of ice in the other. Her Jeep idled in the driveway belching smoke in the cold morning air.

"How is she?" Lois asked.

"She has a sprained ankle but no other injuries. Come on in, Lois."

He showed her into the bedroom where Grace perched on the side of the bed. While she recounted their adventure of yesterday to her friend John took the cell phone into the living room and placed his phone call to the airline. He returned to find Lois wrapping an ace bandage around the swollen ankle.

"Do you think she should go to the hospital for an x-ray?" John asked.

"I don't think it's necessary," Lois replied. "I felt the bone carefully and she can bear some weight on it. We'll just keep the leg elevated and apply ice to the ankle." She fixed Grace with a wicked smile. "I have my Jeep outside and can take you back to the lodge. Or would you rather stay here until Marvin comes for John?"

"I just called Delta and changed my reservation to Sunday," John hastened to say. "I'd feel better if I could look after her today."

Lois shook her head. "The problem is all of my guests are leaving and both vans are completely filled for tomorrow. I couldn't get another person in either one. I'm afraid you will have to let Marvin take you into Denali today. Unfortunately, he had to leave just now without you. Now you have missed your train."

"Lois, you must be very busy today with check-outs," Grace said. "You don't need this additional worry. When Marvin comes back why don't you have him pick John up? Then, he can drop me off at the lodge and I'll stay with you tonight."

"Good idea," Lois said. "You're right . . . I am busy. In the meantime you need something to eat. I'll send someone down with some coffee and muffins. It will probably be close to noon before Marvin returns to take John to the train."

With a jaunty wave she left.

While Grace dressed, her clothes still damp from yesterday's soaking, John placed a phone call to the Princess Lodge and was able to secure a room for the night.

A maid soon arrived with the welcome goodies and instructions to be ready to leave around eleven o'clock. After settling Grace on the couch with an ice pack John pulled up a chair and they hungrily devoured the muffins and steaming coffee.

They made small talk, John launching into a tale about a tent camping trip with his two young boys when it rained every day for a solid week. Grace tried to explain Ben's possessiveness, that he had never seemed to sever the umbilical cord, while Susan was just the opposite—independent as all get out. No mention was made of last night and conversation lagged. John brought his packed grip and jacket from the bedroom and laid it on a chair beside Bandit's traveling cage. Although the sun was bright and all signs of yesterday's storm gone, the room was chilly. John tucked an afghan around Grace, built a fire and brought them books from the bookcase. Bandit, stretched out on the floor beside the couch, whined in a doggy dream.

John tried to read but couldn't concentrate. His face grew pensive. He glanced at Grace, her face soft in the reflected firelight. The chemistry between them was volatile, threatening to burst into flames, but damn it all—he did not have a match to light that fire. And that worried him most of all. In his day to day life he was not bothered by his impotence. Never thought of it in fact. But if he were to allow himself to continue this romance with Grace, who was undoubtedly still capable of copulation, he would face constant humiliation at his ability to reciprocate. He could not face that. Last night had been wonderful—holding a woman in his arms, caressing her, kissing her. But he would be a fool to deny the inadequacy he felt at his inability to get an erection and make proper love to her.

She looked up. "Thank you for last night, John. I'll always treasure it. I needed to be held."

"So did I." A small frown appeared between his brows. "I . . . I feel guilty about leaving."

"Don't," she said. She twisted a ring on her finger. "And don't worry," she added. "When you leave, I'm not going to chase you back to New York."

John winced. "I almost wish you would. I thought I knew

exactly where my life was going. You've thrown a hitch into it."

She smiled archly. "As you have in mine."

A horn sounded in the driveway. Bandit bounded to the floor. John put his book aside and leaned down to kiss her on the cheek. "Marvin is here. I must be going."

He worried that she might break down and cry, instead she put her chin up and smiled bravely.

"We'll keep in touch," he promised.

She nodded.

He walked out the door.

BOOK TWO

CHAPTER THIRTEEN
Seward, Alaska
Two Months Later

Grace had been extremely lucky to secure Lois's lovely room in the bed and breakfast run by Mrs. Benoit. It was small but offered a full size bed, small kitchenette, two easy chairs and a private bath. Peter's cello, recently shipped by Susan, leaned against a tall walnut what-not in the corner.

Grace ripped open the letter from John and read it eagerly, her heart thumping wildly as she read that he was anxious to see her and was delighted with her plan to meet him in New York over the coming holidays when she visited her family.

She had a Red Hat chapter meeting in less than an hour so she stuffed the letter in the pocket of her parka to reread later and hurried out into the dark, still cold of an Alaskan December. Grace walked along the Seward beachfront, stopping now and then to throw a handful of stale breadcrumbs to hawking seagulls and screeching ravens. Snow scrunched beneath her boots, about a foot had fallen overnight, and her nose and cheeks tingled from the cold.

She wondered what the weather was like back in Pittsburgh. Well, she would know soon enough. Next week she would join the hordes of people traveling home for the holidays. She was anxious to see her children. She worried about Ben's marriage, suspecting that once the children were on their own he might leave Emily. And in her letters Susan mentioned a new love interest, Jason Davis, an architect with Lando Associates, a large commercial builder in Pittsburgh. Jason had children by a prior marriage and they would be spending Thanksgiving with him. He wanted Susan to be there, therefore Grace would spend that holiday with Ben, Emily and the grandchildren. Lord, how she missed the kids. Teddy wrote that he was a starter on the basketball team and that he now preferred to be called Ted. *In the blink of an eye they grow from childhood to mature adults*, she thought wistfully. She delighted that her grandson found the time to write to her yet felt an acute pang of guilt. Ted and Kelly were growing up without her and she was sorry for that.

She fingered the letter from John deep in the left pocket of her parka. She was still floating on a cloud from his endearments and the message she had been hoping for. He would like to meet her in New York between Thanksgiving and Christmas.

A brazen gull swooped low and tried to pluck the bag of crumbs from her hand. Angrily she swatted him away and the bird scolded her with loud squawks and furious flapping of wings. The tang of salt air was sharp in her nostrils. She hated to trade all this for the gaseous fumes of Pittsburgh and New York.

Grace emptied her bag of crumbs, then turned uptown to the Senior Center where the "Happy Hoofers" Chapter of the Red Hat Society was holding its monthly meeting. She had made no attempt to find a winter job in Seward, electing instead to read and study about the Alaska she had chosen to adopt.

She entered the large, cheerful room where three tables of women were bent over various craft projects. Grace waved, but made her way to the far end of the room, next to the fireplace, where a half dozen women, dressed in purple dresses and red hats, were gathered.

She pulled a chair next to her new friend, Joanna Wilson. Joanna was reading the quarterly bulletin from Sisters of Mercy Hospital in Anchorage and she waved it under Grace's nose. "There's a lecture in January, entitled Senior Sexuality. A large grin spread across her face. "Something all us widows need to know about, don't you think?"

"Who's giving it?" Grace asked.

"Dr. Jane Mackay, a Doctor of Gerontology from Alaskan University. Why don't we see if any of our Red Hatters are interested in going to hear her. You'll be back from the East by January, won't you?"

"Yes, two weeks with each of my children will be enough for all of us I imagine."

Grace didn't mention that she planned to see John during that time. Her heart did a flip-flop at the thought of seeing him again.

How wonderful it had been that night in the cabin when they hugged and cuddled each other. It was only in his arms that the feeling of yearning and sensuality overcame her. Maybe this lecture could answer some of her vague concerns.

"Find out more about it, Joanna. Why don't you send for some brochures, then we can see who might be interested in going. We can have dinner first, then go to the lecture."

"It sounds like fun," Joanna said.

Fun? Grace thought amused. *Well, maybe.*

It was Thanksgiving and two inches of snow covered the Pennsylvania countryside. Thanksgiving had always been Grace's favorite holiday, a relaxed, family time, without the frenzy and commercialism of Christmas.

Ben stood at the head of the table, carving knife in one hand, long fork in the other, a look of determination directed at the succulent turkey.

As Grace watched her son tears welled in her eyes. The older he got the more he looked like Peter.

Ben bent down and began to carve.

"I want a leg," Ted said.

Grace looked at him in amusement. He had some type of stickum on his red hair that made it stand up in spikes.

"I'd like a leg too, Dad," Kelly added. "I only like dark meat."

Ben looked bemused. "Since this bird only has two legs I guess that doesn't leave one for any one else. Do you think that is fair?"

Ted and Kelly cast guilty looks at their grandmother.

"I actually prefer white meat," Grace said with a wide smile. "We old folks have to watch our cholesterol."

"You aren't old, Grandma," Kelly said. "Anyone who can go traipsing off to Alaska and become a wilderness guide isn't old in my book. When I told Michael he simply couldn't get over it"

"And who is Michael?"

"My new boyfriend. He's pre-med."

"Where is this new boyfriend, today?" Grace asked.

"With his family. They live in South Carolina."

Emily picked up the bowl of candied sweet potatoes and passed them to Grace. "I'm so glad you came home for the holidays,

Mother. It wouldn't be the same without you. I hope it's the beginning of a tradition. Plan to come next year, won't you?"

"A tradition it is," Ben said. He gazed affectionately at Grace. "From now on you will spend every Thanksgiving with us . . . regardless of where you live." He smiled. "Although, I also think Christmas should be with us, not Susan. After all, we have children and a large house. She can come here."

Grace smiled weakly, but did not answer. *Still the same old Ben,* she thought. *Still making decisions for me like I haven't a mind of my own. Just like Peter always did.*

Plates were piled high, thanks given, and everyone began to eat. Emily was a marvelous cook, she had actually taken lessons at a prestigious culinary school in downtown Pittsburgh. When Grace had been the hostess, with the family dinner at her house, she always felt a little inadequate. Cooking was not one of her favorite pastimes.

Conversation flowed easily as Grace recounted her experiences in Alaska. Ted was fascinated by her stories about the wolves, then to everyone's delight she retold the story about the grizzly bear asleep at the side of the road during her wilderness tour of Denali.

"I can't believe you actually have a job there, Grandma," Kelly said.

"Sometimes I can't believe it myself."

Ben grunted. "Nor can I." Everyone fell silent. Then Ben loudly cleared his throat and said, "Mom, I don't know why you want to run off to New York. It cuts into your time with us and New York is no place for a woman alone," His eyes narrowed and he gave her a penetrating look. "I assume you are going to be alone."

"Of course, dear."

"I'd go with you, Mother," Emily interjected, "but I'm involved in the Christmas pageant at church."

Grace felt a moment of panic. The last thing she wanted was Emily tagging along when she met up with John.

"Thanks, dear, I'd enjoy your company, but I already have single tickets for two Broadway shows. I plan to do some shopping and look up an old friend who is living in Weehawken, New Jersey. She was recently widowed." The lies flowed off her tongue like melted butter. She was ashamed of herself—but not ashamed enough to tell the truth.

Plates were refilled and conversation drifted around the table. Emily told Grace of her plans to remodel the kitchen. Grace glanced at Ben who was listening with a stoic look on his face. How can they pay for a new kitchen if they are maxed out on their credit cards, Grace wondered.

"What do you think of Jason, Susan's new friend?" Ben asked his mother.

"I only met him briefly when they picked me up at the airport. He seemed very nice." She laughed. "In the cab they couldn't stop touching each other. I think they're in love."

Kelly nodded. "She told me she was . . . ah . . ." She stopped a-bruptly and lowered her gaze.

"Ah, what? Ted asked.

"Nothing."

"He is somewhat older than Susan," Grace commented, "and I understand he is divorced with three grown children.

"Susan would probably want to have children of her own," Ben said.

"She'd better hurry. Her biological clock is running out," Emily replied with a slight smirk.

Grace fell silent. She wondered what Kelly had been about to say. She desperately needed some private time with her Susan over Christmas. They had so much to discuss. It would be fun—girl talk, like they used to have when her daughter was a teenager.

It would be the perfect opportunity to tell her about John.

John hung up the phone and turned to find Bandit watching him with pricked ears. Could the dog possibly have heard her voice and recognized it?

"Yes, fella," he said, "that was Grace. She's in New York and I am going to see her."

At Grace's name, Bandit cocked his head. He issued a soft whine.

John laughed. "I know, I feel the same way. I may not groan with pleasure but I can feel this old heart of mine kick up a notch or two. She's uptown and I'm going to pick her up this evening for dinner and a show."

Bandit thumped his tail.

"She's staying at The Plaza. That's a pretty ritzy place." He reached down and scratched Bandit under the chin. "I'll admit I've missed her and it sure will be good to have someone other than you to talk to, old boy."

Bandit jumped up on the couch beside him, plopped his head in John's lap and looked at him with soulful eyes.

"No, offense, fella."

John had told Grace he would pick her up at 5:30. Curtain time was 8:30, that would leave plenty of time for dinner.

He hopped into a cab to keep his black business suit from wrinkling with the hoards of humanity on the subway. That soon proved to be a mistake. Traffic was bumper to bumper, horns blared, taxi drivers swore at one another. His stomach began to churn.

At long last he arrived, only fifteen minutes late, at the door of Grace's room. With bated breath he nervously knocked. The door opened and there she stood, her soft green eyes smiling radiantly. He swallowed hard at the sight of her. Without hesitation she held out her arms and he embraced her. Then he stepped back, framed her face firmly in his hands, and kissed her hard. My God he had missed her.

Heat flushed her face. "Well, hello," she stammered.

He was ready to settle his lips on hers once more, when she pushed him away with a laugh. "You'll be wearing all of my lipstick. Behave yourself and have a seat while I get my coat and purse."

Grace looked lovely. Her hair was cut even shorter and was held back from her face with two pearl-studded combs. She wore a black cocktail dress adorned with a single strand of pearls. The dress was of some type of silk material, and clung to her in all the right places. It was all he could do to keep from crushing her in his arms.

She reached into the closet to withdraw a black wool cape and handed it to him with a warm smile. He caught a whiff of her familiar cologne as he settled the cape on her shoulders.

"You look stunning," he murmured.

"And you, sir, look quite handsome." She gave him an impish

grin. "I've never seen you in a suit and tie."

"Guess not. It wasn't quite appropriate for the Alaskan wilds." He walked her to the door. "Now, I get to show you what life is like in civilization."

Grace found herself mesmerized by the fabulous city.

After dinner at Sardi's and the hilariously funny musical The Producers, John suggested a nightcap in the Plaza lounge. He chose an intimate booth in a quiet corner and ordered drinks, wine for her, a whiskey sour for him. Soft candlelight washed their faces and Grace leaned against John, her thigh touching his. She really didn't want to talk, she wanted him to kiss her again. Truth be told, she wanted him to take her to her room, throw her down and make love to her. Her blood heated. Whatever had gotten into her? She'd better get a handle on things or she would make a fool of herself.

"Thanks for sending me a clipping of your article, John," she said fighting for composure. "It was very thought provoking. Have you had much feedback?"

"Quite a bit. Not all of it favorable, I'm afraid. Although I tried hard not to be biased my sympathy for the ecological impact logging has on the rain forest did show through."

"All of the talk, nowadays is about global warming. What do you think? Is there a real problem or are the alarmists exaggerating the danger?"

"I certainly believe it is happening, and faster than the scientific community is ready to admit."

Grace smiled at him coyly. "Maybe you can talk your paper into sending you back to Alaska to write an article about the effect of global warming on the salmon industry."

John swirled the contents of his whiskey sour, his fingers trembling slightly. "I don't need an excuse to go to Alaska, I have a very good friend who lives there." He winked flirtatiously. "Would you like it if I showed up at your door?"

"I'll admit I've missed you."

"And I've missed you . . . much more than I want to admit."

They fell silent. Neither seemed to know what to say next. He ordered another drink and they made small talk, carefully avoiding anything of an intimate nature.

"I hope you don't have plans for tomorrow, Grace" he said. "Since you've never been to New York I'd like to pick you up early and show you around the city."

"I'm ready and eager. You say early . . . how early is early?"

"Eight A.M.? We can have breakfast here before we take off for the day."

"Then, I had better get upstairs and into bed. It's been a long day."

At her door John gathered her into his arms and lowered his lips to hers. His mouth was exploring hers, his hands pulling her to him. Her body seemed to melt into his and her pulse skittered crazily. He pulled her tighter and kissed her harder and longer. "I've been wanting to do that all evening," he whispered into her hair.

Gently, she placed two of her fingers on his lips and pushed him away. "I'm glad. Now, goodnight, John. I'll see you in the morning."

"Wear comfortable shoes. New York is a walking city. There's no better way to feel the pulse of this humming city than on foot."

"Thanks for the tip. I'll do that."

With a sinuous sway of her hips, she slipped into her room.

CHAPTER FOURTEEN

Thursday passed in a blur as John gave her the grand tour of New York. After a light breakfast at the Plaza, they walked to the nearby Apple Retail Store, an unbelievable modern building built entirely of glass and housing every computer gadget known to man. John was beside himself and Grace had to tear him away. Next they visited the famous FAO Schwartz toy store where they spent over an hour, then down Fifth Avenue, past the Museum of Modern Art, stopping to visit several elegant little shops. They strolled hand in hand, mingling with the crowds, going with the flow, while people zipped along beside them never missing a step. The air was bracing and the curbs were piled with freshly plowed snow. Walking close to the buildings protected them from a nipping breeze noticeable only at intersections. If the lights were with them, they crossed without discomfort. They laughed as they tried to time the crossings to avoid the gusts. Fifth Avenue had become less a casual stroll than a hustle to find a warm place to settle in.

They turned west on 44th Street with Grand Central in mind. Although it was still early, John said he'd already worked up an appetite for lunch and the Oyster Bar, below level in Grand Central, would be perfect.

They peeked into the high domed dining area with its red-checkered tablecloths but it was crowded and noisy so they opted for the bar, large and roomy with soft leather swivel chairs. Grace ordered a Maine Lobster Roll with Jicama slaw and John indulged in a fried oyster Po'Boy.

After lingering over lunch, with conversation both meaningful and mundane, John glanced at his watch. "Good Lord, it's twelve-thirty. We'd better get going—we still have a lot to see."

"Where next, Mr. Tour Guide?"

"Upstairs. Grand Central Station itself and its famous Information Booth Clock." They ascended the steps to the cavernous terminal, teeming with people, and John led her to stand beneath the clock. He pointed upward "For decades thousands of people have met each other, through war and peace, under this clock. Now look at the ceiling. It's painted to imitate the night time sky. The only problem," he continued, waving his arm skyward, "is that the sky and constellations are backwards. The manuscript that was used to paint the mural showed a reflected view from the Middle Ages. Most people, simply think that the artist reversed the image by accident, but Mr. Vanderbilt, when he learned of the error, excused it as simply God's view of the sky."

Grace was transfixed as she stared up at the ceiling, turning around and around, until she was dizzy. "Oh, look, John. There's the Big Dipper, and, over there," she pointed, "the Little Dipper. When the children were small we used to lie on our backs in Schenley Park on a clear night and point out the constellations to the children. This is wonderful. I could spend hours here."

"Sorry honey, there is a lot more of the Big Apple to see." He took her arm, leading her to the other end of Grand Central where they boarded the first downtown bus to Battery Park and the ferry terminals. Along the route, Grace began to see changing neighborhoods—some the original dwellings that housed the immigrants in the 1920s—and others "gentrified" by the influx of young professionals who scramble to New York after college and love the convenience of bus and subway to commute.

As they continued south another change began to take place. They were obviously entering Chinatown. Block after block of shops displayed colorful dragons on their signs and their windows displayed everything from Chinese kimonos to sausages and fresh poultry.

Grace leaned forward to peer out the bus window, her eyes shining. "Oh, this is fascinating. Can't we get off here?"

John looked at his watch. "Sure, why not. You want to see New York and this is New York as unchanged as you will find." He pressed the buzzer and the bus continued to the next corner. The driver opened the door for them to step down. "I'm as close to the curb as I can get," he apologized.

John gallantly scooped her into his arms to lift her across the slush-filled curb. Several people on the bus applauded. He beamed. Grace kissed him on the cheek and laughed light-heartedly.

They spent over an hour touring the streets of Chinatown. It was fascinating, each street different, characterized by their ethnic stores and restaurants.

They strolled slowly, stopping often, John an enthusiastic tour guide. "Chinatown's rich history not only tells the story of the Chinese-American experience, but also that of early Irish, Jewish and Italian immigrants, a unique historical experience not found anywhere else in the world."

"I love it," Grace said. She was rosy cheeked and excited. All of a sudden, her hand flew to her mouth and she stopped dead. "John, look at those naked ducks hanging in the window of that store."

John laughed. "Prepare yourself, honey. You'll see all sorts of strange displays in Chinatown butcher shops." He looked at his watch. "We need to hurry along if you want to visit a few gift shops. I'd like to catch the next Staten Island Ferry."

Carrying a few small shopping bags filled with souvenirs, and a bag of popcorn for the gulls, they stood at the curb for the next bus. One came along in minutes and they continued their trip to the ferry where they joined the crowds commuting to and from Staten Island.

Grace was overcome with the awesome movement of tugs, commercial fishing boats, cruise ships, and military vessels; more ships than she had ever seen in one place.

"Let's go stand on the front deck, I want to feed the gulls," she said.

"It might be too breezy. I don't want my girl to get cold."

"Still, the sun is glorious and we might just be chilly enough to cuddle." She looked up at him with a mischievous smile.

They worked their way past the parked cars to where gulls strutted on the railings, shaking their feathers and turning their heads to watch them with beady eyes. Grace threw popcorn into the air, laughing as the gulls dived and screeched overhead. John put his arm around her pulling her close as they gazed across the river at the breathtaking Manhattan skyline.

"This ride is so romantic, I can't believe it's free," she said. "Why would it be free?"

"Well, it's part of the Metropolitan Transit system and in the beginning the trip cost a nickel. Tourists loved it and the price stayed that way for a long time. Ultimately the fare was raised to a quarter and that was still a good deal. Then subways and busses went up to well over a dollar a ride and the Ferry would need to completely overhaul turnstile, equipment, toll booths, attendants, and so forth to compete, so Mayor Giuliani decided it should be free. It attracts tourists and is quite a novelty." He tweaked her nose and grinned. "That's why, Miss Curiosity."

By the time they arrived back to the ferry landing they were chilled to the bone. The huge terminal, with its jostling crowds, smelled like wet wool and their wet boots squished on the marble floors. John had planned to tour Wall Street but it was just too cold and getting dark. Instead he bought two hot chocolates from a vendor and they waited for the uptown bus.

As they rode through the darkening city Grace stared up at the lighted skyscrapers. "You know, John, although I spent all of my life on the fringes of a big city, I've forgotten the crowds, the traffic, the massive height of the buildings. It's so different from where I live now. I never want to live in the city again."

John gave her a shameless grin. "And I love the vitality . . . the excitement of New York. It is alive, it has a presence of its own."

"You would miss it, wouldn't you?"

"Yes, I would. I never want to leave."

As they exited the bus Grace spotted a little café on the corner and pulled at his sleeve. "John, I'm cold and terribly tired. Do you think we could just have a bowl of hot soup and a sandwich and call it a night?"

"Are you sure?"

"Positive. My feet are wet and I yearn for a hot shower. I really don't feel like changing to go out for dinner. It's been a full day." She smiled ruefully. "This ole gal ain't used to running around the city like a teenager."

He looked disappointed, but said, "Whatever my girl wants. A bowl of minestrone and a Reuben sounds good to me."

An hour later, he kissed her goodnight at the door and a weary but happy Grace fell into bed.

The next day it snowed. John gave Bandit for a quick run then took a subway uptown to meet Grace at the Plaza. They had breakfast before walking over to Bloomingdales where Grace loaded up on Christmas gifts for her family: a cashmere sweater in a new shade of boysenberry for Susan, a fish-finder for Ben's boat, the latest gourmet cookbook for Emily, a New York Yankees sweatshirt for Ted, and a nightshirt with a funny saying for Kelly.

On their way back to the Plaza Hotel to unload their packages and have lunch Grace noticed a horse and buggy parked at the front entrance of the hotel. "Oh, look," she cried plucking John's sleeve. "I've always wanted to take a ride through Central Park. Do we have time?"

"Sure, let's do it. It's the perfect day for a carriage ride. The road is clear and the park is beautiful in the snow." John hustled over to the driver and made a reservation for two o'clock.

After a tasty lunch of Quiche Lorraine and fresh fruit at the Plaza they climbed aboard the carriage and settled themselves on the gold-plush seats. A fringed passenger canopy offered scant protection from the falling snow but Grace laughed with delight watching the white flakes settle on her long woolen skirt. The driver tucked warm lap robes over their knees, then climbed up to his open perch at the front of the carriage. The white horse, resplendent with plume and fancy black leather trappings, clip-clopped onto Fifth Avenue, bells jangling, nostrils snorting in the cold, crisp air.

The carriage rolled through the park, past the Wolfman ice skating rink, carousel, pond and zoo. Silvery fluffs of snow clung to the branches of tall hemlocks, bending them low, chestnut vendors were on every corner, a nutty fragrance wafting on the fresh air. At Cherry Hill, a secluded alcove overlooking the lake, the driver pulled up and stopped briefly. He surreptitiously looked back at them—it is a well known spot for marriage proposals.

John gazed at Grace, snow dusting her thick-lashed green eyes, her cheeks pink. He put his arm around her and pulled her tightly against him. Under the blanket his hand dropped to her knee and caressed her leg. She looked up at him with surprise then gave him a small smile of acceptance and snuggled closer.

Love, in all its inexpressible glory, shattered him. This was impossible. He'd never imagined it possible to love again—not like this—not with this intensity. He kissed the tip of her nose, then her mouth, then her neck. She responded with surprising fervor.

The driver, apparently sensing passion but no proposal in progress, studiously ignored them. He clicked to the horse and slowly resumed his trip.

At Sheep Meadow the carriage once more rolled to a stop to let some laughing children run across the path. Snow balls were flying, dogs barking, children shrieking with glee and throwing themselves in the virgin snow on the ground to make snow angels.

"Oh, John," she said, her face beaming. "This is perfect. A storybook memory I'll always hold close to my heart. Thank you."

"I hope you know I ordered the snow just for you," he joked. "I didn't want you to be homesick for Alaska."

The ride ended all too soon back at the Plaza.

"Where are we having dinner tonight?" Grace asked as they entered the luxurious lobby.

"For you, my lady, Central Park's famous Tavern on the Green," John answered with a mock bow.

"How delightful. I've read about it and always wanted to go."

"This is a very special night. When you first wrote that you would be coming I made the reservations. I was lucky enough to get us a window seat. The snow today is just an extra bonus."

"What time is our reservation?"

"I made it for seven-thirty. After this carriage ride I have to go home. I have some business to take care of, but I'll change and pick you up, at seven."

True to his word, he was at her door promptly at seven. The doorman signaled a waiting cab to drive forward and in less than five minutes they were around Central Park South and pulling up in front of Tavern on the Green, overlooking snow-covered Central Park. It looked like a fairy wonderland.

John turned to the *maitre d'*. "Hathaway," he said.

They were welcomed and Grace grasped John's arm as they followed the *maitre d'* through the dimly lit room to their table by the window. Moonlight was pouring through glass walls reflecting on elegant, etched mirrors while candlelight flickered on every table. The windowed wall looked out at trees adorned with thousands of tiny Christmas lights.

As John accepted the wine list, he glanced at Grace. "Would you like some wine?"

"That would be nice."

He surveyed it carefully, smiled up at the sommelier.

"The Cosign-Montrachet."

"Yes, sir.

They sat quietly sipping their wine. "It's lovely," Grace said. "Look at those gorgeous crystal chandeliers and all the stained glass. This room reminds me of books I've read about the Gaslight era when couples dressed for dinner every night and danced all night."

"I thought you would enjoy it. The room fits you, Grace. Elegant and beautiful."

She blushed.

The meal was delightful: Lobster Bisque, followed by Roast Chicken Provencali, ending with the best New York cheesecake John said he had ever tasted.

They lingered, savoring the ambience of the room, finishing the bottle of wine, making quiet conversation. Grace wanted to see the ladies room—it had to be elegant—so she excused herself while John settled for the meal.

She doubted anything could surpass the dreamlike quality of this day. But then it wasn't over yet. A hot wave swept into her belly. It wasn't over by a long shot.

They exited Tavern on the Green into a cold, star studded night. "I have the perfect nightcap," John said with a salacious wink. "You can't spend a romantic evening without going to the top of the Empire State Building. It's fabulous at night. The city is aglow with lights."

"That sounds good. Can we walk?"

"No, it's too far. Let me hail a cab."

Grace stood with head back, staring in awe at the tall building soaring into the heavens. The bottom floors were flooded with Christmas lights of green, the top floors with red. It looked like a giant Christmas tree.

They entered the spacious Art Deco lobby, lathed in marble. John stopped to purchase tickets. Fortunately, both observation decks were open tonight and, holding hands, they entered the elevator which whisked them to the eighty-sixth floor. John put his arm around her waist and steered her out to the circular deck. Grace stood spell-bound, gazing upon millions of glimmering lights. The scene literally took her breath away.

"We call this the Cathedral In The Skies and aptly so, I think." As they strolled slowly around the deck John continued his commentary. "That funny looking building down there is the Flat Iron Building, and over there is the Chrysler Building."

"Look, I can see the lights of the Christmas tree at Rockefeller Center."

"Yes, and further uptown, honey, is your hotel and Central Park." They continued to circle the deck until they were facing west. "That's Macy's at Herald Square, and the lights of Times Square." They leaned on the rail looking down on New York in all her throbbing vibrance, then John took her by the arm.

"We're not finished. Another elevator is going to take us up sixteen floors to the 102nd floor observatory."

They exited and walked out onto the smaller deck to gaze once more at the glittering city. "It is gorgeous," Grace said. 'Thank you for sharing this with me." There were tears in her eyes.

As she looked out at the city he loved, John marveled at the sweetness of her expression and the easy way she showed her emotions. There was simply nothing false about Grace Maguire.

Later, after returning to the Plaza, they sat in the Oak Bar for hours, nursing a few drinks, talking, talking, talking. The room with its dark-sable oak walls and commodious maroon leather chairs, enfolded them like a warm cocoon. Soft music brought back memories of youth and love—not with someone else but with the emotions they remembered poignantly.

That night when they reached the door of her room he took her hand and pulled her close. His kiss soft at first became hot and demanding and she trembled under the heat. He tilted her head back and looked deep into her eyes. John took a deep breath. "May I come in? I want to hold you tonight."

She wavered for only a second. "And I want to be held," she said, handing him her key.

•   •   •

Grace had fantasized about this night for months. After fixing John a drink, she took a quick shower, using the fragrant body wash the Plaza lavishes on their guests and slipped into the new, black satin nightgown she had bought just that morning. Hesitantly she removed three thick, scented candles from her suitcase and placed them on the end table beside the bed and folded back the comforter.

She could feel John looking at her across the room. His tie was off, his white shirt open at the neck, the cuffs turned back. She swallowed dryly, her blood aflame with desire. She wanted this man with every fiber of her being. He walked to the window, and opened the drapes to the glowing lights of the city. "I want to be able to see you," he said turning to gaze at her, his smoldering eyes traveling up and down her body.

She moved toward him and put her hands on the windowsill. He stood behind her, with the shadows of the room playing across his face. She heard the tinkling sound of the elevator beyond the door, the muted voices of people walking along the corridor.

"You are beautiful," he whispered, his voice choked with emotion. He put his hands on her hips, running his hands up and down the satin smoothness of her nightgown.

"I want this to be more than sex, John."

"It is, darling. I want you, I love you. You know that, don't you?"

She nodded, gliding into his arms. He led her across the room and she slipped into bed, watching as he deftly unbuckled his pants and let them drop to the floor. He kept his back turned and she was quietly amused by his apparent modesty.

He was beside her in moments, crushing her to his chest, kissing her deeply, nuzzling her neck, her ears, her breasts. Her head nestled on his shoulder, her fingers stroked his thigh softly. Gradually she realized that something was not as it should be.

John groaned and grabbed her hand, crushing it in his, pushing it away.

Sensing his roiling emotions, she tugged at his hand. "What's wrong, John?"

"Nothing," he answered.

"Something is wrong. Something just changed."

He lay silent for a few seconds, then cleared his throat. "Grace," he murmured, "there is something I must tell you. I should have told you sooner but I hoped tonight would be different."

She twisted toward him, searching his face in the flickering light of the candles. Anxiety clouded his dark-brown eyes. He grasped her hand and twined his fingers around hers.

"I'm unable to make love to you," he blurted, his voice racked with pain. "I . . . I've lost my manhood."

Oh, dear, she thought. *Oh, dear!*

His hand squeezed hers so tightly her ring cut into her finger. "I feel so at a loss," he moaned. "I can't . . . I can't . . . I just can't go all the way with you. You don't understand how devastating it is to a man, Grace. I feel so inadequate . . . so inferior."

What can I say? What does he expect?

She gave him a half-smile. "Inferior? Inadequate? Oh, no . . . not you. Your problem is a part of aging, John, not inferiority." She kissed him softly, slowly moving her hand up to stroke his chest. She touched his lips with her finger. "This doesn't come as a complete surprise to me. But, darling there is something much deeper between us, something much more involved."

He enfolded her in his arms and she moaned with the feel of him near her—the heat of his body. More than flesh to flesh, it was soul to soul. His warmth and strength flowed into her and she sighed with contentment. "It's not that important," she murmured. "Maybe it would have been when we were younger. Not now. Let me fall asleep in your arms. I'm content with that."

John moaned softly and kissed the top of her head. "Sweetheart, there is nothing more I would like to do than make love to you."

"Do it then," she whispered.

"But . . . I just said . . . ."

"Let me show you. Love can be expressed in many ways, John."

CHAPTER FIFTEEN

Grace slowly opened her eyes, temporarily disoriented to hear a man snoring. She was curled, spoon like, against his back, her hand on his shoulder.

The white light of a snow-covered day shone through the window and pigeons cooed on the windowsill.

She kissed his shoulder and he stirred but did not wake.

She lay quietly, thinking about the past year, about the life she had chosen to live. Had her former life been a lie? She had always been content in her marriage, absorbed in her role as wife and mother. She had never craved another life. Why, then, did she need to be liberated now, to be her own person? Why did she want to muddle her life with a man? And there was no denying that things were getting very involved. She was deeply in love with John Hathaway.

Beyond the window she could hear the muted sounds of honking horns, the faint whine of ambulances and fire trucks careening down Fifth Avenue. Her gaze roamed around the room, admiring the high ceilings and classic wainscoting. The room had cost her a small fortune but it was worth it for these few days. The legendary Plaza Hotel, which had spent much of its 100-year history packed with guests like the Vanderbilts and the Beatles, would be closing soon for a renovation and conversion to part hotel and part condominium. She was glad she was here now, while the halls still echoed with the footsteps of all who were here before her.

Her thoughts drifted to John's revelation. She could not help but wonder if part of his problem was psychological. That he felt he was betraying his love for Mary. Would time, or perhaps medical treatment, provide an answer. She was content just to have him in her life, to hold and touch and cuddle. But was he?

John rolled over.

"Good morning, pumpkin," he said.

"Good morning."

They lay quietly, holding hands, murmuring endearments.

All of a sudden Grace's eyes clouded with concern. "I just thought about Bandit? You didn't go home to let him out. The poor dog must be in distress."

John laughed. "He has a doggie-door."

"Good"

"He will be worried, though. His master has never been out all night."

Grace chuckled. "Good, again."

John pushed back the thick down comforter. "Unfortunately, I don't have a doggie-door. I'd better get up."

When he returned he sat down on the edge of the bed beside her. "I have an idea," he said. "The New York Athletic Club is only two blocks from here. While you shower and dress why don't I run over for an hour's workout."

Grace raised an eyebrow. "Are you a member?"

"Oh, yes . . . have been for over thirty years. I usually work out there three days a week." He grinned. "And I still remember how long it takes a woman to do all the girlie things . . . like makeup and hair, and choosing the right outfit."

"Go ahead, then. I'll meet you in the coffee shop." She pretended to pout. "Just in case it doesn't take me as long as you think to do all those girlie things."

Eager for a quick workout John jogged to the club and headed for the exercise room.

"John, of all people." The voice came from Doctor Chad Phillips, John's roommate from NYU, a longtime friend and the doctor who had taken care of Mary during her long illness. Chad was fit and jovial, hand outstretched as he walked toward John. "I've missed you. I hope you haven't given up on regular exercise."

"No, no, Chad. I've been away, to Alaska, on assignment for the *Times*."

"There are two stationary bicycles, side by side, over there in the back row. Let's grab them and we can talk. It makes the time go faster."

John settled himself on the bike, his mind racing. How propitious was this chance meeting? They talked briefly about his article on the Tongass, which Chad had read, before John brought up the subject uppermost in his mind.

"Chad, do you have time to slip into the lounge for coffee after we finish? I have a personal problem and I hate to explain it to your receptionist when I call for an appointment."

"Sure, John. I'm off today."

After finishing their workout they headed toward the lounge. Their strides were quick as both men stepped down the three carpeted steps into the darkened member's lounge. It was almost empty so they slid into the upholstered banquette along the wall.

"What's the problem, John?"

"Well Chad, I met this lady . . . her name is Grace . . . and in spite of the passion I feel, in spite of the yearning, the desire, there is nothing in the way of follow through."

"John, this is not unusual. How long have you been seeing this woman."

"Off and on for several months."

"Give it time. Quite often the problem with impotence is psychological. You and Mary were a very serious, loving couple. I often envied your total commitment to each other. I think she is still with you."

"What do you mean? What does Mary have to do with this now? She's been gone for three years."

"I've talked to men who couldn't perform in the bedroom because they felt guilty . . . as if they were betraying their 'wife,' although she is now their 'late wife.'"

"That has never entered my mind. I was always faithful to Mary, and she is never far from my mind, but I feel no guilt over my attraction to another woman now that she is gone. Besides, this problem started before Mary died."

"Oh, well, then come into the office and we'll run a few blood tests. I'll have my nurse set up an appointment."

"Thanks, Chad. Now, before my girl wonders where I am, I'd better get back to the hotel."

"So, you two are sharing a hotel room." He gave John a salacious wink. "I'd better make your appointment STAT."

•   •   •

When he arrived back at the Plaza, Grace was just exiting the elevator door.

He gave her a quick kiss. "Why don't I drive you down to Greenwich Village to see my house," he suggested. "It's still early. I might even take you to McDonald's for breakfast. You could meet all of my cronies."

"I'd love to. And I would get to say hello to Bandit."

"Let's go, then. You said your plane leaves at three. We have plenty of time."

John's house was not what she expected. The neighborhood was sedate, solid brownstones standing at attention along the sidewalk like staunch Republicans. The street had landmark status, the winding staircases, window trim and massive front doors designated by the historical society to remain the way they were. Most of her contact with John had been in Alaska in very informal settings. Her thoughts of him these last two months had placed him in the cabin at Denali. This was certainly different.

He opened the elegant front door and was almost knocked over by the exuberant dog that jumped up to plant both paws on his master's shoulders. Bandit's tail swung wildly banging into Grace's leg. Suddenly aware of her presence he gave an excited yelp and transferred his attention to licking her face.

They were both laughing as John grabbed Bandit's collar and tried to calm the excited dog.

"What an introduction," Grace said as she wiped the saliva from her face.

John took Grace's coat and placed it in a hall closet. "Come on, I'll give you a short tour before I change out of this suit into something more comfortable. I'm afraid if I appear at McDonald's in this attire it will lead to all type of speculation."

Proudly, John took her from room to room pointing out the high windows, the fireplaces, and Mary's antiques. Grace smiled a lot and tried to look impressed but secretly she didn't care for it at all. Most of the furniture was very ornate, the colors muted, the decor definitely that of a different era from her own and a very different woman.

When he opened the door to his bedroom her gaze flew immediately to the large four poster bed. She felt a lurch in her stomach and quickly looked away. John seemed to sense her discomfort and did not linger.

He settled her in what he referred to as the parlor and went back upstairs to change. Bandit came over for a rub. Grace reached down to stroke his silken head and looked around the room with interest. Dignified wallpaper covered the walls, heavy drapes hung at the windows, an ornate gold framed mirror hung above a couch of pale brocade. Two Windsor chairs and several Queen Ann end tables flanked a tiled fireplace. Her own taste ran to what Susan referred to as Early American—lots of wicker baskets, gingham pillows, warm colors, and pine wood.

When John reappeared, bearing her coat and hat, she was relieved. He had changed into tweed wool slacks and a brown turtleneck that mirrored his chocolate eyes. He held a leash in his hand and Bandit eagerly jumped to his feet.

As they walked along the street John gave Grace a brief commentary on his neighbors and the men they were about to meet. It was obvious that he was very content here—completely within his element. It unnerved her.

After securing Bandit to the leg of the picnic table John escorted Grace into McDonald's. Surprise, then warmth were reflected in the eyes of a cashier named Gladys. John introduced Grace and after placing their order for sausage biscuits and gravy they took a table on the fringe of the group of men. Conversation died and ten pairs of eyes bored into them. John gave her a general introduction and several stood to shake her hand. Slowly the men resumed their dialogue, then, each in turn, surreptitiously cast a glance at Grace.

"I'd love to be a little mouse and hear the comments after we leave," John whispered.

"I'm not sure I want to. Where to next, Mr. Hathaway?"

"I thought we'd take a spin around the neighborhood." He grinned. "I'll show you all the famous landmarks . . . you know, like where I went to school, where I shop, where I go to church, where my boys live."

"That's a great idea. I guess neither of your son's would be home. I'd like to meet them."

"No, they would be at work."

"Does Adam's wife work, too?"

John looked a little flustered. "No, but I wouldn't want to drop in unannounced. Maybe, later."

Grace gave him a long searching look, then changed the subject. "What's on the agenda for lunch?"

"Well, we have to take Bandit home so I thought maybe I'd fix lunch for us. I'll let you kick off your shoes and treat you to some of John Hathaway's gourmet minestrone soup."

"Wow."

John grinned. "I've got to send you back to Alaska with lots of good memories."

"I've already got them. And they aren't about eating."

John leaned over and gave her a kiss on the cheek. He winked and her heart dropped to her shoes. "Me, too, sweetheart. Me, too."

As they left, with Bandit's hamburger in hand, John took her arm and silence once more descended on the group in the corner as all watched them walk out the door.

By two o'clock they were standing at the entrance to Airport Security. John could go no further with her and their goodbye's had been said in the privacy of the cab.

Grace's stomach contracted to a tight ball. "John, I'd like you to meet my family," she said, her voice edged with tension.

He frowned.

"I mean . . . I don't want to hide my relationship with you. I want to be honest with my children. You know I have promised to spend Christmas with Susan and her boyfriend. My son Ben, Emily, and the grandchildren will come over in the afternoon to exchange gifts. I'd like to invite you to dinner with everyone."

"You mean come to Pittsburgh?"

"Yes."

"But honey, I always spend the holiday with my boys and granddaughters."

"Then, how about New Years? I could arrange a family dinner on New Years Day. Is that doable?"

"I guess." He picked up her hand and kissed it. "Besides, I've been trying to figure out how to spend New Year's Eve with my girl."

Grace heaved a sigh of relief. She remembered being dishonest with Ben and Emily at Thanksgiving and it bothered her. She pursed her lips. But why should it? She was not a devious woman but, by God, she was a grown woman. If she wanted to have an adult relationship with a man her children would just have to get used to it.

"That's settled then," she said, "and, since I have a date for New Year's Eve, I have a perfect excuse to go shopping for a new dress."

"Something red and sexy," he teased. "I'll teach you to tango!"

Grace blushed. *Me! Sexy. Well now.*

CHAPTER SIXTEEN

It snowed on Christmas Day, covering Pittsburgh's sooty drifts with a fine powder of fresh whiteness. Grace and Susan, up early and eager as children, carried their coffee to two chairs facing the lighted tree and handed each other gaily wrapped packages.

"Open the red box first," Susan ordered with a grin.

Carefully Grace removed the ribbons and paper, folding them neatly to reuse next year.

"Oh, Mom, Susan moaned, "you haven't changed a bit. Hurry up."

Grace lifted the lid and started to laugh. Inside was a pair of one-piece red, flannel longjohns, complete with a flap in the back.

"I thought they would be perfect for Alaskan winters," Susan giggled. "I ordered them from the Country Store in Vermont"

"They're precious. Now open yours."

Happily they exchanged their gifts, Susan ripping her packages open and throwing the paper in a heap, Grace continuing to fold hers neatly. She had bought Susan an exquisite polar bear pendent of carved ivory, a fisherman knit sweater, a gift box of smoked salmon and a brilliant sun catcher she had bought in Mrs. Benoit's intriguing stained-glass shop. In addition to the longjohns, Susan gave her a warm terry bathrobe and pair of jade earrings.

Ben, Emily, Ted and Kelly arrived at Susan's laden with packages in mid-afternoon and they spent the next hour drinking eggnog, laughing, and exchanging gifts. Susan brought out deli trays of cold cuts, cheese, potato salad, and a veggie tray.

One package still lay under the tree ignored. Ted could stand the suspense no longer and walked over to place his hand atop it. "Grandma, aren't you going to ask what's in this box?"

"Well, I have been wondering. There's no name on it."

At a nod from his father Ted picked up the gift and placed it on her lap. "It's from all of us."

Carefully she peeled back the Christmas wrapping and lifted out a fat, leather bound book. "MOM" was etched in gold on the cover and with a gasp of surprise she opened it to reveal her wedding picture on the cover page.

Ted was beaming. "It's a family album—all our pictures are in it. Dad and Aunt Susan spent hours going through all their old photographs to make it for you."

Everyone crowded around her as she thumbed through the pages, laughing and exchanging memories of their lives growing up. Grace felt as though her heart would burst. It was the nicest, most thoughtful gift she had ever received.

Ben looked at his watch and whistled. "Wow, its past six o'clock. They are predicting three more inches of snow tonight. We had better get going."

Coats were retrieved, hugs and kisses given, and a lovely Christmas Day was over.

That evening, Grace and Susan, both in pajamas, sat curled up on the sofa, mugs of hot chocolate cupped in their hands ready for "girl-talk."

"This reminds me of my high school years, Mom," Susan commented nostalgically. "Remember all the times I poured out my heartbreak over a crush on a boy who wouldn't look at me—or worse still, over a breakup that I was certain I would never recover from?"

"I remember, honey."

"I just don't know what to do about Jason. Like me, he has been burned by a bad marriage. He doesn't want to go down that road again."

"But, he is still pressing you to move in with him?"

"Yes. We are very much in love . . . we want to be together all the time." She ran her hand through her blond hair. "I'm as much afraid of getting hurt as he is. I don't think I could live through another divorce"

"And you don't think you would hurt as much if you were just living together and broke up?"

"At least we wouldn't have all the ugly financial settlements that can turn love into hate."

"What about children?"

"That's another problem. Jason has three to support and put through college. He doesn't want any more. I always wanted a child of my own, but I didn't want to bring one into a bad marriage and I wouldn't want to have a baby if I wasn't married. That wouldn't be fair to a child either." She raised sad eyes to look at Grace. "Maybe I am beyond the age where raising a family is important. Maybe I should be content with the children I am privileged to teach."

Grace desperately wanted to help her daughter, but advice eluded her. She knew that many young couples used the high divorce rates as an excuse not to commit themselves to marriage. But when problems arose, without that total commitment, it was simply too easy to walk away. Marriage involved concessions that it seemed the "me" generation did not wish to make.

"What about his children? I assume he has visitation rights. Can you love them? How will they react to your living arrangements? And don't forget Jason's financial burden. It will indirectly affect you, too."

"I've thought of all that, Mom. I have spent time with the children and they seem to like me. Of course, we always do fun things when they come to visit."

"Susan, I don't know what to tell you. I honestly don't. I believe wholeheartedly in marriage. However, if you want to find out if you are compatible, if your love is strong enough to ride out the storms . . . and there will be some I assure you . . . then I won't interfere."

"Thanks, Mom. I think I am going to give it a try, Jason's way. My lease is up next month, his condo is closer to my school, and it will be cheaper for both of us. Now, while we have been talking our hot chocolates have gotten cold. Let me nuke them in the microwave."

While Susan was reheating their drinks Grace reached over to the coffee table and picked up the fantastic memory book the children had given her.

Susan returned to find her leafing through the pages. "That was a combined effort, Mom. I contributed what pictures I had and Ben found an old shoe box filled with camping photos."

"It's a wonderful gift, honey." She paused at a picture of Peter kissing her at a New Year's Eve party. It brought tears to her eyes and she grabbed a tissue from a box on the end table.

"You loved him very much, didn't you?" Susan said softly.

"Very, very much."

"Have you thought of dating again? You must be lonesome."

Grace swallowed. This was it—the perfect opening to speak of John. She looked intently into Susan's soft-green eyes. "I have begun to see someone," she said, relieved to finally say the words.

Susan's mouth dropped open. "You have? Who? When?"

Slowly Grace recounted her chance meeting with John in Anchorage and the way fate kept bringing them together. When she told her about almost drowning in the flash flood Susan squealed with horror. Grace did not tell her that they had slept together that night in his cabin.

"What now," Susan asked, her eyes bright with curiosity. "You said he returned to New York." Her hands flew to her mouth. "That's what you were doing in New York last week." She chuckled. "You rascal."

"I'm afraid so. We spent several wonderful days together." With glowing eyes she told Susan about the grand tour of the Big Apple, Chinatown, Central Park and Tavern on the Green. "You'll get a chance to meet him, soon. He is coming next weekend to meet the family."

"That sounds serious."

"No, we are just going to spend New Years Eve together before I go back to Seward. I want everyone to get to know him. I don't want to go behind your backs, Susan, and I'll admit I didn't like lying to you and Ben about last week."

Susan giggled. "What an evening this has turned out to be . . . Mother and daughter discussing their love lives."

New Year's Eve ended in bitter disappointment. Near blizzard conditions in New York caused a cancellation of John's flight and he didn't arrive in Pittsburgh until New Years Day.

Grace met him at the airport and they went directly to Oakmont. She held firmly to John's elbow as they mounted the front steps of Ben's two-story Colonial.

"I don't know who is the most nervous . . . you or me," she said.

"It has to be me," John replied tightly. "How much do they know?"

"Not much. Only that I met you in Alaska and that you live in New York and I spent some time with you there."

The door flew open before Grace had a chance to ring. Ben must have been standing behind it waiting. As she introduced John to Ben the entire family came trouping into the hallway—Emily, Ted, Kelly, Susan and Jason. Grace was so flustered she almost forgot their names.

John, to her surprise, looked very self-assured as he shook hands and smiled warmly.

After introductions were made, Emily directed everyone to the living room. "We have time for a drink before dinner," she said. "Ben, why don't you see what they want while I check on the potatoes."

The men all chose beer while the women opted for wine. Ben took a long swig of his Iron City and gave John a slow, appraising look. "I understand you work for the *New York Times*."

"I'm actually retired from the *Times*. Sometimes I do special articles for them. That's why I was in Alaska."

"Have you always lived in New York," Susan asked.

"Always. I was born there and raised my family there. In the same house as a matter of fact."

Kelly chimed in, "Grandma said you are a widower. How many children do you have?"

"Two boys. Both live in New York." His eyes glinted with pleasure. "And I have three lovely granddaughters, all about your age."

Emily poked her head through the door. "I don't like to rush everyone but I wanted to have dinner early so you boys could watch your football games. Kelly, I need you in the kitchen. The potatoes are ready to be mashed."

Grace and Susan both jumped to their feet. "We can help," Grace said as she followed her niece to the kitchen.

She hated to leave John alone but she was glad to be free of the interrogation.

The last dishes were removed from the dining room table and

while the women loaded the dishwasher and transferred leftover pork and sauerkraut to the refrigerator, the men eagerly retired to the family room to watch the football game.

Grace felt a sudden stab of anxiety. The initial introductions and dinner had gone well but she could imagine the grilling Ben was giving John now that they were alone.

Susan gave her a playful nudge. "Wow, Mom, John is handsome. And charming. I wouldn't let him get away."

Emily set her lips in a tight line and busied herself at the dishwasher.

Grace gave Susan a grateful smile. "He's just as nice as he is handsome."

"And that gorgeous silver hair. It's unusual for a man that age to have such a full head of hair.

Emily looked up. "How long have you actually known the man, Mother?"

"Six months, or so. I told you we met in Alaska." She turned away anxious to change the subject. "Here let me help you dry those, honey" she said to Susan who was washing the pots and pans in the sink. "I like Jason. He seems very attentive."

Susan cleared her throat and looked at Grace with shining eyes. "Thank you Mom." Her face grew pensive. "I may as well tell everyone, now. When my apartment lease runs out I'm going to move in with him."

"Move in? Before you get married?" Emily sputtered.

"We aren't talking marriage. Maybe some day. Just not now."

"But . . . Susan. . . ." Emily's voice trailed off, her brow knit with concern.

Susan ran her fingers through her hair with an impatient gesture. "Please don't start, Aunt Emily. It's a changing world. Today's generation is not looking for conformity . . . they're looking for change. To try things out first before committing to the long haul."

Emily gave her a scorching look, her face mottled, red with anger. "It's a sin, young lady. Sex without marriage is a sin." She glared at Grace. "Did you know about this?"

"Yes." A spasm of irritation crossed Grace's face. She took a deep breath and swallowed. The conversation was taking a dangerous turn—this was not the time or place for it.

Fortunately, Kelly interrupted. "If you want my opinion, I think

Susan is right," she said, avoiding looking at her mother. "The divorce rates today are staggering. I think it's smart to find out ahead of time if you share the same values, if you are compatible in the big decisions. You know, like how many children you want, where you want to live, whether you get along with each other's families."

"Kelly . . . that's enough," Emily snapped. "You better never bring those ideas home to your father and me."

Susan gave everyone a shaky smile. "I'm sorry. I didn't mean to start a family feud. And Mom, I'm very impressed with your friend, John. He seems very intelligent and it's obvious he really likes you."

"Me too, Grandma. I'm impressed," Kelly said.

Susan laid her dishrag aside and pulled Grace into a tight hug, staring earnestly into her eyes. "I admire what you are doing with your life, Mom. Finding a meaningful relationship is only adding dimension to it. Don't let happiness pass you by."

"I won't. I promise you, that."

"And Mom . . . please . . . please . . . don't hesitate to love again."

During half-time in the football game, Jason and Ted went outside for a smoke.

Ben regarded John critically. "Mom tells me you are partial to the conservationists in the logging industry dispute."

"I suppose you could say that, but I tried hard not to reflect it in my article. I tried to be fair to both sides."

"From everything I've read the cessation of logging has cost a lot of men their livelihood."

"That's true, Ben, but timber jobs account for less than one percent of the region's employment. I'm not against logging, *per se*. What I do favor is intelligent land management in the sensitive rain forest, not indiscriminate clear-cutting of millions of acres." John chewed on his upper lip, unsmiling. "You may think I sound like an environmentalist, but I'm just a guy who hates to see rape and pillage and waste. Alaska needs a lumber industry. But there are ways to get wood out of the forest that don't wreck the environment. Everyone I talked to, bankers, townspeople, loggers agreed that the rainforest can have a future that supports both wildlife and the logging industry. What is necessary is a commitment from timber lease holders to build fewer roads, leave large blocks of uncut forest intact, and do more to ensure that logged areas grow back."

"Aren't the lumber mills required to reforest?"

"Reforestation in the Alaskan Tongass is different from what you think of here in the lower forty-eight. For example, second-growth cedars will have no value for at least eighty years until they begin producing the chemicals that give cedar its natural preservative. And it will be centuries before second-growth resumes the stature of landmark trees favored by the Asian market for its grain." John noticed a questioning look on Ben's face. "Grace tells me you are quite the outdoors man, interested in hunting and fishing," he added.

Ben nodded.

"As a conservationist I guess my main interest is the impact clear-cutting has on Alaskan wildlife."

"Yeah, I know. You guys get all excited about saving the spotted owl and goshawks."

John smiled. He didn't want to antagonize Grace's son. "It's a lot more than saving a few birds from extinction, although that is important too. I hear you love to fish. Salmon need undisturbed watersheds to spawn and it will take generations for the spawning streams to regenerate. The towering shade of the big trees keep streams cool and fallen trees slow down currents. Most people don't think of that."

Ben was listening now and John was on a roll. He leaned forward in his chair. "Old-growth is important for hunters, too. Woodland nutrients fertilize the food chain. Grizzlies and black bear favor old-growth stands for hibernation. The thick canopy of old-growth branches keeps heavy snowfalls from burying winter provisions vital to black-tailed deer, and the black-tails are the mainstay of the wolf. It goes round and round—all part of the ecological chain."

"But," Ben interrupted, "Alaskans need logging jobs. I mean aren't people more important than fish and animals?"

"Of course, they are," John said, anxious to be understood. "I'm not talking about eliminating logging altogether, only eliminating clear-cutting, which denudes thousands of acres at one time and takes decades to restore. Community leaders in Southeast Alaska predicted economic disaster when the large pulp mills closed. But, what actually occurred, Ben, was worker dislocation and training . . . more painful for some than for others . . . followed by a surprising economic rebound. Today, tourism drives the economy and small-scale mills flourish."

Seemingly anxious to change the subject Ben pulled a bottle of beer from the cooler in front of the TV. "I must say, I'm surprised that Mom is so taken with Alaska," he said. "I was hoping the winter would turn her off."

"She seems quite excited about her new job. I assume she has told you all about it."

"Yeah." Ben gave John a piercing look. "How do you like it there? Do you plan to go back?"

"Nope, I'm a New Yorker, through and through."

"Help yourself to a beer," Ben said pointing to the cooler.

John walked over to pull one from the ice. Just as he did so his gaze fastened on an album lying on the coffee table with "MOM" emblazoned on the cover in bold gold letters.

Ben saw his glance. He jumped up and handed the book to John with a flourish. "Our Christmas gift to my mother. Feel free to look at it."

"Oh, I don't know. It must be personal."

"No . . . look at it. It's a memory book, filled with pictures of her and my dad and us kids growing up."

John felt his face grow warm. He really did not want to see pictures of Grace and her husband. Neither did he want to appear to reject looking at the book.

He picked up the album and carried it over to the couch where he began to leaf through the pages. Ben watched him with narrowed eyes.

John knew he shouldn't feel jealousy when he looked at the old photos but he did. This was another part of the woman he loved, a part he could never match. Her first love, her wedding picture, her childbearing years. In one picture she was heavy with child and he realized that he could never place his hand on her stomach and feel the movement of his own baby. Up until that moment he'd done a good job of not being jealous when she talked about her husband.

He finished leafing through the album with reluctance, glad when he could turn the last page and put it aside.

Just then the patio doors slid open and Jason and Ted returned from outside, flapping their arms, their noses red with cold.

The rest of the afternoon passed quickly. Midway into the third quarter of the football game the women rejoined them bearing bowls of popcorn and peanuts. Grace settled on the couch beside John and he folded her hand in his. He caught her scent and pressed himself closer to her. He saw her glance at the memory book and quickly away.

"I like your family," he whispered into her ear.

She smiled gratefully.

What he didn't say was that he didn't think her son liked him.

After Grace left to take John to the airport Emily pulled Ben aside. "You and your sister have to get together and talk. I think this relationship between your mother and Mr. Hathaway is more serious than you realize."

A stress line creased Ben's forehead. "It's really none of our business, Emily. I mean, what do you propose we do about it."

"I don't know. But I think you and Susan should talk to her. How well does she know this man? He could be up to no good . . . interested in her money."

"Honey, I think he has excellent credentials of his own. I'll admit I'm not crazy about him. But I want Mom to be happy. Besides, at least for now, they live in different parts of the country. How serious can it get?"

Emily smiled derisively. "Talk to Susan. See if she didn't detect the same thing I did when they looked at each other. Mark my words, Ben. This affair could spell trouble."

Grace and John sat side by side in a booth in a darkened lounge at Pittsburgh International Airport waiting for John's flight back to New York. Their thighs touched and Grace had an almost uncontrollable urge to rest her head on the broad shoulder pressed against hers. Two drinks sat untouched before them.

Music was playing softly in the background— Frank Sinatra

singing "September Song." The words drew her attention. She looked at John. He, too, had caught the words.

When the autumn weather turns the leaves to flame,
One hasn't got time for the waiting game.
Oh, the days dwindle down to a precious few,
September, October, November!
And these precious days I'll spend with you.

"It's going to get complicated, Grace," he said. "I've fallen in love with you."

"Love is always complicated."

"But, Good Lord, I live in New York and you live in Alaska!"

Tears began to form in Grace's eyes. *He has admitted love. Can I? What can our future possibly be?* She squeezed his hand. "And I love you, John. I'm sure you know that. Maybe, for now, we should just let it rest at that. My father always referred to the *tincture of time.* Let's see where this love leads us."

John swirled the amber liquid in his glass. Then he turned and looked deeply into her eyes. "You're right, dear. We should not rush things." He looked at his watch. "I must go. I don't know how long it will take to get through Security."

Grace made a move to get up, but he put his arm around her and gave her a deep kiss. "I don't want to say goodbye at the gate amid a crowd of people." He leaned back and cupped her face with his two hands. "I want to remember you like this. Just you and me, your lips soft from my last kiss, a look of love on your face."

He rose and walked away, his tall frame soon disappearing into the crowd.

CHAPTER SEVENTEEN
Seward, Alaska
January

Grace had been home for two weeks and had received only one letter and three phone calls from John. During the phone conversations she thought he sounded distant and rather formal, as though she were a very good friend—not someone with whom he had been intimate, to whom he had professed love. She was disappointed and hurt.

Could it all have been as fleeting as that? Was he having second thoughts about their relationship? But then wasn't she was the one who suggested they give it time. It was all very confusing.

Wistfully, Grace picked up a book entitled 'The Wolves of Mt. McKinley' and settled herself in a cozy lounge chair beside a good reading lamp. She tried to read, it was part of the research material she had to learn for her job this summer, but she simply couldn't concentrate. Her thoughts kept drifting back to John and the time they had spent together in New York.

They were in love with one another—there was no doubt in her mind of that. But what about the future? She had heard many stories from her friends about the pitfalls of second marriages. One of her fellow Red Hatters had confided that her second husband still kept his first wife's underwear in his dresser drawers and would not allow a single item in the house to be changed. He even refused to let her replace the plants in the flower beds. And Grace wondered why John had made no real attempt to introduce her to his sons while she was in New York. Did he anticipate animosity from them? She certainly could not dismiss the fact that her own son did not accept John.

Restlessly, she jumped to her feet and went to the closet to retrieve her parka. Maybe a good brisk walk along the beach to her favorite restaurant would lift her spirits; that and a hot bowl of

Cristo's fabulous crab soup.

Snow, pushed into piles higher than Grace's head, lined the street leading to the Anchorage train terminal where she was meeting Joanna, Barbara and Eileen.

Determined not to let her unhappiness show, she greeted her friends with a warm smile.

"I just heard from Lois. She's already at the hotel."

"I'm anxious to meet her," Joanna said.

Grace hailed a cab and they sped through the busy city where streetlights still lit the afternoon dusk.

That evening the four of them lingered over dinner, bringing each other up to date on their activities since their last meeting in November. Grace did not mention John, although they all knew of him. She was not yet ready to confide that she had spent time with him in New York.

The lecture started at ten o'clock and by nine-thirty the auditorium was packed. Grace was amazed at the interest.

"Look," Lois said, "the first three rows are filled with seniors in wheelchairs. It goes to prove interest in sex doesn't end with age or disability."

Grace settled back in her seat and studied the program. Dr. Jane Mackay lectured extensively to seniors and at spiritual conferences. After a glowing introduction she stepped up to the podium. She was attractive, with short graying hair and appeared to be in her late fifties or early sixties.

She began her speech with a smile. "The other day," she said, "I saw a funny cartoon that I believe says what this lecture is all about: a couple looking to be in their seventies—he is bald, she is wearing a shawl around her shoulders—are sitting on a park bench holding hands. Another younger couple has walked by and the boy says, with furrowed brow and raised eyes, "You don't think they . . . I mean . . . they're much too old, aren't they?""

Everyone laughed.

Dr. Jane, as she preferred to be called, nodded sagely. "I think that pretty much reflects the attitude of the general public toward our senior citizens.

"There's a popular perception that older people aren't as interested in sex as younger people. That simply isn't true. Sexuality in later life is acceptable and natural; it is an important and integral part of life. And when I say sexuality I mean much more than the word sex implies. Sexuality can be as simple as holding hands, as touching, as expressing words of love and caring."

Dr. Jane smiled warmly. "Older people are really just younger people later in life. There's no reason to believe they give up the basic human desire for love and intimacy and the kind of pleasure that comes from an intimate relationship just because they have aged.

"Younger people, and unfortunately many physicians, underrate the extent of sexual interest in older people. In a random sampling of women ages fifty to eighty-two nearly fifty percent of the women reported an ongoing sexual relationship. In another study reported by *USA Today*, twenty-six percent of men seventy-five to eighty-five years of age were sexually active.

"Understanding that sexuality is normal and natural in old age is an important step to realizing and becoming at ease with one's own self."

Grace listened with more interest than she would have felt a year ago.

Dr. Jane paused for a moment and gazed at the audience intensely. Then she said, "I repeat, there is more to sexuality than just intercourse. There are many other forms of intimate expression ranging from holding hands, to kissing, to masturbation, to oral sex. Understanding that these options are available and acceptable can enrich sexual expression greatly.

"What is sexuality? It's a simple question, but there are many answers. It is a lifelong behavior with evolving change and development. It begins with birth and ends with death. The notion that it ends with aging is inherently illogical. Sexual desire remains intact. Even if the desire or ability to have sexual intercourse is no longer present, the desire for hugging, touching, kissing, fondling, caring, sharing, being needed, being respected, receiving and giving affection, persists."

How well that fits my feeling for John, Grace thought. *I would*

like to have intercourse with him, but in the absence of that I am
content to express my love in other ways.

Dr. Jane continued. "It is important to let older men and women
know that sexual desire, and dreams are normal as long as we live.
There is no reason for guilt, discomfort, or shame. The elderly, sick
or well, need to be hugged and cared for as much as young people.

"Masturbation is not a dirty word. I happen to prefer the word
'self-stimulation' but that is beside the point. For some older
people, it may be the only convenient and available form of sexual
activity. It is appropriate for physicians to suggest this method to
seniors.

"Let's examine the subject of aging a little further." Dr. Jane
continued. "Sexual problems do increase with age, and the rate of
sexual activity fades somewhat. But interest in sex remains high
and the frequency remains surprisingly stable among the physically
able who are lucky enough to still have partners. Given the
availability of a partner, the same general high or low rate of
sexual activity can be maintained throughout life despite age.

"Women, as they age, often find intercourse painful because of
vaginal dryness. This can be helped by the use of a variety of
jellies and creams on the market. After menopause or a hysterectomy some women experience decreased desire.

"In men there are four changes associated with aging: it takes
longer to achieve full erection, there is a decrease in the volume of
seminal fluid in the ejaculate and there is a reduction in the demand
for release of sexual tension. All men experience temporary
periods of impotence at some time in their lives, and these need not
cause alarm. Over ten million men suffer from more extensive
impotence and of those fifty percent are over the age of seventy-
five.

"These changes, while of immediate importance to men, are
important to the female partner as well. A woman may react to
these changes by questioning her own sexuality, and the result may
be unfounded fears and reactions on both sides of the equation.

"Men who develop erectile dysfunction, now called ED and
previously referred to as impotence, often feel embarrassed,
ashamed, and frustrated. The availability of good treatment and
society's new openness have removed some of the stigma, but for
men, ED is still a heartbreaking affair. But if men . . . and their

doctors . . . don't recognize ED as an important medical problem, the consequences may include a truly 'broken heart.' That's because a man's ability to have an erection is often a barometer of his cardiovascular health."

The doctor spent the next half hour discussing various types of sexual problems—erectile dysfunction, premature ejaculation, vaginitis, surgery, phobia after a heart attack, alcohol use, certain prescription drugs, diabetes, hypertension, weight problems, performance anxiety, decreased arousal in women, and hardening of the arteries. She went into great detail about the various medications used to treat hypertension and their possible side effects.

She ended that part of her lecture by saying, "It should be kept in mind that all individuals are susceptible to dysfunction when they resume sexual activity after a period of abstinence . . . such as the death of a spouse . . . and this is even more of a problem with the elderly. Perhaps the most important ingredient in reversing this problem is the cooperation and understanding of a patient partner. If there has been a previous pleasurable sexual life, this period of dysfunction responds readily if addressed promptly."

That may be the only problem with John, Grace speculated. *Mary was quite ill for a long time before she passed away. Maybe all we need is time.*

At this point in the lecture Dr. Jane removed her microphone from the podium and walked to the front of the stage. "What I am about to say next may be distasteful to some but it is important that it be said.

"Institutionalized elderly have another source of difficulty. The staff in retirement and nursing homes often accuse their patients of having sexual problems. The problems most often include exposure of genitalia, masturbation and sexual talk. Ladies and gentlemen these sexual problems only indicate the need for closeness, tenderness, and warmth. Sexual segregation in institutional homes is nothing but a barrier to natural and comfortable relationships. The elderly do not lose their capacity for love and fondling, especially the need to be touched and to touch. Families of elderly parents should look for nursing homes where living is more family-like, more conductive to normal relationships. The key is a staff that understands and supports sexuality, especially the components of loving and feeling.

"I'd like to read part of an article from the *New York Times*, dated June 4, 2002.

"Not long ago while doing morning rounds at the Hebrew Home for the Aged in Riverdale, the Bronx, Edna Adams, a nurse's aide, knocked on a resident's door. As was her habit, when she didn't hear an answer, she pushed it open, and found two of her patients—each over eighty—exchanging intimacies.

"With barely a hint of surprise, she did exactly what she was supposed to: she whispered 'excuse me,' closed the door and made a mental note to come back later.

"Mrs. Adams knew to let nature take its course, thanks to a highly unusual set of policies and procedures concerning sexual expression introduced at the Hebrew Home in 1995."

Grace felt tears well in her eyes. Thank God there were such caring, compassionate homes for the elderly, and people willing to speak out about the need for love no matter their age. She had heard a few snickers from the audience but for the most part there was a look of understanding on the faces of those around her.

Dr. Jane walked back to the podium. "In closing I would like to touch on a recent startling statistic. Approximately one-fourth of all new cases of HIV/AIDS diagnosed currently are among those fifty years and over, with many over sixty-five years of age. The sad fact is that those in that elderly population developing HIV often develop into full-blown AIDS more quickly than a younger population because of weakened immune systems, thinning of the vaginal wall, and so on."

There was a discernable gasp from the audience.

"Hard to believe, isn't it? But realize that condom use appears to be very uncommon among older adults. Women no longer fear pregnancy. And men often seek out professionals.

"There is very little talk about female condoms which are responsible for preventing the virus, yet their use in third-world countries have produced an amazing lowering of female HIV statistics.

"We need to understand better how to best prevent sexually transmitted diseases among older couples. Calling a local HIV hotline, easily accessible in all the US by calling 411, could provide much useful information about condoms—male and female approved by the appropriate authorities—testing, and general preventive measures."

Dr. Jane concluded her lecture to a rousing applause.

As the women in Grace's group donned heavy coats and filed out of the auditorium she noticed thoughtful, serious looks on their faces. This was a subject usually kept tucked away from general conversation, yet very much a part of their lives, as they moved into their senior years.

The lecture was not really "fun" as Eileen had predicted. It touched each of the women in a different way—widowhood, aging partners, their own secret desires and fantasies.

Joanna, Barbara, Eileen, and Grace stopped at a franchise restaurant for decaffeinated coffee and pie and although they talked about the lecture in general terms Grace was glad that no one voiced any off-color jokes. They were about ready to leave when Barbara spoke up, "I find the statistics about HIV hard to believe. Surely very few men with erectile dysfunction would go out looking for sexual partners. It would be too intimidating."

In the silence that followed her comment Joanna cleared her throat and spoke up. "I believe it. When my sister's husband started having problems he blamed my sister. He said she was overweight and didn't make herself attractive for him anymore. He started looking for sex elsewhere. I guess it helped at first. Then, when he had more and more erectile failures he had to accept responsibility. But it was too late." Joanna swallowed, then forced herself to finish the thought. "He got HIV and gave it to my sister."

Grace reached over and placed a gentle hand on her friend's arm. "Thank you for sharing that. It helps all of us to understand the problem."

CHAPTER EIGHTEEN
New York City

John laid aside his book, yawned, and stretched. He simply couldn't concentrate.

Ever since Grace had returned to Alaska he was at odds with himself. Up one moment and down the next. His life—once simple—had grown complex. He was in love and resentful of the complication it presented. He didn't understand why he was choosing to tear apart the tapestry of a life that had been comfortable and predictable. He had not fallen in love at first sight. He had not been looking for love. Grace had been just another woman, attractive but not enchanting. The feelings he had for her now were unimaginable when he first saw her at the airport in Anchorage.

He missed her so desperately his gut hurt. The laughter, the companionship, talking to someone he could open his heart to, the feeling of her warm body next to his. He remembered his hands on her breasts, remembered stroking her thighs until she trembled, remembered kissing her in all her private places as she writhed in pleasure. His body grew warm with desire as he remembered her own ministrations to his need. Their love had shown no inhibition.

But marriage? Somehow he knew that Grace would not accept any lasting relationship that did not include marriage. Still, the obstacles were obvious. He had heard all the horror stories from widowers like himself. Family squabbles over money, children who could not accept a substitute partner for their parent, adjustments to long established living patterns. And obviously the biggest obstacle to any relationship with Grace was geographic. He lived in New York—Grace lived in Alaska.

And then, of course, there was the problem of his impotence. It had been a factor in his life ever since he first realized it with Mary, but it had been a dormant worry after her death, buried in his subconscious. Now it was very much a concern.

Grace had been very understanding—requiring no more from him than he could give—but what about the prospect of spending years together without full culmination of the sex act? Would she regret her decision later on and perhaps seek a relationship with another man who could satisfy her needs. That would destroy him.

John groaned in dismay, then brightened. He had an appointment to see his doctor tomorrow. Maybe something could be done.

Chad finished studying the results of the John's blood test, leaned back in his chair and gave his friend a professional smile. "We talked a little about this at the gym, John. Before the term ED became common, doctors called your problem impotence. Physicians viewed it as a psychological disorder. Now we know that sixty percent of impotence has a physical basis, which is a sign of a medical problem. After talking to you I do believe that your problem is physical not psychological."

"I'm glad to know you don't think I'm a nut case."

Chad grinned. "I take it there's been no response since our little pep talk."

"Nope. But Chad, if it's physical there must be a medical solution."

"Yes and no. As you know our examination of your prostate indicated a slight enlargement, however I don't think surgery is an option at this point."

John gave a sigh of relief. "Good."

Chad smiled. "I've been treating you for years for hypertension with blood pressure medication. Your present regimen seems to be controlling that and I suggest you stay with the same dosage."

"Several of my men friends blame their blood pressure medication."

Chad shook his head. "Not at all. Recent studies at Harvard Medical School report that anti-hypertension medication is not the cause of ED. Don't stop taking it." He pushed his glasses back on his nose and studied the sheaf of papers he held in his hand. "According to this report there's no sign of diabetes. But your testosterone level is very low."

"Um."

"I'm going to get a little technical here, but bear with me." He scooted his stool next to John and handed him a drawing. "The physical mechanism that makes an erection possible includes two unique blood vessels that are filled with spongy matter. These cigar-shaped vessels flank the underside of the penis. Two sets of valves regulate the flow of blood. One allows blood to be pumped into the vessels, changing the penis from flaccid and pendulous to hard and erect. An erection can increase the size of the penis anywhere from twenty to two-hundred percent."

"I remember that reaction with much fondness," John commented.

Chad's face softened from his professional demeanor to that of a good friend. "Don't we all. But John, that's how the new drugs on the market work. They all act to widen narrowed arteries."

"You mean Viagra?" John said.

"Among others. Viagra, Levitra, and Cialis all work the same way. I'm going to give you a few Cialis to take home with you. Try them. But John, I am going to be honest with you. Considering your age, and the labs we have received, you may be in the category of those men we cannot help. I wish there was more we could do, but age is the strongest risk factor you face."

"That's not very encouraging."

"I know. But let's give the pills a chance. And there are other things we can try if they don't work. I recommend a small, hand-held vacuum pump, easy to use and quite successful." He laughed at the look on John's face. "First you climb in bed and get the lady all worked up. Then, when you are both ready, you slip into the bathroom and use the device. It only takes minutes and she need never know. You will be amazed at the size of the erection you get."

"God!"

"Men don't talk openly about their sexual inadequacies but there are literally thousands of these devises in use. We carry a sample in the office that we rent to our patients on a trial basis. But, first let us see how you react to the pills." He drummed his fingers on his desk. "Please, don't be disappointed, John, if they don't work. They are not as successful as the TV ads suggest. And they do have side effects. Read the label carefully."

John left the office with a packet of pills tucked in his pocket, more than a little depressed. *Age—Pumps—Injections.* He certainly hoped the pills worked. What he hadn't mentioned to the doctor was the difficulty in trying them out.

Grace was now three thousand miles away.

Valentine's Day arrived with a vengeance and twelve inches of snow. John's driveway was drifted shut, his yard man a day behind schedule. He had managed to shovel a path to the bird feeder in the backyard where tufted titmice, chickadees, and a pair of cardinals shared their bounty with several squirrels. He enjoyed looking out his window at the drifts of white powder and that evening he drew up a chair by the fire, pipe in hand, and dog by his side. He closed his eyes. This was home. A home he never wanted to leave.

Try as he might, however, his thoughts kept drifting to the phone call to Grace that morning. He had wired her a dozen red roses and he thought he detected a trace of tears when she thanked him.

After her return to Seward he had purposefully kept his contact with her as light as possible. He did not want to remarry. Live with her—maybe. He grimaced. He was a Deacon in his church. His pastor would have a fit. Still, he missed Grace.

Missed the way you miss someone you've fallen in love with. He could dance all the way around that statement, soften it somehow, say his emotions were on overdrive, claim that it was nostalgia for a time long past in his life, but the fact remained. He liked being with Grace. Liked the way she made him laugh, liked the way she made him feel young. Liked being in love. It was as simple as that.

She had sent him a funny Valentine and he drew it from his pocket and looked at it for the dozenth time that day. A row of X's and O's were penned across the bottom of the card.

That night he patted the bed and invited Bandit to sleep beside him.

One thing in John's life he insisted remain unchanged was the daily trip to McDonald's. The next morning they set out beneath a chicory blue sky, boots screeching on the surface of the snow, Bandit leaping in the snow, barking joyfully.

Of the usual gang at McDonald's, only Arnold had braved the weather. He greeted John with a salute of his cup, slopping coffee across the fish emblazoned on his sweatshirt.

"By God, I thought I was goin' to be the only one here this morning," Arnold said.

"What is it they say . . . *neither rain nor snow*. . . . But you weren't a mailman, were you? You were a fireman."

"Same thing applies."

John draped his wet jacket across the back of the chair and sat down with his breakfast.

Arnold winked. "You're looking a little peaked . . . haven't seemed yourself since Christmas. Couldn't be mooning over that lady you had in here, could you?"

"Only teenagers moon over girls."

"Well now, I don't know about that."

John took a careful bite of his breakfast sandwich. It was good. The coffee was good, too. He sipped slowly. "What ever happened to that lady you were telling me about last fall? Are you still seeing her?"

Arnold looked a little confused. "You mean Lilly? Ah—that didn't work out. I think she was after my money. She kept asking me about my investments and picking nothing but the most expensive restaurants."

"I do miss Grace," John admitted. "She returned to Alaska."

"That's what you call a long-distance relationship."

John swirled the steaming liquid in his cup. "I . . . I'm thinking about the pro and cons of getting married." He raised the cup to his lips and swallowed hard, almost choking on the hot coffee. *There he had said the words! And at McDonald's of all places! And to Arnold of all people!*

Arnold stared at him. "Married! Man, you are serious, aren't you?"

"I guess I am."

"How well do you know her? You were only in Alaska for a month or so. And you said she was only visiting New York for several days."

"I know her well enough."

"What does your family think? Do your boys like her?"

"They haven't met her."

"Where do you plan to live? Will she move to New York?"

"I haven't asked her. Look, I didn't mean to say anything. I've been thinking and thinking about her and it just popped out."

"Off hand, I'd say you're rushing things, John. I mean there's nothing like an old fool who thinks he's in love. Have you thought about just living together? Trying things out before you take the bit in your mouth?"

"I have thought of cohabitation," John admitted, "but there is the moral issue and I don't think Grace would go for it. She's a real lady."

Arnold nodded. "Hell, I'd want to see how the wind was blowing before I made things legal. I had a buddy say that after he married a widow he noticed a fancy wooden box sitting on her bureau. Turned out it held the ashes of her dead husband. She wouldn't remove it and he said he felt like the guy's ghost was watching everything he did in bed. Put a real crimp in things. I'd at least insist on a prenup. It'll protect you financially and give your children peace of mind if you tell them they are protected. I hate to say this but a lawyer friend of mine stated that money is the biggest problem in second marriages. Kids won't admit to it, but deep down they resent the fact that someone else might inherit the money that their mother helped their father save."

"I think I'd find it hard to ask Grace for a prenup. Money is a sensitive subject."

"At least you'd have a better idea what kind of woman she is."

"I've never seen her show the slightest interest in material things. Just the opposite. In fact, only recently, she confided that she thinks her son's marriage is in jeopardy because her daughter-in-law is somewhat of a spendthrift."

"How many children does she have?"

"Two . . . a son and a daughter."

"Have they been receptive to you?"

"Yes and no."

Arnold shook his head. "Gotta be one or the other. Look John, I think you'd better get a clearer picture of this whole thing. Seems like there are a lot of loose ends."

John jumped to his feet. "Look forget I said anything, okay? I've got to get going. Bandit is tied out back and he'll freeze to death."

John practically ran out the door. What ever had gotten into him?

CHAPTER NINETEEN

During Grace's stay in the east she had come to realize what she so blessedly escaped by living in Alaska—the pressure of time, the press of people living and working close together. Thursday morning, she rose at daybreak and set out for the beach. She preferred to get her exercise early before starting the day. The morning air was crisp and cold and fog lay close to the ground, thick as gauze. She walked at a fast pace to warm up. Along the bike path the trees were ghost like, shrouded in fog. Beyond that the sea tumbled and churned. Grace almost bumped into a woman tossing breadcrumbs into the air. Gulls were wheeling in from all directions shrieking with excitement. Grace slowed to a strolling pace, letting her thoughts wander to the letter she had received from John.

The letter had come in yesterday's mail and she still hadn't recovered from the shock. He was flying into Anchorage on Friday. He missed her and wanted to talk about their future.

Oh, my, she thought. *Oh, my.*

Future?

What could their future possibly be? What about the geographic question? Where would they live? "Hold it kiddo," she muttered under her breath. "Maybe I'm reading more into his message than I should." She was assuming that he meant marriage—spending the rest of their lives together. But perhaps she was jumping the gun. Perhaps all he wanted to talk about was keeping the status quo, within the bounds of a simple commitment to one another. And wouldn't that be the more sensible way to go?

Or, heaven forbid, maybe he meant that he realized the futility of a long distance romance and wanted to end it cleanly.

She drew a deep breath of the crisp-cold air. Despite the perpetual February darkness she could see the outline of the mountains rising in the distance. Even in the icy moonlight they were magnificent.

She fondled the letter tucked in her pants pocket. He had linked missing her with their future together, hadn't he? What would she do if he asked her to marry him? How would she feel if he didn't?

She had a lot of thinking to do. There were a million reasons why she didn't want to get married again. And a million reasons why she did.

Always, when she and Peter had to make a major decision—like what car to buy or what college would be best for one of the children—they listed all of the pros and cons on a sheet of columnar paper. She could do that, but this decision involved the heart and emotions and love. Those feelings did not belong on an analytical sheet of paper.

Friday! That gave her two days to agonize over what she really felt for John Hathaway.

Friday evening she was waiting anxiously outside the security gates at Anchorage International. The plane was an hour late and she was a bundle of nerves. Then she saw his tall frame striding toward her, his gaze searching the crowd of people for her. After a hurried kiss they took the escalator to the lower level baggage claim.

"Do you sense a feeling of déjà vu?" John teased. "This was where it all began."

Grace chuckled. "Little did I know what lay ahead when I followed a tall, silver-haired man through this very terminal."

"Let's just hope we don't have a repeat of the lost luggage syndrome."

Fortunately, John's bag was one of the first out of the chute and he grabbed it on the first go round.

"What about Bandit? Do we have to claim him?" Grace asked.

"No. I left him home. My housekeeper agreed to go over every day and feed him."

So he didn't bring the dog, she thought with a jolt. *He must not be expecting to stay long.*

John took her elbow and began to lead her toward the exit door. "I'm starved. You don't get enough to eat on planes nowadays. What do you say we go directly to the hotel and have dinner."

"That's fine with me. You said you made reservations at the Marriott?"

"Yes." He looked at her anxiously. "I only booked one room . . . a suite. Is that all right with you?"

Grace felt a rush of heat to her face. "I guess," she mumbled, unable to meet his gaze. She simply wasn't used to this way of doing things. The idea of checking into a hotel with a man that wasn't her husband was discomforting to her. Somehow the circumstance of the other nights they had spent together were different.

John apparently realized her discomfort because he quickly changed the subject.

They made small talk during dinner, bringing each other up to date on their activities since Christmas, carefully sidestepping the subject that had clearly brought John to Alaska. The room was crowded, a noisy group of four couples were seated across from them, one woman with a raucous laugh.

Finally, John reached across the table and took her hand in his. "Honey, I want to talk to you, and this obviously is not the place. Can we go up to our room?"

Grace gave him a shaky smile and simply nodded yes.

John ordered a bottle of wine delivered to the room and after the waiter left they settled themselves on the sofa. Grace took a small sip of her drink. It was a delightful Pinot Noir with a faint flavor of oak. "Um," she said. "This is good."

John slipped his shoes off and settled back against the cushions. The heating unit clicked on with a small whoosh of air and through the sheer drapes they could see the lights in dozens of skyscrapers. The muted sound of traffic played in the background.

"Did you know that over two hundred thousand people live in Anchorage . . . more than half the entire population of Alaska," Grace commented.

"So, I've heard."

"As you know during the winter it's dark most of the time. And cold too."

John gave her a crooked grin. "Honey, I didn't come over three thousand miles to talk about the weather." He slipped his arm around her and pulled her to his chest. Gently he tilted her head back and settled his lips on hers.

She dissolved like warm butter at his touch, returning his kiss deeply, their lips becoming warmer, almost savage in intensity. She heard him groan as his hand caressed her back, crushing her against him.

"God, woman. What you do to me," he whispered, his eyes dark and smoldering.

Grace had to admit he did the same to her, her carefully banked desire fanned into fire. She hadn't dreamed she could ever again feel this deep, demanding love. All of her arguments over the past two months, to remain free and unencumbered, flew out the window.

She wanted love. She needed love.

John issued a deep sigh. "After you flew back here it was if my whole world went dark. For a while I tried to talk myself into believing that it was for the best. We hadn't spent more than several weeks together, really didn't know each other that well. I don't want to give up my home and family and move to Alaska to live; you've made it perfectly clear you want to be here. It seemed an unsolvable dilemma." He winked at her salaciously. "That worked until I began to miss you miserably."

"And I missed you. I've gone over all the same arguments, John. What are we going to do?"

"Suppose I stayed here for now. We could live together . . . get to know each other better. See if we can work out the geographic differences."

Grace felt a flash of anger. "Live together? What would our children think of us?"

"They have their lives . . . we have ours."

"I don't buy that argument, John. I'm well aware that the rules of society have changed. It would be more of a problem for me than for my children."

"In what way?"

A thousand reasons flew through her mind. She wasn't a prude, she liked to think of herself as a modern, well-informed woman. Yet, it would be a problem for her.

"I . . . I guess I'm just old-fashioned. It would go against all my moral principals." She gave him a pitiful look of appeal. "I would be ashamed."

"Then forget I asked. I never want you to be ashamed of our love. I only mentioned it because it seems our culture today accepts different mores from those we grew up with. Many seniors have reasons for taking this route . . . loss of pensions, reductions in social security benefits, or other reasons . . . like the objections of their children."

"I know all that."

"Grace, I'm in love with you. I don't want to live without you in my life. There's no reason to analyze it further."

"Are you saying you want to get married?"

"I guess this isn't very romantic." John's mouth curved in a half-smile. "I'd get down on my knees but at my age I'm afraid I wouldn't be able to get back up."

Oh-my-God, he was proposing. She swallowed hard to ease the tightness in her chest. *Do I really want to marry again? To assume the daily duties of a wife? To give up my newfound independence— my dream? Suppose I get sick and John is faced with caring for another invalid wife.* Her heart was pounding. But she loved him!

"Say something," John said.

"Where would we live?" she stammered inanely.

"We can work something out. What if we built a life together that's divided between New York and Alaska? I would be willing to compromise. When your job ends in September we could leave Denali and spend the winter in New York, then return in the spring."

"It might work."

"Would you be willing to try?"

Grace looked into his anxious brown eyes. "I love you John— have no doubt about that—but do I have the right to disrupt your life this way? You're at an age when you should be settled in one place, not running back and forth across the continent twice a year to satisfy my desire to become a guide and live in Alaska."

"Darling, you forget I have been a journalist all my life. Traveling is nothing new for me. I wouldn't have accepted this last assignment if it were."

He pulled her closer softly nuzzling her neck, running his hands through her hair. She pressed against him and locked her lips on his. The kiss was hard and demanding and ended with both of them breathless. This time when they parted Grace knew the answer. Love erases all logic. She reached up and traced the outline of his lips with her finger. "I love you, too. With all my heart and soul. You came to me like a whisper in the night. And I do want you to be a part of my life."

"Is that a 'Yes' then?"

"Yes."

After giving her a long kiss John poured himself another glass of wine and took a deep swallow. "There are some other things we need to discuss, though."

"I know. Your sons haven't met me. Do they even know about me, John?"

"Yes. Before I flew out here I had both families to the house for dinner and told them all about you."

"How did they react?"

"They were surprised. They didn't know I had been seeing anyone. Of course, I didn't indicate that I was thinking of getting married. Both boys said they understood the need for companionship and wanted me to be happy." John drummed his fingers on the stem of his glass. "Adam seemed a little upset. He kept mentioning his mother. And my age. I think he was hoping I'd confide that I am too old for sex." He smiled ruefully. "As far as that goes, children can never picture their parents having sex. I don't know how they think they were conceived."

Grace laughed.

John laughed, too, then grew sober. "And I'm afraid I may have a little trouble with your son, Ben. He seems very possessive of you. Given a little time, I hope both of our boys will come around." His heavy eyebrows furrowed and he looked down at his clasped hands. "But while we are talking frankly I think we need to discuss our mutual finances."

"You needn't worry about supporting me," Grace replied curtly. "Peter left me a large insurance policy and we had enough savings to see us through our retirement years."

"I didn't mean that. After you are my wife I will support you. That's a husband's responsibility." He looked away, his eyes not meeting hers. "Please don't get angry. I think we should have a prenuptial agreement. Our estates, prior to our marriage, should go to our children."

"By all means. I want my estate to pass to Ben and Susan."

John put his arm around her shoulder and pulled her to him. "I think I am a very lucky man."

Grace grinned dreamily. "And I think I have just been proposed to."

John laughed. "That you have. Now all we have to settle is where and when. I know one thing I want it to be fast and private. "

Grace reached up and caressed his face, rough with stubble. "Honey, you must be dead tired, it's been a long day for you, you flew coast to coast, and it's past midnight, Why don't we wait until tomorrow to talk about the details?"

"I am tired," he admitted.

She gave him a soft smile. "Then, let's go to bed. Tomorrow we can talk about the where and the when."

John ordered their breakfast from room service and, surprisingly, the hot cakes were hot and blueberry syrup perfect. With a second cup of coffee in her hand Grace wandered over to an end table where she picked up a magazine. "John, look at this." She waved the magazine in front of him. "It's about getting married in Alaska. There's a really great article entitled 'Saying I Do in Rubber Boots'."

John looked askance.

She plopped down on the edge of the bed and began to read. "Honest, honey. It says Alaska is only one of five states to use marriage commissioners to perform weddings. These are ordinary people, like cruise operators or lodge owners, who can get a one-day permit to marry you. They'll take you anywhere . . . up on a glacier, beside a remote lake, out in the wilderness. According to this article, during Alaska's early days when the closest minister or judge could be several days away it became the custom to use marriage commissioners."

"So, what do you want to do . . . get married on a glacier?"

Grace broke out in a gay laugh. "You must admit it's a novel idea."

"I wouldn't put it past you."

"Seriously, though. I would like to get married beside a lake or someplace special. It's a shame not to take advantage of all this natural beauty."

"You're right. How about the beachfront in Seward with Resurrection Bay in the background?"

"That's a lovely idea, John. Something like that would be perfect. Let's think about it. I want you to read this article. It sounds like a quick, uncomplicated way to get married."

John poured another cup of coffee and settled himself on a chair to read the magazine.

Grace lay down across the bed deep in thought. This could be fun. Different. Hadn't the article indicated that marriage commissioners could be lodge owners? What about Lois? She jumped up in excitement and ran over to John. "Why not have Lois marry us at Wonder Lake? At the base of Mt. McKinley."

"Wow . . . you've really grabbed hold of this idea, haven't you?"

"It's perfect. Oh, John let's. Lois would be thrilled."

"We have to find out more about this marriage commissioner proposition, though." John's face grew serious and he laid the magazine aside and joined her on the edge of the bed. He took her hand in his and stroked it gently. "Grace, I know I said I wanted it to be quick but it's still winter up here and I need to go back to New York. We mentioned a prenuptial and I'd like to have it prepared in New York by a lawyer who has been a long time friend of our family. Of course, before you sign it you will want to run it by your attorney. Plus, this is March. I need to get my income tax prepared. And I have to take care of Bandit and spend some time with my family to tell them my plans."

Grace felt a flush of disappointment, then chagrin. Of course, he was right. She was letting her emotions run amuck. She, too, needed to talk to her children. Susan would be fine with the idea of her marrying again but Ben was a different story.

"We'll go back together," she said. "I'll consult the lawyer in Pittsburgh who handled Peter's estate. I've also been wanting to set up trust funds for my grandchildren." She grinned. "And I need to tell Susan and Ben that their mother is getting married."

"Once our legal affairs are taken care of we could get married in New York and wait until the first of May to return here and get settled at Big Bear Lodge," John suggested.

"If we get married back east we will have to invite all of the children and things will get complicated. I'd rather return here and get married without a lot of fanfare."

"That's fine with me. I will have to close the brownstone and I want to talk to my editor at the *Times*. Maybe he can give me another assignment in Alaska. Do you need to go back to Seward first?"

Grace nodded. "I'll need more clothes than I have with me. I only packed an overnight bag. I suppose we should expect to be gone several weeks."

"At least. Attorneys, even friends, don't work quickly. Where will you stay?"

"With Ben and Emily." Her lips pursed. "Susan has moved in with Jason. I couldn't stay there. I would be in their way."

While John placed a phone call to the airlines Grace began to pack. John's mention of the brownstone had caused her a wave of dismay. She would have to get used to the idea of living there for six months of the year. Surely John would let her change things, give it her imprint, make it more like her home.

Mention of their respective children also gave her pause. She wondered how John's sons would accept her. She knew from talking to other widows who had remarried that often children, who were quite receptive to their parent dating someone for companionship, reacted quite differently when marriage entered into the equation.

I hope I am doing the right thing, she worried, suddenly unsure of herself. *Am I letting my heart rule my judgment?* Actually, I don't know John very well. I wonder what he likes to eat, if he is hard to cook for, if he is ever moody or has a temper. I wonder if he is receptive to change—or set in his ways. I know his house was tidy but he has a housekeeper. What about religion? He has never mentioned his faith.

Maybe Susan was right—maybe it was smarter for couples to live together for a while and get to know one another.

No! It was against everything she had been raised to believe. She loved him—things would work out for them.

John set out for a run. The train for Seward didn't leave for an hour and he needed time to clear his head. Things were happening awfully fast. When Grace said she would be ashamed to just live together he had had to scrap that idea in a hurry. And there were private worries that he hadn't discussed with Grace. The idea of dividing his time between New York and Alaska did not really appeal to him. He was getting too old to pack up every six months and move despite his reassurance to Grace. But it did seem to be the only solution to their geographic problem. Maybe she would tire of being a naturalist guide and settle down into a normal retirement. Then again maybe she wouldn't. He had seen her independent side, her zest for life, and wasn't that what he admired in the first place?

He also worried about the acceptance of their children. The idea of a second marriage was completely foreign to him. It frightened him. Then he remembered Grace's merry laugh, her independence, her willingness to step out in life with no preconditions. With a half-smile, he shook his head and chuckled, shrugged, sighed and stepped up his pace.

Three days later Grace and John boarded a plane for New York. Their plan was to introduce Grace to Adam and George, then Grace would backtrack to Pittsburgh to present the news to her own family.

Much to John's disappointment the pills had not had the desired effect. In addition to being of no avail they made him sick to his stomach and when he confessed why he was ill, Grace refused to let him try again. She was such a sweetheart and so understanding, insisting that she was content just to be held and caressed. To be loved in other ways. However, he wasn't ready to throw in the towel just yet. When he returned home he intended to consult Chad again to discuss other options.

Once they were airborne, and served with soft drinks and peanuts, Grace turned to John. "Tell me more about your boys," she said.

"Well, Adam was the first born." John grinned. "I think Mary got pregnant on our wedding night because, to my parents consternation, he was born a scant nine months after we got married."

John's face grew reflective. "He was always somewhat of a mama's boy, quiet, uninterested in sports, an 'A' student both in high school and college. He loved animals and always had a pet of some sort."

"Where did he go to college?"

"NYU. Both boys did. Adam went to work for the Chase Bank in Manhattan right out of college and is still there. He met Becky at work and they dated for several years before they got married. They have three children, Sharon, Gail and Margaret.

"Margaret is the oldest. She is twenty-nine and a secretary at a brokerage house on Wall Street. Gail is a social-worker and engaged to a young medical student. Sharon is still in college. She's an Art major." He smiled proudly. "They are wonderful girls. We had the two boys and Mary always wanted a daughter so the girls spent a lot of time at our house. Mary adored them and they adored her."

"You said your boys live nearby. Where exactly?"

"In Englewood, New Jersey, an upscale town three miles west of Manhattan via the George Washington Bridge. They have a lovely four bedroom Colonial that is much too large for them now that the girls are grown and leaving home. After Sharon graduates they would like to sell and move into the city—closer to Adam's work."

"And George . . . what about him?"

"Just the opposite from Adam. A hellion when he was a young-ster, lettered in basketball and football. He was a playboy and almost flunked out of college. George was also the best looking of the two boys—tall and stocky with curly black hair and long eyelashes that Mary swore drove the girls crazy. He isn't married and I worry about that sometimes."

"Why?"

"Oh, afraid that he might be . . . you know . . . ." John's voice faltered.

"And if he is. What would your reaction be?"

"Disappointment. I wouldn't disown him if that's what you mean. He's my son." John ran his hand through his hair. "I really don't think I have to worry, though. He has dated a number of girls over the years. When I question him about his single status he simply says he can't find a girl as great as his Mom."

"That's sweet," Grace said primly.

John shot her a questioning glance.

Grace changed the subject. "You know you have never mentioned your faith, John. What is it?"

"Lutheran. In fact I am a deacon in my church. Does that surprise you?"

"It does."

"I missed going to church while I was in Alaska. I was always on the move. How about you, honey? I don't remember you mentioning any particular church affiliation."

"Peter and I belonged to the Presbyterian Church where both of our children were confirmed. Ben converted to Catholicism after he married Emily and both Ted and Kelly went to parochial school. Susan still belongs to the Squirrel Hill Presbyterian Church where she attended Sunday School." She frowned. "I'm afraid I'm not a very faithful church goer."

"We'll change that. You'll enjoy my church. We can join after we get married."

Grace bristled. *Was he already making decisions for her?* When a stewardess approached them with offers of pillows and lap robes she was glad for the distraction. John reached under his seat and removed a book from his carry-on. She glanced at the title—"Bill Clinton, My Life."

"Are you a Democrat," she asked.

"Yes. You?"

"Republican."

"Hmm."

Grace pulled out her own book. She seldom read non-fiction, preferring English mysteries. Her face grew pensive. This little "get to know each other" session wasn't going too well.

John reached over and folded her hand in his. He winked and raised her hand to his mouth, kissing her fingers one by one. All of her misgivings dissolved at his touch. Democrat or Republican, Lutheran or Presbyterian, fiction or non-fiction—what did it matter? She loved this man.

CHAPTER TWENTY

It was warm for March, gloomy and raining. New York City was awash in a downpour when the plane landed at LaGuardia, the wait for a cab interminable. Grace began to develop a headache which quickly grew worse after John gave the driver the address of his home in the Village. She could not believe she had not given thought to where she would stay while in New York.

"Aren't you dropping me off at a hotel, first?" she asked anxiously.

John blinked with surprise. "I . . . I assumed you would stay with me . . . in my house. Come on Grace, it's foolish to stay in a hotel. Besides, as you know from your stay at the Plaza, hotels are terribly expensive in the city."

"John, what impression would that give your family? I think we have to ease into this. It's going to be enough of a shock when they find out their father is planning to get married. I don't want them to think we are living together."

"They needn't know where you are staying. I was planning to take everyone out to dinner . . . tomorrow if possible . . . to introduce you."

Grace's mouth tightened into a stubborn line, her head throbbing. "I'm not ready to move into your home. I want to go to a hotel."

"If you insist. But honey, it's late. At least come home with me tonight and make reservations tomorrow morning."

Grace sighed. Nodded. "I suppose I am being silly, but honestly you took me by surprise. I do think I should stay in a hotel, though. I want to make a good impression on your sons. And there's my family to consider. I need to call and let them know where I am. They will ask where I am staying and I can hardly say I am staying at your house."

"I think you'll find that the younger generation is less judgmental than we are."

"Perhaps, but you don't know my daughter-in-law." She nestled her aching head on his broad shoulder. "She's Catholic," she added as though that explained everything.

They arrived at the brownstone, tired, wet, and more than a little disgruntled.

Bridget had been by earlier to feed Bandit, but the dog was so excited to see them he refused to calm down. Despite the rain and the hour John drew on a yellow slicker and took him for a quick run while Grace prepared a late supper from items in the freezer.

She moved about the kitchen, peering into the pantry, opening and closing cupboard doors, examining the silverware tray. Meals were apparently all served in the dining room because the kitchen, long and narrow, afforded no place to eat. The cabinets were old fashioned, high with dark paneled wood and brass pulls, the walls cream, the floor oak. She shook her head in dismay at the stove, it had to be of 1950's vintage, with gas burners. She hadn't cooked with gas for many years, although it had recently come back into vogue.

A fairly new microwave sat on a counter beside the sink and Grace sighed with relief. She plopped in a frozen lasagna and studied the dials. After touching a few pads that beeped furiously but did not seem to turn it on she finally got things humming.

She found the dishes and silverware and carried them into the dining room. An oblong walnut table with a fluted center pedestal graced the middle of the room. It was covered with a lace tablecloth that, although it showed a few stains, was still elegant. She needed place mats and pulled opened the drawers of a buffet but found only more tablecloths and napkins. A sterling silver tea set was centered on the gleaming walnut surface flanked by silver holders with tapered candles. Dried flowers in an etched glass vase sat at one end and a silver framed picture at the other. Her gaze settled on the picture. She picked it up. It showed a young John in dress navy whites and a pretty girl in a white wedding gown. Grace felt a lurch in her stomach. Up until this moment she had kept the green-eyed monster at bay but it overcame her now. This was the love of his youth, and this was the home Mary had made for him and their children.

Her chest tightened. She was coming into this relationship at the bottom of the totem pole. She had sold everything she owned—everything of a material nature that is, except Peter's cello. She could bring nothing to this house to make it her home.

The front door opened to a whirlwind of dog and rain. Grace hurriedly replaced the picture and retreated to the kitchen. Bandit ran to her for a quick ear scratch before John grabbed him by the collar and moved him out to the laundry room.

The microwave began to beep. "Dinner's about ready," Grace shouted.

"Just a moment," he called over his shoulder. I need to towel this mutt off and clean his paws before he gets mud over everything."

She lifted the bubbling pasta from the microwave, set it atop the stove. John snuck up behind her and nuzzled her neck. "Um, I don't know which smells better, you or the lasagna," he said with an exaggerated groan.

"It better be me." She gave him a quick peck on the cheek. "Where do you keep the place mats and hot pads."

"He pulled open one of the cabinet drawers next to the sink. "Here."

"Oh, I thought they would be in the buffet, next to the table where you eat."

"No, Mary always kept them here."

"Hmm."

"Can I help?" John opened the refrigerator door. "Good, I see Bridget followed my instructions and picked up a few staples." He pulled out a loaf of bread, butter and a carton of milk.

"Bridget?"

"My housekeeper. You'll love her. She's as Irish as they come. A big, red-haired woman with a heart of gold. We've had her for years."

Grace did not miss the use of the word "we". She realized with a jolt she had a lot of adjusting to do, then silently reprimanded herself. She had to get over this. He was a widower. What had she expected?

The lasagna was delicious and despite their fatigue their plates were soon clean.

"I don't know about you but I am exhausted," John said as he helped Grace load the dishwasher. "What do you say we get to bed?"

She swallowed a lump in her throat as the impact of what he was proposing struck her. Of course, he expected her to share his bed. The same bed he had shared with his wife. She simply couldn't do it.

"John," she stammered, "I don't know how to say this but I . . . I just can't. It's the room and bed you shared with Mary. I mean somehow I think her presence would haunt me."

John's face paled and he looked completely bewildered. "But this is my home. Are you saying you don't want to live here because of Mary? We agreed . . . ."

"I know," Grace interrupted. "Honey, I'm not saying I don't want to live here. I just need a little time to adjust. To give it my imprint, to make it my home too. This is a big house, we could move our things into another room, maybe the one that faces the back. The one you pointed out as Adam's room."

John's eyes grew stormy. He looked confused and exasperated.

"Please, try to understand and help me with this," she implored.

"I don't understand . . . but if it's that important to you, go ahead."

"It is. Why don't you put my things in that room for tonight? We are both tired. I have a headache and could use a good night's sleep. We'll talk about all of this tomorrow."

Grace woke at first light and hopped out of bed, eager to explore the house before John woke. She tiptoed past his door, reassured that he was still asleep by heavy snores emanating from the room. Bandit trotted behind her and she started exploring in the front of the house spending an hour strolling through the high-ceilinged rooms. One thing became clear to her. The heavy, dark feeling had to be lightened. This could be done by painting the moldings and the mantles for the seven fireplaces white. They were beautiful examples of Victorian architecture and would stand out even more in gleaming white. The heavy drapes had to go. She would hang the deep windows with the finest of sheers.

She returned to the kitchen and Bandit, after looking quizzically at her to see if she wished to examine his yard, exited his doggie-door. The kitchen baffled her. She liked the homey feeling of eating in a kitchen and this long, narrow room did little to suggest a solution. Maybe they could knock the wall out between it and the dining room. She smiled inwardly imagining John's reaction to all this.

Just then she heard footsteps overhead and scurried to the refrigerator to see what Bridget had left them for breakfast.

The first thing John noticed when he awoke was that it was still raining. He swung his arm across the bed expecting to find Grace's warm body. It was empty. Of course, it was. She was down the hall in Adam's old room.

He considered going back to sleep but thoughts about last night crowded into his subconscious. He really didn't understand Grace's reluctance to share his bed. This was his bed now, had been his alone for years, freshly made up by Bridget. He shook his head in frustration. Sometimes there was no understanding a woman.

He could hear her moving about downstairs. He sniffed. The smell of freshly brewed coffee wafted upstairs. Breakfast was underway.

His stomach churned. He couldn't wait to get down to the kitchen, and not just for the food that awaited him. He couldn't wait to be with Grace, to touch her, and see her lovely smile. He jumped out of bed, showered quickly, drew on a pair of jeans, and bounded down the stairs. The kitchen smelled like heaven. Frying sausages sizzled in a skillet.

"Good morning," he said. "Did you sleep well?"

Grace smiled sweetly. "I did, it's very quiet in the back of the house." It was simply said as she went about cooking breakfast, humming to herself.

John went to the coffee maker to fill his cup. He pulled a stool from beneath the counter and perched on it. "Where did you find sausage?"

"In the freezer." She smiled, turning them over in the pan. "Your housekeeper has the refrigerator pretty well stocked too."

"She's a real gem. I can't wait for you to meet her."

"I'm looking forward to it." She took eggs and broke them into a glazed, stoneware bowl.

John started to tell her that the bowl was strictly decorative, not dishwasher safe, but thought better of it. He intended to tread softly until he found out the lay of the land.

She poured the eggs into the skillet. "I hope scrambled is okay."

"Just fine." He also didn't say that he always ate his eggs sunny side up.

"Take your coffee to the dining room. The eggs will be ready in a minute."

"Darling," she said as she set a plate of eggs, sausage, and toast in front of him. "I phoned the Hilton Hotel and made a reservation. It's in mid-town, right across from Grand Central Station."

After piling butter on a piece of toast he looked at her seriously. "I plan to call both Adam and George this morning and see if they are available for dinner tonight. Is that all right with you?"

Grace smiled, biting into her own piece of toast. Her eyes, softly green and mellow met his. "The sooner the better . . . I'll admit the whole prospect of meeting your family fills me with panic. But I guess you felt the same way when I dragged you off to Pittsburgh."

"Pure, unadulterated terror."

Just then the doggie-door in the kitchen banged and Bandit came skidding into the dining room. He immediately stopped beside Grace, his tail swishing wildly.

"Oh, oh. Bandit smelled the sausage," John said.

"Do you feed him from the table?"

"I'm afraid so." He tried to look appropriately apologetic. "Mar . . . ah, the kids spoiled him rotten."

"I see. Before you got up this morning he and I toured the house. I have a few ideas to brighten things up if you don't mind."

"Certainly. I want you to make it your home—to put your imprint on things. Are you thinking of new furniture?"

"That, and a few changes in wallpaper and paint. The mantles and woodwork would look lovely painted white." Her voice grew hesitant as she noticed the frown on John's face, but she hurried on. "And what would you think of taking down the wall that separates this room from the kitchen? It would make it much more convenient and easier to use."

"Honey, that would destroy the integrity of a brownstone. These homes have historical significance." He pushed his empty plate aside and rose. His handsome face was anxious, his silver hair rumpled as he repeatedly ran his fingers through it. He twisted the platinum wedding band he still wore. "We'll talk about this later, Okay? Right now I want to go to the den to make my phone calls. If we can work it out I'll call and make reservations at Sardis. We had a good meal there last time."

As he moved to make his phone calls he admitted to a feeling of panic. *Paint the beautiful oak mantles white and tear out walls.* This was a complication he had not foreseen. And now he had to call Adam and George. This was going to be a shock to his family.

"You mean she's with you? Here in New York?" Adam barked. "I don't understand, Dad."

"Look Adam, when we see you tonight I'll explain."

"I'll have to call home and see if Becky has plans for this evening. It's awfully short notice."

"I know it is and I apologize for that. But Grace is leaving for Pittsburgh tomorrow and I want you to meet her. I'm going to call George next to see if he can join us. Why don't you call me back after you check with Becky. I'll hold off making reservations until I hear from you."

An hour later John rejoined Grace in the kitchen. "Reservations are made for seven o'clock. It will only be you and me, George, Adam and Becky. My granddaughters can't make it. Oh, and I called my attorney. He has a cancellation this afternoon and can see us at two o'clock. He said it was best to talk to us together to discuss how we want the prenup drawn up. Then he will fax a copy to your attorney in Pittsburgh."

"Fine. That will give me plenty of time to get checked into the Hilton and dress. How far is the restaurant?"

"On 44th Street. A quick cab ride from your hotel. That's why I chose it."

"How did your boys react? I imagine they were surprised."

"I guess you could say that." He walked over and gathered her into his arms. "Everything is going to work out, sweetheart. They will love you."

"And what will you do if they don't?" she asked anxiously.

"Marry you anyway. You are mine, and I love you," he whispered. "Nothing is ever going to change that." He lowered his lips to hers and kissed her, his hands moving down to grasp her bottom and pull her tightly against him.

"I think you've gained a little weight," he said with a grin. "Maybe a pound or so in the butt area."

"John!" she exclaimed in mock horror.

Grace liked Becky immediately She was diminutive, a little overweight, with dimples in both cheeks and blond hair that Grace suspected got a little help from a bottle. She kept watching Grace with a smile, apparently excited at a romance brewing for her father-in-law.

She and John had decided on the way to the restaurant that they should not announce their intention to get married at this first meeting. It would be better to let Adam and George meet her first.

Adam was silent and aloof. After a few polite questions about her background he directed most of his conversation to his father.

George, on the other hand, with a bemused look on his handsome face, kept looking from his father to Grace, to Grace from his father. He seemed to be the complete opposite of Adam. While Adam was serious and thin-lipped, George had an easygoing smile. Adam was fair with light brown hair and a slender frame. George, on the other hand, had thick, coal-black, hair undoubtedly an earlier version of John's silver hair and he had inherited his father's features, from the strong eyebrows that defined his clear, dark-brown eyes, to the tall, muscular stature of his body. He seemed intrigued with Grace's plans to become a naturalist guide in Alaska and she felt an immediate infinity with him. They were soon engrossed is conversation, George asking her question after question about the Denali area.

When Adam excused himself to go to the men's room Becky scooted over next to Grace. "Do you have grandchildren?" she asked.

"Two. Ted is a senior in high school and Kelly is a junior at Penn State."

"I can't wait to have some grandchildren," Becky bubbled. "It's a long time off, though. The girls all want careers and don't seem to be in any hurry to move out of the nest and get married."

"Girls today don't feel the pressure to find a husband that we did," Grace agreed.

"How do you and Dad plan to see each other . . . you living in Alaska and him in New York?"

Grace felt her face grow warm and glanced at John. He had apparently heard Becky's question and reached under the table to squeeze her hand. Silence descended on the table. Apparently everyone had heard the question and was waiting for the answer.

John came to her rescue. "We'll work it out," he said. "I've become quite fond of this dear lady. I'll admit it is a rather long commute between Anchorage and New York City but plane service is convenient. Except for Grace's summer job we are both retired and free to travel. Then, of course, there is the telephone and mail."

Becky beamed. "I think it's wonderful that you've found each other, Dad."

The waiter appeared to remove their plates and take dessert orders. Grace sighed with relief. She felt a little guilty, but she and John still had a lot of details to work out. Foremost, of course, was the prenup. They had agreed on the basic details but it would take time for his lawyer to prepare and forward to her's for approval.

Adam returned in time to hear his father's comments. He gazed at Grace, a deep frown creasing his brows. *He has quirky eyebrows just like John*, Grace thought inanely. She sensed that he was not in favor of her.

"You said you always lived in Pittsburgh. What made you want to leave?" he asked.

She picked up a napkin and slowly wiped her mouth, vying for time to find the right words. It was a question she had asked herself, over and over. "I'm not sure I can answer that, Adam. It was not so much a matter of wanting to leave as it was a feeling that I didn't want to stop living just because my husband was gone. And I wanted to have my life mean something. I'll admit choosing Alaska was an unusual decision but I honestly believe someone, or something, was guiding me. The Alaskan wilderness is unbelievably beautiful and I hope, working as a guide, I can convey my reverence for its majesty and wildlife to others."

She eased back in her chair. John had been studying her face and he smiled now. His look of love was obvious. He leaned over and kissed her cheek.

Becky giggled in delight, Adam pursed his lips, and George laughed.

Dessert was served and the conversation turned to the activities of John's grandchildren.

It was still raining and the temperature had dropped. "This could be ice by morning," John commented as they left the cozy restaurant. They huddled in the doorway waiting for the doorman to hail them cabs.

George had a late night date with a waitress from a nearby club so he winked at his dad, gave Grace a tight hug, and took off running.

Becky kissed her on the cheek. "I know you are going to Pittsburgh tomorrow but please visit us the next time you are in New York. I'll try to get all the girls together to meet you." She grinned wrinkling her nose. "Notice, I said try. Getting them all together at the same time is a real challenge. They are a whirlwind of activities."

Adam's mouth quirked in annoyance. "On the contrary I'm sure they will be eager to assess their grandfather's new companion," he said.

Grace did not miss the sarcasm. This was not going to be easy.

Taxis are always hard to come by on a rainy Friday night so John planned to say goodbye to Grace in the cab, drop her off at the hotel and continue on home. She had an early morning flight, that would get her up in the middle of the night.

They were barely settled in the warmth of the cab when he pulled her to him. His mouth skimmed hers, gentle at first, then hardening as his passion swelled. He moved his lips along her jaw, up to her nose, then buried his face in her hair. "Tell me you'll miss me, Grace," he murmured, finding her lips once more. "That you'll think of me."

"Night and day." Her fingers reached up to caress the side of his face. "I don't want you to leave me. I need you tonight." Her voice was silken and thick.

And he knew, from somewhere deep inside, that he needed tonight as much as she.

"Cancel Greenwich Village," he called to the driver. "I'll be getting off with the lady at the Hilton."

CHAPTER TWENTY-ONE

Grace had explained her return to Pennsylvania by telling Ben and Susan only that she had some unexpected legal business to take care of.

Ben was waiting for her at the security gate. After giving her a bear hug he grabbed her small suitcase and carry-on. His gaze scanned her face, his eyes anxious. "I hope this isn't anything serious," he said. "Not that we aren't glad to see you again so soon," he added quickly.

"Not at all. I'll explain later."

"If you want to wait here at the curb I'll claim the car and pick you up. The parking garage was full. It's quite a long walk."

"That would be good. I'm somewhat tired . . . I had to be at the airport early." Grace fought to hide a smile. That wasn't the only reason she was tired.

Half an hour later they were speeding north on Route 28 toward Oakmont. "Ted's basketball team is playing tonight. It's part of the Regional Tournament at Pitt Field House. I hope you'll go with us. He is all excited about having his grandma see him play."

"Of course, I'll go." She smiled ruefully. "I still remember the first Jaycee game he played in. Your dad was so proud of him."

"It's a shame you weren't here to see all his games."

Grace did not know how to answer the accusatory comment so she remained silent, twisting in her seat to gaze out the window at the slow moving Allegheny River. A tug was headed north pushing a long barge loaded with steel. They chatted idly as Grace explained one of the reasons for her return. "I want to file my income tax return here with my accountant because he is familiar with the sale of my house."

"Susan wants to see you but she has to work tomorrow and she and Jason are entertaining in the evening. They will be over for dinner on Sunday."

Grace looked at him intently. "I have detected an undercurrent in your letters. How are things going between you and Emily?"

"She's not a happy camper, right now. I talked her out of remodeling the kitchen. She was pretty upset but I convinced her we couldn't really afford it. With Ted graduating from high school we will have two in college next year."

"Are financial woes your only problem, son?"

"Not really." He pursed his lips. "I just don't know . . . we seem to be at odds with each other all the time. Maybe when both kids are in college and she is free to get a job and some independence it will be better. Then again, maybe not. I'm afraid the romance has gone out of our marriage."

"That happens sometimes. The financial stress of maintaining a home and educating two children can cause tension."

Ben looked grim. "Right now if Ted and Kelly were out of school I think I'd leave her." He slapped his palm on the steering wheel. "Maybe come out to Alaska and live with you. Start over."

My, oh my, she thought with dismay. Instead she said, "Be patient, Ben. You and Emily were happy once. I believe you can work it out."

They pulled up in front of the house and Ben scurried around the car to open the door for her. He leaned down and kissed her on the cheek. "I love you, Mom," he said.

"I love you too, son."

That night they went to the basketball game between Oakmont and Penn Hills. Ted was a senior starter and played guard, racking up twelve points and three assists. It was an important game between two bitter rivals and the score seesawed back and forth until Oakmont surged ahead with fifty-four seconds left to play and won 78 to 76.

Grace screamed until she was hoarse. She was so proud of this grandson of hers. Twice Ben reminded her that Oakmont had only one loss and might be in the championship playoffs. It would be a shame if she were still in Alaska and did not get to see him play!

Sunday morning she accompanied Ben and Emily to St. Francis

Catholic Church.

"I let Ted sleep," Emily said with a laugh. "He was completely zonked after the game and party. He can go to late Mass."

Ironically, the gospel was on Jesus' first miracle, changing water to wine at the wedding at Cana in Galilee. The priest's homily spoke of both a son's respect for his mother as Jesus honored her request and also the importance of the sacrament of marriage. Grace listened intently. Marriage was very much on her mind as was retaining the respect of her family.

They exited the church into brilliant sunshine, a late winter day of biting cold, frost, and a pale, cloudless sky.

"It looks like snow," Emily commented. "Susan and Jason are coming to dinner. I hope the roads don't get icy." She gave Grace a sour look. "I guess you know they are living together."

"Yes, I know."

"I don't approve, but then what can I say. I'm only a sister-in-law."

"When they feel the time is right I'm sure they will get married," Grace said quietly.

At two o'clock that afternoon the doorbell rang and Grace hurried to answer it.

"Mom," Susan cried, throwing her arms around her. "Oh, I've missed you." A sprinkling of snow dusted her blond hair and her nose was red with cold. She wore fuzzy ear muffs, a Sherpa-lined coat Grace had never seen before and red mittens. She looked lovely.

Jason stood politely beside her and extended his hand. "It's good to see you again, Mrs. Maguire."

Grace showed them into the living room and Ben took their coats. Drinks were served and everyone chatted. The robust aroma of roast beef wafted from the kitchen, a cranberry candle burned on the mantle and a wood fire crackled in the fireplace.

"I'm glad I cleaned out the grate," Ben said as he added a few chunks of wood to the fire. "This will take the chill out of your bones."

"That and some red wine," Susan said. "Now, tell us Mom. What brings you back here so soon? Did the Alaskan winter get to you?"

Grace wavered. Emily was still in the kitchen and Ted had not yet arrived home. She wanted everyone present when she broke her news. "No indeed, I need to take care of my income tax and some unexpected legal affairs," she said instead. "Nothing serious but I wanted to use Bill Schier, the attorney Dad and I had in Pittsburgh."

Ted arrived only minutes before Emily poked her head out of the kitchen to announce that dinner was about ready. Grace jumped to her feet. "Susan why don't you and I go out to the kitchen and help Emily serve dinner."

"That beef was the best I've ever had, Mrs. Maguire," Jason said wiping his mouth on a linen napkin. "Susan is right—you are a fantastic cook."

Emily gave him a thin smile and excused herself from the table. Minutes later she emerged from the kitchen bearing a golden pie. "Our dessert," she said, holding it aloft. "Cranberry, apple. It's a new recipe I found in this month's Country Cooking magazine."

She cut it into eight pieces and passed the plates around the table.

Grace bit into hers and sighed. It was scrumptious with a thin, flaky crust, the tartness of the cranberries merging with the sweetness of apples. "What is your secret?" she asked Emily. "I've tried cranberries and apples together and the bottom crust always gets soggy."

"I cooked the apples for ten minutes in the microwave before I layered them with the cranberries. That got rid of a lot of the juice. I'll copy the directions for you if you want."

"Please. I've discovered that John loves pie."

"Do you see him often enough to bake pies for him?" Emily asked, giving Grace a slow, appraising look.

All eyes turned toward Grace.

She swallowed. *This is it then. This is the time to tell them.*

"John and I have decided to get married," she said.

Susan's fork stopped halfway to her mouth. She gasped, then jumped to her feet and ran to fling her arms around her mother. "How wonderful," she cried. "When?"

"Probably not till May. We haven't decided. We have a lot of things to work out."

Ben's face looked set in stone "Congratulations. I'm glad you finally got around to telling us," he said grounding out the words.

"Cool," Ted said with a huge grin. "That means you'll be coming back here to live, doesn't it Grandma?"

"Sort of, honey, but not entirely. We plan to compromise. We will spend the summer months in Alaska where I'll work at Big Bear Lodge as planned. During the winter we will live in John's home in New York City."

"That's okay. I can visit you both places" He jumped up and hugged her. "Boy, wait till I tell the guys. My grandma is marrying a big time journalist and has a home in Alaska and New York City. They'll be impressed!"

Ben pounded his fist on the table causing everyone to jump. "You hardly know the man. At least that's the impression I've been under." His eyes became narrow slits. "Or have I been under the wrong impression?"

"We have been together as much as geography allows." Her stomach fluttered. It was important that she said this right. "Ben, at our age time is a factor. Each day is a gift . . . a precious gift. We love each other and we recognize that we do not have unlimited years. I want us to be together every moment we can."

"In love! At your age. You're my mother, for heaven's sake."

She looked thoughtfully at Ben. *He doesn't want a mother who is part of today's culture. He wants a mother who is matronly, acting her age, more sedate than daring. He wants me to be a grandmother. And heaven only knows, he doesn't want to picture me in love, or having sex, with a man, other than his father.*

"I am thinking that I am very lucky to have love offered to me twice in my lifetime," she answered.

Ben looked confused. "It hasn't even been that long since Dad died. How can you love someone else?"

"Do you really think that time is a measure of how much I loved him?"

Susan, still standing beside Grace, began to cry. "Enough, Ben. Enough."

Emily hadn't spoken a word. She looked at Grace now, her brow puckered, her eyes cold and speculative. "You said you were here to take care of some legal matters. Does it have to do with your planned marriage?"

"Yes . . . and to meet John's children."

Emily nodded sagely. "I understand most seniors contemplating a second marriage have a prenup drawn up."

Grace noticed that it was not a question but a statement. She bridled, then realized this was typical of Emily. Money would be uppermost in her mind.

"Both John and I agree that our children's inheritance should be protected," Grace said.

Susan had regained her composure and, smiling jauntily, resumed her seat next to Jason. She leaned over and whispered in his ear, "Say something, honey."

"I think it's wonderful news, Mrs. Maguire."

The poor man never seemed to know what to call her—Grace, Mother, or Mrs. Maguire. "Thank you, Jason." She jumped to her feet. "Emily let me help you clear the table," she said, glad to have an opportunity to end the discussion. Tomorrow she would see her attorney and maybe avail herself of the downtown department stores to do some shopping. After all, she had a wedding dress to buy.

CHAPTER TWENTY-TWO

The next morning Grace woke to the sound of Ben's tires screeching on the driveway as he pulled out to go to work. *He's still angry*, she thought sadly.

Last evening had been a silent nightmare. Susan and Jason left right after dinner. Emily picked up a book and settled herself in the love seat under the window while Ben spent the evening watching television, flicking from channel to channel, a habit men seemed to have which always drove Grace crazy. There was no further talk about her pending marriage.

She had planned to spend several days with her son but realized this would be uncomfortable for all of them. Ben needed time to adjust to her news. Maybe she could leave tomorrow.

Today's appointments were with the attorney at ten and the accountant at two. Fortunately, she had made them before she left Seward knowing how long it sometimes takes to schedule a meeting. That would keep her busy most of the day and she planned to have lunch at the Cork and Bottle if it was still there.

Annoyed at her feeling of dread for the evening ahead with Ben and Emily she got up and went in to shower. Standing in the billowing warmth of steaming water she slowly began to relax. Thinking of lunch at the Cork and Bottle had brought back memories of her friend, Shirley, and their many shopping trips to Kaufman's Department Store. Grace turned her face up to the spiky assault of the shower. Shirley was now divorced and working as a receptionist for a furniture store on Liberty Avenue. What was the name of that store? Ah, yes—Colony House Furniture—that was it. Since it was on Liberty Avenue, not far from the accountant's office, she would stop in and surprise Shirley.

Her attorney, Bill Schier, greeted her with a warm smile.

"I imagine congratulations are in order, my dear," he said as he led her to the conference room. "In addition to the trust we are discussing a prenuptial agreement. That means only one thing."

"It does. I'm planning to get married in May."

"Who is the lucky gentleman? Do I know him."

"No, but you might recognize his name . . . John Hathaway. He was an investigative reporter for the *New York Times* for many years."

"Afraid not." He pulled a legal pad toward him and clicked open his pen. "Now, first of all, you indicated you wished to draw up a trust fund for your grandchildren. What do you have in mind?"

For the next hour they discussed her desire to set up trust funds for Ted and Kelly and to leave the balance of her estate—everything that was in her name at the time of her marriage—to Ben and Susan via the prenup which she and John were having drawn up.

As she left the office she glanced at her watch. It was only eleven o'clock. Maybe Shirley would be free for lunch.

Shirley, while delighted to see her, had a noon-time appointment for a manicure. She suggested they spend the evening together instead and catch up on all the news.

Perfect. That way I don't have to sit around forcing conversation with a sullen Ben, she thought with pleasure. She couldn't really fault her son. His role as protector, as the strong man in her life, had been terminated by someone he hardly knew. It was natural for him to be resentful of this intrusion into their lives. Surely, as he got to know John better, he would relent and be happy for her.

After a visit to her accountant Grace spent the rest of the afternoon shopping then, on a whim, decided to treat herself to dinner at Mario's on Fifth Avenue. She called Emily and told her she would not be home for supper and planned to spend the evening with an old friend. She thought Emily sounded relieved.

She arrived at Shirley's around seven and after a short tour of the small, but tastefully decorated, apartment they settled themselves on the couch with cups of herbal tea.

Grace looked at Shirley with sympathy. "Tell me what happened between you and Steven."

Shirley reflected a moment before answering. "You always knew I was unhappy in my marriage. I stayed with Steve until all of the children were gone, either in college or married, then I figured it was now or never." Shirley took a sip of her tea. "He was critical of everything I did. Remember when I took that correspondence course to be an interior decorator?"

"Yes, you were so enthusiastic. I was surprised that you didn't follow through on it."

"He wouldn't let me. In fact he wouldn't give me the money to pay for the course. I had to sneak it out of my grocery allowance." She reached up and began twisting a strand of her hair. "Of course, it was more than that. Toward the end we fought about everything . . . Sam's choice of a college, the Jewish boy Janice wanted to marry, Amanda's poor grades . . . just everything. And although I could never prove it I suspected he was being unfaithful."

"What about the house? You put so much work into it and had it decorated so beautifully."

"Well, since I left him he contested the divorce. He fought me tooth and nail over every piece of furniture and I ended up settling for only one-third the equity in the house. At that point I simply wanted out." She gave Grace a sardonic grin. "I've given most of the money back to the kids. Sam is a wildlife photographer so I invested in a good camera for him. He has a great job with the Pennsylvania Fish and Game Commission and Janice got married so I helped them with the down payment on a townhouse."

"What about Amanda?"

"She went into the military police. I only hope she doesn't get deployed to Iraq." Shirley jumped up from the couch. "Let me get you another cup of tea."

While she busied herself in the kitchen Grace gazed around the living room. It had Shirley's personality. Grace recognized the wicker rocking chair, upholstered in pink and green chintz, and remembered shopping with her for the fabric.

Shirley returned with steaming cups and a plate of cookies and sank down on the couch beside her. "Now, enough of my tale of woe. Let's hear all about this wonderful life you have carved out for yourself in Alaska."

"It is wonderful . . . but I haven't told you the most wonderful part." Her lips parted in a huge grin. "I am going to get married."

Disbelief, then joy spread across Shirley's face. "Oh, baby, that is great," she said. She glanced down at Grace's hand. "I don't see an engagement ring."

"We haven't had time." Grace's eyes clouded. She had wondered about that. John had made no mention of shopping for a ring.

"So he just proposed? Is he from Pittsburgh? Do I know him?"

For the second time that day Grace launched into an explanation of how she had met John and why she was back east. This time, however, she added a glowing description of this man she had grown to love so dearly. Just talking about him brought a warm flush to her face and Shirley noticed it at once.

"You look like a lovesick teenager," she teased.

"I feel like one."

Shirley's face sobered. "Are you sure, though? So soon. You and Peter seemed like such a happy couple, so much in love. I always watched you two with envy."

"It's not impossible to fall in love again, Shirley. It's a different love . . . just as deep but different. One can never recapture the excitement and passion of young love. I know that. This is a solid, mature love for a different phase of my life."

Shirley reached over and patted her hand. "How do your children feel about you marrying again?"

"Susan is thrilled, but Ben went ballistic on me," Grace admitted.

"Oh dear. How are you going to handle that?"

"I hope that time will take care of it. I don't want to be alienated from either of my kids."

"And if Ben doesn't come around? I've hear a lot of widows say that their children's acceptance of a new partner can be a huge problem."

"I . . . I don't know. I knew he might be a little standoffish but I never expected him to be as rude as he was last night."

"Spend some time with him, Grace. Don't let the problem fester. Make him believe your feelings for John in no way belittle your deep love for his father. Tell him what you told me."

Grace leaned her head back against the couch and momentarily closed her eyes. Shirley was right. Instead of running back to New York with her tail between her legs she should stay and work to mend her relationship with Ben. "You're right, she said. "I admire your commonsense. Mine seems to have taken leave of me recently."

"Things will work out. And if I know Susan she will be behind you one hundred percent. Have you set a date?"

"Probably in May. By then the weather is tolerable in Alaska."

Shirley blinked. "You mean you are going to be married in Alaska? You're going to live there?"

"Married, yes. We've agreed to split our time . . . summers in Alaska so I can work and the winters in New York."

"That's going to get old though, honey. The older you get the harder it is to move back and forth. I hear it from a lot of our friends who have given up a second home in Florida. Is he in good health?"

"Yes, he's the most virile man I've ever met. He has no problems that I know of." *At least none I want to discuss.*

"Good, now tell me all about him. All the nitty-gritty details."

Grace brought out a photo that Lois had taken outside the cabin at Eagles Nest. Her heart fluttered just looking at his picture again. She handed the photo to Shirley and for the next hour talked practically non-stop about his family, his background, his home and their time together.

The plate of cookies disappeared and they switched from tea to wine. When Grace thought to look at her watch it was ten o'clock. "Goodness," she cried, "I must get going. I forget you are a working woman."

"One last thing," Shirley said as they walked to the door. "The Red Hats are meeting tomorrow afternoon. When I went back to work I had to drop out, but they still send me notices. You might enjoy seeing all your old friends again."

Grace thought for a minute. She would be available—had decided not to cut her visit short—why not go. "I'd like that. Where and what time?"

Shirley walked over to a calendar and took a folded piece of purple paper from a clip. "Let me give you the notice. They are going to watch a movie at Marjorie Weese's house this month. Tuesday at two o'clock."

"Thanks, hon. Now I've got to be going."

"Call me." She grinned. "I'm always receptive to a wedding invitation."

"Even if it's in Alaska?"

"Even Alaska. It would make a nice vacation."

As Grace walked to her car she tucked the purple piece of paper into her pocket. It would be fun to see everyone again—fun to see the expression on their faces when she announced her engagement.

Engagement. The word sounded foreign to her ears. She had always associated engagement with youth.

The next afternoon Grace borrowed a violet blouse from Emily, donned a pair of lilac slacks she had with her, and found a red baseball cap of Ted's. It wasn't dress-up attire for the Red Hats but it would do. A number of women came in casual attire, socialization was more important than what they wore—just as long as they had some type of red hat.

Marjorie elected to show a classic movie video of Easter Parade starring Fred Astaire and Judy Garland. Coffee, tea, bottles of water, and small pastries were laid out on the sideboard and after watching the delightful musical they filled their plates with refreshments agreeing that it was a real pleasure to sit and enjoy a movie without violence, sex, or profanity.

During one of the silences, when cookies were being passed around, Grace announced her engagement. She almost laughed aloud at the startled looks on half a dozen faces. However, that soon gave way to chattering excitement and shouts of congratulation. Gaily she answered questions as well as she could—a description of John, how they met, their plan to get married in Alaska, and where they would live.

"Have you no problems with the children?" a women named Charlotte asked her.

Grace issued a deep sigh and momentarily closed her eyes. There it was again—the children. "I'm afraid my son has reservations," she answered slowly. "And we haven't talked to John's children yet about marriage."

A small frown appeared between Charlotte's brows. "As you know this is my second marriage and my husband's daughter is a real thorn in our side, but we don't let that spoil our happiness. It is your life, dear, and you'll find that sooner or later the children become so involved with their own lives they are quick to disappear from yours."

"Hear, hear," several women chimed in. "Go for it, honey."

"Does he have a bachelor friend?" Marjorie asked with a twinkle in her eye.

And so the afternoon passed with a few well intentioned jokes and much encouragement. Grace left feeling uplifted and happy. The Sunshine Chapter was well named.

Ben sat in his easy chair, cigarette in hand, flicking the pages of the newspaper, studiously avoiding conversation. Grace doubted he was reading—the pages were turning too quickly.

"I visited with my old friend Shirley, last evening," she said.

"Hmm."

"She was thrilled and happy with my news."

Silence.

"Ben, I really want to talk to you."

He threw the newspaper aside. "What, then?"

Grace's palms grew clammy. "I thought you would be happy for me, too. Happy that I had found someone to share the lonely hours with, someone to care for me."

"Mom, I want you to be happy. I guess I am being unfair. It's just . . . it's just . . . ." His voice choked and trailed off.

"Just, what, son?"

"It's just that it seems like the end of an era. My childhood . . . my memories of you and Dad."

Grace could understand that. She fought to find the right words. "That is a part of your life I hope you will always cherish. Nothing can change that. Remember the memory book you and Emily and Susan made for me at Christmas? Those pictures are proof of the love our family shared . . . that I shared with your father. I will always keep him in my heart."

"Then how can you already be in love with someone else."

Grace's fingers trembled and she pressed them tightly together. "Because this is a love for a later time in my life. Ben, we humans are able to love in many different ways. You love your wife and you love your children. Your love for each of them is intense and personal, but it is a different love. Even with your children . . . you love each one equally . . . but differently. The same is true of many elderly people who lose a spouse and pour out their love on a pet. We all need someone to love, to touch, to talk to."

"We are here. If you didn't want to run off somewhere else we could give you what you need."

"No, you couldn't. It's not the same. It's that different type of love I'm telling you about. Honey, sometimes there's room in our hearts for more than one true love. You know the Red Hat Society theme song uses a refrain from a song by Mark Harline. It goes: *All my life I've done for you. Now it's my time to do for me.* That's why I went to Alaska and that's why I'm going to get married."

Ben made a great business of retrieving the newspaper that had fallen to the floor. He rose slowly and came over to give her a kiss on the forehead. "I want to be supportive, Mom, but John is a senior. He may have health problems we don't know about and if not now he will have later. I saw you nurse, Dad, saw what a toll it took on you. You cared for him day and night for over three years. I don't want to see you go through that again."

"Caring for someone you love is not a chore," Grace said.

"I don't believe that. I saw the strain you were under." He pulled at his lip. "If this is what you really want, I'll try to be supportive. I don't want anger between us. You do know, though, that if all this doesn't work out and you need someone to take care of you, I'm always here."

Grace fought to hide a smile. Ben, always her protector, trying so hard to be the man in her life. "Of course, son. I know that." She lifted her hand to caress his cheek gently. He was trying to be understanding. Maybe it would be all right after all.

CHAPTER TWENTY-THREE

John answered his chiming doorbell to find his granddaughter, Margaret, the wind whipping her scarf in the frigid air, her arms laden with a cardboard box.

"I come bearing gifts," she quipped gaily.

"Come in, come in, honey . . . and Bandit, you behave," he commanded the excited dog. He took the box from her and placed it on the seat of the hall rack beside the door. "Give me your coat and hat." He hung them on a bronze hook and looked at her with quizzically. "What brings you out on such a bitter day? And why aren't you at work?"

"Bring the box out to the kitchen, Grandpa, and I'll tell you." She laughed and reached down to calm Bandit. "You too, fella."

After placing the box on the kitchen counter John put the kettle on to boil and removed packets of tea from the cupboard. Margaret sat perched on a stool watching him.

"Open the box, Grandpa. It's your favorite chocolate cake. I used grandma's recipe."

John removed the cake and sat it on the counter. He noted it was frosted with peanut butter icing, another of Mary's recipes. "Hmm, I can't wait. Why don't you cut it for me. We'll have some with our tea. You know where the plates are, and the cake cutter is in the top drawer next to the fridge." He grinned. "Mind you, make mine a large piece."

While Margaret set the dining room table, John carried in cups and the tea pot. He had a vague feeling of apprehension. This was no ordinary visit.

After sampling the cake and issuing the expected groans of pleasure, he looked Margaret firmly in the eye. "Now, young lady, what is this all about?"

"Mom called me and told me about your lady-friend."

"And . . . ?"

Margaret dropped her gaze. "I was a little upset. Mom said she read between the lines and although you didn't actually say so she suspects that you may be thinking of getting married."

John's face grew pensive. This might be the time to announce his intentions. It had to be done sooner or later and Margaret might make the perfect ambassador. He cleared his throat and made a great business of folding his napkin.

"I am," he said quietly.

"Oh, Grandpa no. You can't be."

"I thought you'd be happy at the news. Glad that I will no longer be alone in this big old house."

"It's not any *big, old house*. It's Grandma's house."

John noted the slight tremble in Margaret's voice. Acceptance of another woman in his life was not going to be easy for his family.

"Sweetheart, it was *our* house, your grandmother's and mine. I'm glad it's full of happy memories for you, memories of love and laughter, of sleep-overs and family. But things change. Your grandma is gone and the house is empty without her. I am lonely."

"But . . . when . . . how soon?"

"Our plans aren't complete. First, we wanted to get acquainted with each other's family."

Are you certain, Grandpa? According to Mom you only met her recently."

"I'm sure." John took a big bite of cake and wiped icing from his mouth. He looked at Margaret intently. "We have known each other long enough to know we want to be together."

"Where will you live?"

"Here, at least part of the year."

"I'll bet your lady-friend was impressed with your house. A New York brownstone is nothing to sneeze at," Margaret said, her eyes bright with curiosity.

"Not really."

Margaret's brows shot up in surprise.

"Brownstones are foreign to Grace. She has no idea of their historical or architectural significance and I think she found this place a bit dark and gloomy."

"But Grandpa, this house is magnificent. The architecture alone. . . ." Her voice faltered. "I mean Grandma fought so hard to maintain its character. I'd give anything to own a place like this."

"And maybe someday you will. I want it to remain in the family." He smiled at his granddaughter. "We'll work it out, honey. Grace just needs time to make it seem less like a New York City landmark and more like her home. It's natural, Margaret. As a woman I'm sure you can understand." John placed a small sliver of cake in his hand and slipped it under the table where Bandit was waiting patiently. "The important thing is that I have grown to love Grace and we want to be together, whether here in this house or in the Alaskan wilds."

Margaret toyed with her cake. "I guess we sort of got side-tracked talking about the house. It's not really my main concern."

"Then, what is?"

"I saw you nurse Grandma for years. You were wonderful to her, pushing her around in a wheelchair, cooking for her, cleaning up after her. I remember your terrible grief when she died. I love you, and I don't want to see you ever have to be a care giver again."

"Honey, Grace is in excellent health. It is far more likely she would be the one to end up being the care giver."

"You don't know that. I mean at your ages anything can happen."

John threw back his head and laughed. "Indeed it can . . . indeed it can . . . and probably will." He noticed the true concern in her eyes and felt immediate remorse at his flip response. "It will be okay, Margaret. She is a lovely person, warm and friendly. You'll love one another."

"I'm sorry I didn't get to meet her. I had other arrangements I couldn't break." She rose and began to pick up the dishes. "It was rather short notice," she added accusingly.

"I know, and I apologize. We do have geographic problems. Besides her living in Alaska and me in New York, her family is in Pittsburgh and mine is here." He put his arm around her shoulder as they walked back to the kitchen. "You never did tell me why you aren't at work today."

"I wanted to talk to you . . . so I took a day of vacation time." She giggled. "Plus, the whole family is dying of curiosity. Wait till I call and tell them you are getting married." She frowned, then looked at him anxiously. "I can tell them, can't I?"

"Of course. You break the ice. Be gentle though. I'm not sure your father is up to the news."

"It'll blow his mind," she agreed.

Grace was in a funk! All of a sudden Ben's objections and her own vague doubts engulfed her. She was building a life apart from her children, ending the era of father and grandfather more than Peter's death had done. Did she have the right? Then here was the loss of her hard-earned independence and the idea of simply being together when they could and enjoying one another's company. Dividing her time between New York and Alaska was fine for now but what about ten years from now when she and John were older. Would they end up living in New York City? She would hate that. And she'd have to accept his home the way it was. He had been visibly appalled at her idea of renovating the brownstone.

What about their children? The idea of a happily blended family was a fantasy. Adam's dislike of her was palatable and although Ben seemed resigned to her marriage that is all it was—resignation.

Other than agreeing to a prenup she and John had never really discussed money. Everyone told her that the biggest problem in second marriages, aside from the children, was financial. Her attorney made it clear that a prenuptial agreement was primarily intended to protect against the consequences of divorce. And he warned that estate laws varied from state to state. Would John have any financial responsibility toward her? Would she have a home if he died before her? He had made it clear that his sons would inherit the brownstone. Would bitter disputes over personal assets ensue? She had heard many horror stories about families being torn apart by fights over money. She didn't need that in her life.

As she sat mulling over her dilemma the phone rang. It was John.

After exchanging endearments he told her about his visit from his granddaughter.

"She is going to break the news to the family," he said with a chuckle.

"Oh," was all she could say.

"Honey, what's wrong. You sound unhappy."

"John, I . . . I've been doing some thinking. Maybe we should give each other some breathing room, take a week to think things over and make sure marriage is right for us."

Her statement was met by dead silence.

Grace began to cry. "Forget I said that," she blubbered. "I'm just having a down evening."

"But. . . ."

"No, please. I'll be all right tomorrow."

Again there was silence on the other end of the line. She heard him sigh. At length he cleared his throat and spoke softly. "Once before you suggested we take more time. Maybe you are right, Grace, maybe we are rushing things. Why don't we take this interlude to be certain of what we want. There should be no uncertainty on either side."

"There is no uncertainty about my love for you," she said.

"Nor of mine for you. That needn't end and it won't." His voice broke. "I'm going to hang up now . . . let's give it a week. I'll call you next Sunday."

The line went dead.

Grace pulled aside the curtain in her bedroom to gaze at gloomy, threatening skies. The leafless tree outside her window whipped back and forth in the blustery March wind. It was early afternoon and she was still in her bathrobe. For the past three days she had moped around the house, not dressing until Ted was due home from school, saying little to anyone. Emily, immersed in the coming Easter Pageant at church paid scant attention to her and Ben watched her with worried eyes but said nothing.

Wearily she picked up a book and curled up on her unmade bed. She tried to read but found herself staring into the middle of the room in silence. Brooding. She had never been so damn unhappy.

This whole mess was of her own doing. Where had the doubts come from? She loved the man. Why not grab at the years they had remaining? She was letting the doubts of others poison the love she and John had found together. Angrily she slammed the book on the night stand. "Maybe I no longer have a choice," she muttered into the silent room. "Maybe my doubts have ended everything. Maybe John has made his own decision."

•　　•　　•

After talking to Grace, John debated whether he should get drunk or go to the athletic club and work out until he was ready to drop. In the end he did neither.

The fact that his girl expressed doubt ran up a red flag on their relationship. There was no room for uncertainty. Not when something as serious as marriage was concerned. Maybe they were just being a couple of old fools, trying to recapture youth.

He tried to remain calm and rational, reminding himself that no final decision had been made. His life was still the same. He was financially secure; he had his home, his friends, his family. He was in good health, had his own hair and teeth.

He walked a lot, and thought a lot. Suppose, after marriage, she decided she wanted to live in Alaska permanently. He loved the vitality of New York—the museums, concerts, theater. There was always a new restaurant to try and food of every nationality to sample, from Chinese to Greek, to Italian and Ethiopian.

He had loved his wife so much that he never dreamt another woman could share his life. For him, this love of Grace, had come as an unexpected gift and he savored it like a fine wine. Yet, as he thought about their conversation he believed he knew what had happened. Ben. Ben and his disapproval. Grace was by nature a kind, nurturing mother. Much as she touted her independence, her children and their opinion of her were of primary importance. She was always bragging about their accomplishments. It was one of the things he loved about her. She wanted and needed their love as much as she needed John's.

He would give her the week to sort through her feelings. If she still had doubts then perhaps their union was not meant to be.

After watching his mother for several days, Ben decided to call Susan. "I don't know what the problem is, sis. Mom is pale, not eating, sitting around staring into space. You need to come over and talk to her."

"Did she and John have a fight?"

"She won't say but I can't think of any other reason for her depression. When I asked she more or less indicated I should mind my own business."

"Jeez, this is a bad time for me. I'm enrolled in a graphics design class at Pitt with classes every night this week and Jason and I are going to a wedding on Saturday. I can come over Sunday, though."

Ben drummed his fingers on the table. He was disappointed and worried. "Can't you cut a class?" he asked.

"No, I really can't. I have an idea, though. She may not feel free to talk to us about what is worrying her. Why don't I give her friend, Shirley, a call?"

"Good idea."

"I'll do it now. Either way, I'll see you Sunday."

On Friday night Shirley and Grace drove into Pittsburgh for dinner at Lombardi's, a popular Italian eatery.

Once they had sipped a glass of wine and placed their orders, Shirley leaned forward. "Now, tell me."

Grace frowned. "Tell you what?"

"What is bothering you?"

Grace lowered her eyes, then picked up her napkin and carefully placed it on her lap. When she looked up she saw Shirley watching her, her eyes soft with compassion. "You've been trying hard but I know something is wrong," her friend said.

"Oh, Shirley, I did a dumb thing. I suggested to John that we give each other a week to think about our decision to get married. I don't know what possessed me. I love him so much and now it may be too late."

"Why?"

"Knowing I am indecisive, he may have second thoughts himself."

"But why did you question your decision? You seemed so happy and sure of yourself."

"I guess I just gave in to all of the misgivings I heard from my family and friends. Most people I have told seem glad for me but a few have made negative comments about second marriages. It isn't always easy to make major adjustments to your life when you are older. It made me begin to wonder if John and I are doing the right thing."

"Surely you didn't hear that from your fellow Red Hatters. I talked to Sylvia the other day and they were thrilled with your news." Shirley grinned. "It gives all the widows hope that there's still a chance for them."

"No, they were very encouraging."

The waiter brought their dinners and for the next few minutes they busied themselves as they settled down to eat.

"Forget what others think. How do you feel?" Shirley asked as she raised a fork of Eggplant Parmesan to her lips.

"I don't want to live without him. All of the silly questions I tormented myself with pale beside my love for him."

"Have you told him that?"

"He's going to call tomorrow." Grace picked at her food. "What will I say if he starts off by saying that he agrees with me and thinks we should wait?" She raised agonized eyes to look at Shirley. "God, what a mess I've made of things."

"Don't give him a chance. Tell him what you just said to me. If he loves you and if this marriage is right then things will work out for you."

Grace gave Shirley a weak smile. "You sound like Lois Yost. Remember, I told you I ran into her in Alaska. She would say it's all in God's plan."

"Good for her." Shirley smacked her lips. "God, this eggplant is yummy. When I fry eggplant, it all falls apart. That's the only thing I miss about my ex. He was a darn good cook."

"Do you think you'll ever remarry?"

"I'd like to. Not all men are bastardly . . . there are some good ones out there. I just haven't had the good fortune to meet one. Did you know Eleanor remarried?"

"No, I didn't." She had been more Shirley's friend than hers. Just before Peter died Grace heard that Eleanore had lost her husband to cancer. "Who'd she marry?"

"Morris Gibble. They were sweethearts in high school, then when they went off to college they drifted apart. Although they each married someone else and raised families they both stayed in the Pittsburgh area and saw each other from time to time at class reunions. He is a retired attorney, seventy-nine years old and quite wealthy." Shirley threw back her head and laughed. "When I asked her how she met up with him again she said, 'I saw his wife's name in the obituaries. I went to the viewing and was the first one at his door with a casserole'."

"That sounds like Eleanor. She was always the life of the party."

Shirley nodded. "She's quite a character. When she came over to console me after my divorce we opened a bottle of Jack Daniels and got drunk. When she told me of their first sexual encounter she had me in stitches. He is incontinent and was wearing a diaper and she has dentures that she takes out at night. He didn't know what to do with his protective wrapping and she didn't know what to do with her teeth."

Grace laughed until tears ran down her cheeks. She could just picture the consternation on their faces as they assessed the situation. "You know, Shirley, it isn't easy entering into a relationship when you are older. There are physical changes to your body that you are painfully aware of. A married couple grows old together and their body changes occur in harmony with each other. A man may develop a sizeable potbelly and his hair thins, a woman's breasts begin to sag and she may have a tummy of surgical scars and stretch marks. But in the familiarity of day to day life it is hardly noticed." Grace's face grew sober and she took a gulp of wine. "It can be a bit of a shock when two seniors see each other naked for the first time."

Shirley swiped a tear of laughter from her own cheek. "I did some volunteer work at the nursing home for a while. I heard a lot of funny/sad stories. One lady I talked to told me her new husband wouldn't let her replace a single item in the house, including the flowers in the garden."

"On the other hand," Grace commented, "I talked to a Red-Hatter in my Happy Hoofers Chapter who always speaks of her new husband as 'sweet Charlie' and you never see them together that they aren't holding hands."

Shirley toyed with her spoon. "Do you have any problems with jealousy? By nature I'm a very possessive person and I've often wondered how I would react. I mean, when you divorce like I did, there is usually bitterness toward the former spouse. But when a spouse dies and there is no animosity it's different. When John relates stories and happy memories about his wife, does it bother you?"

"Sometimes," Grace admitted. "I realize that I can never share the passion of his youth." Her face grew warm. "In fact, there is a physical intimacy that I can never share, but I won't go into that

. . . it's not that important. I can love him without . . . you know physically loving him. I do think, though, the thing that saddens me the most is that we can never have children together. I can never have him place his hand on my stomach and feel the throb of a new life that we have created together. I will never see that special look on his face when he watches me hold his child to my nipple."

"I know what you mean, but I certainly don't want any more children, even if I could still have them. Speaking of children, is Ben still giving you a hard time?"

"Not really. We did have a long talk and he wants me to be happy. I think Ben will accept him in time. John is a fine person, very patient and understanding and he is a strong family man."

Shirley smiled. "Then put all those crazy doubts and fears aside. Remind yourself why you fell in love with him in the first place. I believe the tragedy of 9/11 reminded all of us that life is fleeting. Grab at the happiness being offered you."

Grace took a final bite of her pasta and pushed her plate aside. She felt light and relaxed. The shared laughter and conversation had been good for her. For the first time in a week she couldn't wait for John to call. Her philosophy had always been that if you want something to happen you have to make it happen. He would hear no doubt in her voice—only boundless love.

Early Sunday morning John picked up the phone to call Grace, his fingers white-knuckled and trembling. He could wait no longer. He loved her and missed her too much. His whole future depended on this call.

It only rang once. She must have been sitting beside the phone, waiting.

"Hi, pumpkin," he said.

"Hi, sweetheart."

"I hope I didn't get you up."

"Not at all. I hoped you'd call early." John heard her draw a deep breath. "Before you say anything more I want to tell you that I've been a silly goose and I'm sorry. I let other people cast doubts when all that really matters is our love for one another. At our stage of life time is precious. Our years together may be limited but love isn't measured by time. It lives forever. We've been given a second chance to reach out and grab the gold ring and I almost blew it."

"Are you saying . . . ?"

"That I love you and want to marry you."

John felt giddy with relief. His had been a week of hell, confident one minute and despondent the next. He almost shouted into the phone. "And I want to marry you, darling. Tomorrow, if possible."

Grace laughed, a gay laugh he would recognize anywhere. "Well, I'm not sure about that. There are things a gal has to do."

"Like what? What could be more important than getting married?" he teased.

"Oh, you know . . . buy a dress, get my hair done. All sorts of things."

"Seriously, Grace. No more doubts?"

"None." He heard her pause. "Sweetheart, we're bound to encounter a few problems. Life is like that. But none that we can't handle together. How about you? I haven't given you a chance to say what conclusions you came to . . . how you spent this past week."

"Agonizing over your answer. I suspected that the problem might be opposition from your son and mine but, honey, when our children are around us and feel our love I'm sure they will be more understanding." What he didn't tell her was that the day after her call Adam had appeared on his doorstep full of indignation. John shouldn't be running back and forth across the country. Adam had said he needed to stay in New York, close to his family and friends. He didn't need to exchange vows just to have a relationship with this woman. Adam worried about the brownstone getting out of the family hands. If his dad insisted on getting married he wanted to buy the brownstone. On and on he went— one argument after another. John promised to give each careful thought. And he had, but they didn't sway his conviction that he wanted Grace to be a permanent part of his life.

"Honey," he said, "we can't let our children deprive us of happiness just because it disrupts the pattern they have set for us. It's our life and our decision."

"I know."

"Now, when are you going to get that pretty little butt of yours back here so we can make plans? I had Bridget give the house a thorough cleaning this week so all we have to do is close it up and I want to talk to Ed Sinclair, my former boss, about another assignment in Alaska. Global warming is a hot subject right now and it might be interesting to investigate its possible impact on Alaskan salmon."

"We do have a lot of decisions to make," Grace admitted. "Where to live until May, the courses I still have to take, flying versus driving back. You'll need a car during the summer. What do you want to do?"

"I've thought about that. I think it would be cheaper to rent a car for six months than drive back and forth twice a year. Besides, my BMW is ten years old."

"I agree. Another thing—isn't it foolish for me to fly back to New York and then retrace my steps through Pittsburgh. Why don't you finish up what you have to do, then book a flight with a stop-over here and I'll join you." Her mouth lifted in a half smile. "It also solves the problem of where I stay while in New York."

John frowned. She was right, of course. He desperately wanted to see her but it would be a lot simpler that way. When they returned to New York in the fall—fait accompli—where she slept would no longer be a problem.

"I miss you," he said plaintively, "but I guess I can handle a few more days."

"I miss you, too. How long do you think it will take?"

"At least a week. I'll call the airline today and see how the flight can be handled. I don't know if they have a stop-over in Pittsburgh. If they don't I may have to completely deplane because of Bandit. I don't want him to get separated from me. And I'll see how soon I can get an appointment with Ed Sinclair. My attorney called and he has the prenup ready. I'll fax it to your attorney to review."

"That sounds fine."

"Then, let me get busy on the phone. I'll call you later and let you know what kind of reservations I can get."

"I'm going to my old church in Mt. Lebanon this morning but I'll be home after lunch." Her voice grew soft. "I need to offer some special prayers of thanks."

"Me, too, sweetheart. Me, too." He coughed. "I have a slight cold. Nothing to worry about, though. I'll see you in a few days. I can't wait much longer than that to hold you."

CHAPTER TWENTY-FOUR

Grace spent the next few days in a whirlwind of activities. She visited her former hairdresser for a cut, got a thorough check up from her doctor, and had her teeth cleaned. Then, she and Susan went shopping together, giggling like a couple of kids over her trousseau.

Ben surprised her by saying that he planned to arrange for some vacation time. He insisted he wanted to walk her down the aisle. She reminded him that it would likely be a pine covered path beside a lake and he grinned with pleasure saying he might have the ring in one hand and a fishing rod in the other.

Everything was falling into place. Now all she had to do was call Lois and set the wedding date.

When Grace asked Lois to perform the marriage ceremony she was thrilled. Grace insisted she wanted the vows to be presented in a simple ceremony—one that would incorporate a poem she had received from a good friend. Lois agreed that Reflection Pond would be a perfect setting and they chose May 14th as the date. The weather should be moderating by then, it would give all the children time to make plans if they wanted to fly out, and she and John would have ten days for a honeymoon before she started her new job.

John was due to arrive in Pittsburgh Saturday morning. Delta had no flights to Anchorage with a stop in Pittsburgh so he and Bandit would fly directly to Pittsburgh on a red-eye commuter where he would meet Grace. An hour later they would board Delta for the nine hour flight to Anchorage.

He called nightly. His cold had worsened, his voice horse and raspy, but he insisted all he needed was a hot toddy and a warm body next to him. He assured her it would not delay his travel plans and he would be with her soon.

When he did not phone Thursday evening she began to worry

that his cold might have worsened. She waited until ten o'clock then called him but got only his answering machine.

She called Susan who only laughed off her concern. "His friends are probably giving him a bachelor party. Don't be such a worry-wort, Mom."

"Surely he would have mentioned it."

"Maybe it was a surprise. Come on over. Jason is taking his son to a football game and I'm alone. We'll pop some corn in the microwave, kick our shoes off, and watch one of the videos I picked up at Blockbusters today. Wait and see . . . he'll call tomorrow full of apologies."

But John didn't call the next day, nor did he return her messages. By Friday evening Grace was sick with worry. She did not have a phone number for either Adam or George and was on the verge of calling information when the phone rang.

"Grace, this is Adam, John's son," a quiet voice said.

Her hand shook so hard she almost dropped the receiver. "What's wrong?" she cried.

"Dad is in the hospital. He's stable but he has bronchial pneumonia."

"How . . . when . . . ?"

"Bridget always goes in to clean on Thursday. She found him in bed burning with fever and unresponsive. She called 911 and then called me."

"But you say he is stable?"

"Yes. He's in intensive care, though and still on oxygen. He's been asking for you. When they move him to a regular room he'll have a phone. I'm at home now but George and I will go in tomorrow morning. The hospital has my number and will call if there is any change."

"What hospital is he in?"

"Memorial Sloan Kettering. It was the closest."

"Who is his doctor?"

"Dr. Banner. He's an excellent pulmonary specialist and has treated Dad before. He's familiar with his history."

"History? What do you mean?"

"Dad has a long history of severe chest infections. Twice they have landed him in the hospital." Adam's voice became strained. "That's why I objected to his leaving his doctors here in New York to traipse off to the wilds of Alaska. Maybe this will make him stop and think."

Grace did not miss the implication. John had never talked about his medical history. He was so strong and robust looking she simply had not questioned his health.

Adam gave her his phone number, promised to call her immediately if there was any change, and hung up.

Instinctively, Grace knew what she had to do. She called Delta for a flight to New York. One left at 6:20 A.M. She made a reservation then called Susan and told her what had happened. "I was so rattled I forget to cancel our reservations to Alaska," Grace moaned.

"Get packed, Mom. I'll handle the details."

Within minutes Susan called back. "I cancelled your Anchorage reservations, called the hospital to check its location and asked about nearby hotels. One of the ones they recommend is the Hotel Greenwich Village so I made reservations for you for a week's stay."

"Thank you, sweetheart."

"Now try to get some rest and call me the minute you find out how he is."

"I will."

But she tossed and turned all night unable to sleep, worried about John, wondering how this would affect their plans, cringing at the accusation in Adam's voice.

Maybe this changed everything.

The sky was streaked with the first rays of crimson when Ben drove her to the airport and miracle, of miracles, her flight was on time. They had a good tailwind and it seemed they were hardly in the air before the wheels set down. Grace checked into her hotel first, then caught a cab to the hospital.

John was still in intensive care, but when she identified herself as his out of town fiancée they allowed her to go in for a fifteen minute visit.

He was sleeping, attached to an IV, an oxygen tube in his nose. Grace pulled a chair close to his bed and sat watching his face.

It shattered her to realize it was possible to feel this overwhelming love for a man she hadn't even known a year ago. She placed her hand atop his and he opened his eyes.

"Grace," he whispered. "Oh, honey . . ." He tried to raise his head but it sank back on the pillow.

"Shhh. Don't try to talk, sweetheart. I'm here with you."

"Kiss me," he whispered.

She cupped his face in her hands and placed her lips on his.

He smiled. "You don't know how much I needed that."

"Adam called me last night."

"I hope he didn't frighten you. I'm going to be fine. You didn't need to fly to New York."

"I wanted to. I want to be with you." She reached up to smooth his hair. "I have to make sure they are taking proper care of my man."

He smiled ruefully. "I thought it was just a bad cold. I guess I neglected it too long."

A nurse appeared to change his IV and politely suggested that he needed his rest. "Dr. Banner is on the floor making rounds if you wish to talk to him after he has seen Mr. Hathaway. You can wait outside in the hall."

The doctor emerged from John's room and greeted her with a firm handshake. He was a middle-aged, heavy-set, handsome man with wavy brown hair graying at the temples.

"How long will his recovery take?" Grace asked. "We . . . ah . . . we are making wedding plans."

"Several weeks, if all goes well. Have you set a date?"

"Not specifically, but we were hoping for mid-May."

The doctor pursed his lips. "That should work unless there are unexpected complications. John is strong and except for being prone to chest infections has the physique of a man half his age. I'm happy to hear he is getting married again. Will the wedding be here in New York?"

"No, Alaska."

"Oh, my."

"Will travel be a problem?" she asked anxiously.

Doctor Banner tapped his pen on his clipboard before answering. "It's really too soon to say. Let's wait a few days and see how he is doing."

"It doesn't get as cold there as most people think," Grace replied. "The average March temperature in Anchorage is in the thirties—not much different from New York. But, whatever you say, Doctor. John's wellbeing is the most important thing right now. We can adjust our wedding plans if we need to."

"Good. I'll keep you informed." He shook her hand and strode down the corridor.

An hour later George found her in the waiting room, surprised but seemingly delighted to see her. He gave her a big hug.

"Let's go to the coffee shop to talk," he suggested.

As they walked down the corridor George told her he had just had a brief visit with his father and that he seemed to be in good spirits. They carried mugs of coffee and two cheese pastries to a table and sat down.

George beamed at her. "First of all, let me say congratulations."

"Thank you, George."

"Dad says you plan to be married in Alaska but arrangements are still incomplete."

Grace nodded. "Nothing is ever simple. My new job requires certification in CPR and a class B commercial driver's license. I'm enrolled in two courses in Anchorage starting April 1st. That's a little over a week from now."

"Can't you postpone them?"

"Not really. The commercial driver's test is only given once a month. Big Bear opens for the season the first of June. I will be putting Mrs. Ross in a real bind if I fail to take the job. I don't want to do that." She sighed. "I'm a born procrastinator. I could have taken the tests last fall but at that time marriage was not on my horizon."

George's eyes twinkled. "Nine months ago none of us even remotely suspected that wedding bells were in our future." His face sobered. "Dad will be all right. This is only a bump in the road. He may not recover quite as fast as he has in the past—he's older now—but I don't believe wild horses could keep him from getting married. I can tell how much he loves you when he talks about you."

Tears formed in Grace's eyes. "Thank you, George."

He reached out and squeezed her hand. "I must be off to work. I want to pop my head in Dad's door once more and say goodbye. I'll be back around six. Are you free for dinner?"

"Of course. I plan to stay here all day. The doctor said they may move him to a private room later."

"Good, they have an excellent restaurant right here in the hospital." He rose, leaned down and kissed her cheek. "I'm glad you are here. See you later."

John was still very weak and heavily medicated so Grace spent most of her short visits with him merely holding his hand. Adam came in once, but didn't stay long. At four o'clock they moved John upstairs to a private room.

While they were getting him settled Grace went back to her hotel to take a shower and freshen up. It had been a long, exhausting, day. When she returned to the hospital John was sitting up in bed and George, Adam, Becky, and Gail were all there. Becky greeted her with a big smile but Adam was his usual cool, reserved self. Gail was a delight and Grace warmed to her immediately.

To avoid over tiring John, George took Grace downstairs to eat while Adam and his family visited. When they returned the room was empty and John had his eyes closed.

"I think we should say goodnight to him and let him rest," Grace suggested.

At the sound of her voice John opened his eyes and smiled weakly. Grace leaned down and kissed his cheek. George did the same and John grabbed his hand. "Please see that she gets safely to her hotel," he pleaded. "She's very precious to me."

"I will, Pop. I'll deliver her right to her door."

And he did just that.

Now if she could just win Adam over, things would be so much easier.

The next morning when she entered John's hospital room she was delighted to find him sitting up in bed, running his electric shaver around his chin.

"My, don't we look dapper," she said as she gave him a warm

kiss.

He grinned. "More," he said.

She kissed him again, slower this time and deeper.

"You have a wonderful mouth, Grace." He winked at her. "I've been away from it too long."

"Well now, I'd say my man is much better this morning."

"Much better." He withdrew his hairbrush from the bed table. "I have to look good for my girl."

She reached across him and took the brush. "Let me do that." She began to draw the brush through his hair. "You have gorgeous hair," she murmured. "So thick with shades of silver and white." It shocked her to realize how intimate it was, how arousing, to tend his hair. She trailed her fingers behind the brush, pushing hair back from his forehead, cradling his head to brush the back of his head.

"Um, that tingles," he said.

More was tingling than John's hair. Grace sat down abruptly, shocked at her reaction.

"Dr. Banner was just here," John said. "He is quite pleased. My temperature and blood pressure are close to normal. He wants to keep me for a few days while I'm on antibiotics." He wrinkled his brow. "What day is this?"

"Saturday."

"My, God. Did you think to cancel our plane reservations?"

"I did." She got up and walked over to the window. "I didn't book a later date, John. We have to wait to see how you recover."

"We still have plenty of time." He closed his eyes, obviously tiring.

Grace didn't think it wise to remind him of her classes and job commitment. He was still ill—better to wait a few days. In the meantime she planned to go back to the hotel at noon, place a call to Mrs. Ross, who was still wintering in Anchorage, and fill her in on the changes in her life. She also had to call Lois and warn her that the wedding might have to be delayed.

She came back to John's bed and pulled a chair close. "Let me lower your bed so you can take a nap. I have a book with me. I'll sit here and read."

"I'd like that." He lifted her hand and kissed her fingers. "You won't leave me, will you sweetheart?"

"Never, dear. Never"

•   •   •

John was released from the hospital on Tuesday, but the doctor made it clear that it was unwise for him to leave for Alaska for several weeks. That would be too late for Grace to begin her driver's course, pass her test and get her commercial license. The best solution was for her to go back by herself and take care of her commitments. When he was completely recovered he could join her. Their wedding plans need not be changed. He reluctantly agreed.

To some extent it was a relief to Grace. Much as she wanted to be with him she had been concerned about their living arrangements until their marriage. True, they had already slept together but she was old fashioned enough to want to wait now, to make their final union more honest and meaningful.

With George's help she got John settled at home. He still tired easily but insisted he was able to care for himself. Grace went grocery shopping and loaded the freezer with easy to prepare dinners. Bridget offered to stop by every day to check on him and help where needed.

Friday, Grace said goodbye and was once more on a plane headed to Alaska. *I guess I'm no longer a novice traveler*, she thought as she casually pulled a pocket novel from her carry-on and leaned back in her seat. *I'm really piling up the frequent flyer miles. In less than a year this is my third flight over the United States.*

That night she stayed in a Holiday Inn close to the airport, planning to spend Saturday looking for a place to stay in Anchorage for two weeks until she got her necessary certifications. The next morning she called Lois, who was still in town at her winter lodging. Lois volunteered to let her use her sleep-sofa but Grace assured her that she would be more at ease and able to study in a place of her own. Lois mentioned a nice rooming house for nursing students, run by a Mrs. Keefe, close to the hospital where Grace was enrolled in the CPR class.

"When you get settled, give me a call," Lois suggested. "Maybe you would like to go to church with me in the morning then come back to my apartment for lunch. A lot has happened to you since we parted last fall. I'm dying to hear all the details and discuss your wedding plans."

"That sounds great. What time is church?"

"Ten forty-five."

"I don't have any dresses with me. Are slacks okay?"

Lois laughed. "Honey, this is Alaska. You can wear mukluks and deer skins if you want. Slacks are fine. I think it best if you take a cab direct to the church and I'll meet you there. Let me give you the address."

"Better still, give me directions. I plan to rent a car."

After getting directions to Living Hope Methodist Church in suburban Anchorage Grace called the rooming house Lois had suggested. Mrs. Keefe had a vacancy she would be willing to rent short term. Next, she called Enterprise and arranged for a Toyota Camry to be delivered to her motel. They promised to be there within the hour.

It was a gorgeous April morning in Anchorage with bright sunshine and temperatures expected in the fifties. Grace drove slowly, admiring the lovely city's parks framed by the ever present towering mountains on the horizon. She located Mrs. Keefe's home with no problem and found it perfect for her needs. It was reasonable, bright and clean.

She moved in immediately and walked to a nearby diner for a light lunch, then returned to her room and settled down in a cushiony chair with her book. Within minutes she was fast asleep.

Sunday, Grace met Lois and after church they returned to her friend's small apartment. Jill had a good job and had moved out only last week. Over lunch they discussed the way they would handle the wedding service and reviewed the vows Lois had drafted. The cabin John had rented last summer would be cleaned and ready for his use when she and John arrived on or around May tenth. The lodge itself was scheduled to open for the season on the fifteenth so the wedding would take place on Friday, May 14th.

Everything seemed to be falling into place too smoothly. Too perfectly. Grace pondered that thought. Life didn't usually unfold so effortlessly. It almost seemed as though God had a hand in things.

With the lunch dishes cleared Grace settled back against the cushions of Lois' sofa with a deep yawn. "I slept most of yesterday," she admitted. "I guess I'm still suffering jet lag. I'm bone weary."

"I'm not surprised. You've really had quite a time of it. John's proposal, another trip to the east coast to meet his family, then the fright of his illness. That's enough to tire anyone."

"I feel like I've been in perpetual motion ever since I left Pittsburgh last summer. I'll admit I'm tired of eating in restaurants and hopping from place to place. I'm ready to land somewhere and settle into this new life I've chosen. I wonder though, Lois, do you think I'm kidding myself—that I'm too old to take on this job at Big Bear?"

"Not at all, but it will certainly be a challenge to master a new career *and* a new marriage. How does John feel about it?"

"He has not pressured me but it's obvious that he'd prefer I not work. Once I enter the training I owe it to Mrs. Ross to stay at least several years. Do I have a right to commit him to that? I'll concede I feel guilty. True he has traveled a lot but realistically he has spent his entire life in one house, now I am moving him all over the place."

"But I feel you are so well suited for the job as naturalist. I would hate to see you give it up.

"I know. Somehow I feel I am being called to this vocation."

"You are. It is a way of returning the gift you have been given."

Grace frowned. "Gift?"

"Your very life is a gift and you are a gift to others."

"I guess I never really thought of myself as a gift."

"Grace, take a look at your life, starting from the beginning. Are you the cause of your own existence? Of course not. You are here because in their union your parents were gifts to each other. You received the gift of your mother's body from conception to birth, you were fed by her, given the gift of a sheltering home, the opportunity to go to school. Later you were given the gift of a loving spouse and a gift of children. You have enjoyed the gift of smell and sight—of life itself." Lois smiled sweetly. "Remember some time back I mentioned your spiritual wellness? Your soul? Now, you have the opportunity to teach adults and children to see and understand another gift. The gifts of nature around them."

Grace took a deep breath. "I guess you are right. From the very beginning of this quest of mine I have been looking for something more but I didn't really know what it was or how it could be found. Thank you Lois."

They talked long into the afternoon and when Grace eventually returned to her room she felt renewed and ready to accept the challenges of the next few weeks.

Grace had no problem with her driver's test. She had driven a school bus for an entire winter in Pittsburgh traffic and the skill easily returned to her. She also received her CPR certification and at the end of two weeks she said goodbye to Lois, packed her suitcase one more time, and headed south to Seward until the time John could join her.

CHAPTER TWENTY-FIVE

John recovered quickly. He spent hours at the gym building up his strength and by the end of the month regained the ten pounds he lost while ill.

One day, just as he was finishing an especially grueling workout, his doctor, Chad Philips, approached him. "I haven't talked to you for awhile—we must be coming in at different times," Chad said. "How did the pills work out?"

John winced. "They didn't."

Chad pursed his lips. "I don't have any appointments till after eleven. Do you have time for a coffee?"

"Sure. I'm ready to quit now."

"I want ten minutes on the barbells. Suppose I meet you in the lounge after we shower.

"Great. I'll see you then," John said with a grateful smile.

John was nursing his second cup of coffee at a corner table, when Chad sat down with a steaming Cappuccino. "I think I'm addicted to these darn things," he said placing his cup on the table. "Now tell me what happened . . . or didn't happen."

"I don't know, maybe part of it was nerves but the pills made me terribly nauseated and they didn't do what they were supposed to do. I tried twice."

"An upset stomach can be one of the side effects. Chad puffed out his cheeks and sighed. "John, I'm your friend as well as your doctor so I am going to be frank. As I told you in my office the pills do not work for all men. If it's that important to you—and I assume if you are getting married it is—I'm going to recommend the vacuum pump."

"Oh, I could never. . . ."

"Of course you can. You, as well as lots of men, have a total misconception of what it involves. You and your girlfriend. . . ." He cocked his head. "What's her name again?"

"Grace."

"Yeah. As I explained before, when the time is right you excuse yourself, go into the bathroom and use the small plastic tube you have readied ahead of time. It only takes minutes and is not much different than applying a condom. When you return to bed she may not even know what caused the erection. The act itself is no different than it would be without the extra help."

John's face grew warm. "Are they difficult to learn to use?"

"No, but it does take a little practice." Chad chuckled. "I'd try doing it in private, though."

"Does it hurt?"

"Not at all. Come to the office and I'll see you get one to try. They come in a small black case about the size of a shaving kit. The cost is covered by Medicare."

"Thanks, Chad."

"Not at all. We men have to stick together. Now, enough medical talk. Bring me up to date on your wedding plans."

John flew into Anchorage on the tenth of May. He had arranged to meet at the luggage carousel. He spotted Grace the second he entered the terminal and she came running toward him. He stopped in mid-stride and opened his arms to her, pulling her close. For a long, quiet minute she remained clasped in his arms before lifting her lips to meet his.

"God, I've missed you," he moaned. "I'm never going to let you leave me again."

"I promise I won't. I thought this month would never end."

Just then the loudspeaker announced the off-loading of John's plane, so hand-in-hand they headed to the proper conveyer. They were so lost in one another they missed his luggage when it trundled by the first time and had to pick it up on the next go-around.

They loaded his two large cases on a cart and wheeled it to a Avis Rental booth. "I think its better to rent a van for the summer here in Anchorage," he explained. "I get a discount through the newspaper and it's easier to return a rental at the airport when we leave for the East in the fall." After filling out the necessary paperwork John pulled their cart to the nearest exit door. "I must claim Bandit," he reminded her. "Why don't you wait here with the luggage for the car until I get the dog?"

Bandit's joy of life was totally restored. Ecstatically he threw himself at Grace, almost knocking her over, his wet tongue giving her face a thorough going-over. Grace tousled his big head and laughed the quick, merry laughter John had grown to love.

"I've booked a room at the Marriott for tonight," he said with a salacious wink.

"Sorry, Romeo."

He looked at her askance. "What do you mean?"

"I mean I plan to be the typical blushing bride. No sex until our wedding night."

"But we've already. . . ."

She put her fingers on his lips. "No buts." Her face turned serious. "Humor me, please."

"You really know how to hurt a fellow," he said with an exaggerated pout.

Bandit's tail was still wagging wildly, banging him against the leg. "Simmer down, boy. Our girl has just presented us with a big surprise. Guess you'll be sharing my bed tonight."

An attendant pulled up to the curb and beeped his horn. Together they piled John's luggage into the trunk and Bandit scrambled into the back seat of the rental van that would be their transportation until September.

"Look at that," John said with a loud guffaw. He pointed to a large sign on the van's visor requesting NO FISH. "I think I'm going to like this place."

On the way to the hotel they stopped at a picturesque restaurant near the sea, and John held her hand across the table, as they watched sailboats rocking gently in their slips. Lost in each other they hardly noticed the waiter, who had to come to the table two times before they even opened their menu.

"I find it hard to believe that within four days you will be my wife," he said softly.

"Forever, John. Or as our vows say, 'till death do us part'."

"Refresh my memory. What is the plan now? When you explained it over the phone it sounded rather complicated."

"Not really. We'll drive down to Seward and pack up all my belongings then drive north to Denali where Lois will pick us up. She has your old cabin ready and I will stay with her until the wedding on Saturday. Ben and the family are flying into Anchorage on Tuesday and they will also rent a car and meet us in Denali. Lois has a large cabin ready for them. That will give us several days to show them around the park before the wedding."

"Have you given any thought to where you want to go on our honeymoon?" John asked.

Grace gave him a coy smile. "I thought Fairbanks would be nice. It's where we had our first date and this time we just might be lucky enough to see the Northern Lights." She grinned. "After all if it weren't for the Northern Lights on the cover of National Geographic I might never have met you."

"It was fate, sweetheart. We were meant to be together." He rubbed his chin. "We may have to go much further north to see them this time of the year. But, let me check the Internet and see what I can come up with."

"We'll have two weeks. I start at the Lodge on the first of June."

"You've made up your mind, then? You are going to work?"

"I made a commitment, John. It just wouldn't be fair to Mrs. Ross to back out at this late date."

John raised his eyebrows but said nothing.

"Besides, I really want to do it," Grace added.

John's lips lifted in a smile. "That's what is important, honey. You want to do it. And I want you to be happy. Now, let's line up our ducks and see where we stand. First of all, once we get to Denali we have to find a place to live, comfortably, until September."

"Mrs. Ross has a cabin behind the lodge we can rent. I'd rather do that. It would be much more convenient. Let's look at it first."

"We'll have to check it out. I want something nice for my bride. If it isn't satisfactory for six months of the year we may have to buy something."

"Oh, John. . . ."

"I'm serious. Owning real estate in Alaska has to be a good investment. But let us not jump the gun—let's look at the cabin Mrs. Ross has. And in order to do that we need to get to the park and touch base with her."

When their waiter approached for the third time John grinned and said, "We'd better order or the dining room will close."

"I'm too excited to eat. I think a Caesar salad will be fine."

"Two Caesar salads," John said to the hovering waiter. "Oh, and two hamburgers to go, without the bun." At his surprised look, John added, "my dog is in the car and probably starving."

"Gracious, I forgot Bandit," Grace exclaimed.

"Don't let him know that. Honestly, I think he's as smitten with you as his master. He moped around the house for days after you left."

"I've grown to love him too. He's part of our family."

John's face sobered. "If I have one regret it's that we are too old to have children together. Somehow I've always equated marriage with the begetting of a family."

"Marriage is much more than begetting babies, John. It begets love. It's loving and caring for one another through all life's up and downs." She smiled tenderly. "Besides we already have a family. A blended family."

John looked at her with reverence, aching with an inner longing. He felt like leaping across the table, grabbing her in his arms and kissing her in front of everyone. "Speaking of loving," he said, "it's been an eternity since I held you in my arms all night. I need you, Grace. Are you sure you won't change your mind. Just this one night?"

He could see the indecision on her face, the yearning, the desire.

"I want that as much as you do, dearest," she said toying with her silverware. "But I made a commitment to myself to wait . . . to make our wedding night special."

John swallowed the lump in his throat. "You're a special person, Grace. That's why I love you. If it's that important to you I can wait."

A vision of snowcapped mountains filled the windshield as John headed south on the Seward Highway, a National Scenic Byway. It was cold for May, the air still and crisp. Snow still covered the ground, plowed into prodigious drifts at the side of the road. John felt himself becoming more and more enamored by the sheer beauty of this land. He turned to Grace with a smile. "You know, I've been reading a lot about Anchorage. It's actually located on a peninsula that juts into the northern terminus of the Pacific Ocean. It has an airport and seaport that are among the busiest hubs on the planet, yet it boasts that it is still a frontier. It's the sixty-fifth largest city in America and growing fast. I could live here. There aren't many places where a man can walk down to the creek on his lunch hour and catch a king salmon before he goes back to work."

Grace did a double take but didn't say anything. Maybe someday John could accept Anchorage over New York City. Instead she commented, "Lois says that large numbers of moose, as well as black and brown bears make the city their home."

"I know. The last time I was here I took Bandit for a walk and we came upon a moose, feeding only feet from the path."

As they left the city limits he mused about what he had just said. Perhaps it was the beauty of the mountains, or the profusion of parks and lakes throughout the city. If traveling back to New York City to spend their winters became too taxing, living here just might be the answer. After all, Adam had made it perfectly clear that he wanted to buy the brownstone. Anchorage had all of the cultural amenities he craved. A relaxed city without the urgency of New York, a place where, on the same day and within the same square mile, a person could catch a salmon or see a symphony.

They drove steadily for the next hour through a deep glacier-gouged valley between soaring mountains, soaking up sun and harmony. Lingonberries, bright red on the sun side, green on the other, ripened among the grass and lichens. The few trees on the vine-covered slopes were small—dwarfish almost—willow and birch no higher than John's waist. The tundra lay dark and wet from a recent rain. A red fox trotted by a nearby lake, its fur soaked, a ptarmigan dangling from its jaws.

At Trapper Creek John pulled off the road to let Bandit out for a run. He bounded across the tundra, a dense carpet of vegetation formed of dozens of species of low-lying plants, toward a small lake which he entered with a splash. Grace pulled a handful of blueberries from a bush, then made a face when she put them in her mouth. They were still too tart to eat. An arctic ground squirrel used to the photographers who came to capture the beauty of Mount McKinley, danced around John's boots. It reminded him of New York Central Park's gray squirrels. John whistled for Bandit. When the dog appeared the little hare issued a sharp "sik-sik" alarm, flicked its tail and took off.

They resumed their journey through Alaska's spectacular countryside passing through the historic mining district where contemporary gold miners still operate claims.

Late in the afternoon John pulled into Seward where Grace spent much of her winter. He was impressed. It was a quaint little seaside town, the area along the waterfront housing warehouses and docks that had been completely rebuilt after being destroyed by the earthquake in 1958. Dozens of boats lay at anchor along a new marina and a seven-acre waterfront aquarium overlooked beautiful Resurrection Bay.

"I'm getting hungry," John commented as they drove along the beach. "Where's a good place to eat?"

"I like the Gray Goose. It's in the marina with a fantastic view of the bay and the seafood is great. Why don't we park the car at my B&B and walk along the beach. It will give Bandit some exercise."

Mrs. Benoit, a romantic at heart, had reluctantly given John a room not normally rented to guests. Bandit, however, would have to be content with an outdoor dog house.

Since they would only be staying one night John left his luggage in the van and took only an overnight case upstairs. They decided to eat first, then load Grace's belongings for the trip north.

They strolled along the beachfront trail to the restaurant, the clean, crisp spring wind ruffling Grace's hair. There was a woodsy fragrance to the gentle breeze, the scent underscored by the faint suggestion of wood smoke. Only a steady low hum of insects permeated the stillness.

"Some people would give anything to experience this isolation, this wealth of nature at their doorstep," Grace said, her eyes glinting with pleasure.

"Yeah, but the Chamber of Commerce brochure says that 35,000 people descend on this isolation every Fourth of July for the Mount Marathon race."

"I know. It attracts over eight hundred runners. Mrs. Benoit says this entire beach is covered with camping trailers and motor homes during the run up the mountain."

Bandit started to nudge John's pocket as they walked, looking up at him with pleading eyes.

"You want to play, fella?" John withdrew a battered tennis ball he always carried in his jacket pocket. "I guess maybe we can accommodate that." With a heave he threw the ball in the direction of the bay.

For fifteen minutes they played throw and retrieve until the exhausted dog flopped near a park bench. John pocketed the sandy ball and sat down. The bench was wet with salt spray, but with a shrug of resignation Grace followed suite.

John folded her hand in his and they leaned back, the sun's rays warm on their faces. Out in the harbor gray pelicans floated, biding their time, waiting for prey. In the distance bell buoys sounded their mournful cry, a ship sounded its horn, the tide lapped gently at the shore. The air smelled of fish and salt—not exhaust fumes and industrial waste. She felt at peace here in this Land of The Midnight Sun. She remembered the talks she and Lois had about developing one's spiritual wellbeing. Without question that's what her work at Big Bear Lodge would do for her. She couldn't wait to begin, it's why she came to Alaska in the first place.

Bandit came over to squat in front of her and rest his wet nose on her hand. She idly scratched his ears, then turned to John. "Before I get involved in my new job there is something I really want to do," she confessed. "I would like to go salmon fishing."

"Wow! Another side of this woman I'm just getting to know. You like to fish?"

"Love it."

"Well, I understand there's no better place than the Kenai right here at Seward. Can we take an extra day?" John asked.

"I told Mrs. Benoit we would be leaving tomorrow."

"I can probably get us a half-day trip. We could fish in the morning, then start north early in the afternoon."

"That should work."

"Why don't we pack all of your personal belongings from your room into the van tonight. That way we can leave quickly after picking up Bandit when we return from fishing," John said.

"First we have to eat."

"Right. Let's go."

Grace and John sat side by side at a table on the deck of the Gray Goose where they could watch the activity in the harbor crowded with sailboats. Farther out in the deepest water several large yachts and a Holland American cruise ship lay at anchor. John nursed a whiskey sour, Grace had an iced tea. A lime green T-shirt that did wonders for her eyes was tucked into khaki walking shorts. She saw him looking at her and put her hand on top of his. He raised her hand to his mouth and kissed her fingers bringing a smile to the waitress' face as she brought their lobster salad and refreshed their drinks.

"Please bring me a hamburger, without a bun, before we leave." John said. The waitress looked puzzled. "My dog is outside," John explained with a smile.

"Susan called yesterday," Grace said.

"And?"

"She can't get much time off this close to the end of school but she doesn't want to miss the wedding. She's going to fly out on Friday and return Sunday. Jason isn't coming because of the quick turnaround."

"It's a shame she can't come with Ben and his family. He arrives Thursday, doesn't he?"

"Yes, but his flight was already full when she made her reservations. She will get here just in time for the wedding." Grace took a sip of iced tea, and grinned at him as she put her glass down. "Besides she isn't that fond of Emily, long term."

They concentrated on their lobster salad full of large hunks of succulent lobster. The Gray Goose had become Grace's favorite place to eat, friendly, smoke free, with a picturesque view of the harbor.

When they finished eating they claimed Bandit, fed him his treat for *staying*, and John took Grace's hand as they strolled along the brick-lined waterfront. Street life was sparse, the tourist season not due to swing into action for another two weeks. Old houses with birds-eye glass windows, weathered siding, widow's walks and weathervanes were set well back from the beach. Windows in the houses they passed were lighted for the evening, and people sat watching television or reading, some together, many alone. Grace always wondered what their lives were like, what problems or happiness they were experiencing. Someone behind one of those windows could someday enter her life and become her best friend. She didn't have the words to express those thoughts so she did not voice them as she and John walked, their footsteps faint in the heavy sea smelling air.

"Can you believe that in just a few days, you will be mine forever?" Grace said.

"No regrets?"

"None."

In their walk they had made a slow loop along the waterfront, up into the town and down a darkened street to Grace's B & B. They tied a pouting Bandit to his doghouse and entered the front hall of the boarding house.

It did not take long to pack and move all of Grace's clothes out of her room. Some things were still stored with Susan as Grace had not yet settled permanently. When she handed him the large cello case John's thick quirky eyebrows raised a notch.

"Peter's," she explained shyly. "I . . . I simply could not sell it. Do you mind?" She searched his eyes for a reaction.

"Of course not. There are a lot of Mary's personal things in my house that you will have to get used to. I'm glad we rented a van, though."

When everything was stowed away John turned to Grace with a grin and a provocative wink. "Sure, I can't sneak into your room, tonight?"

For a moment she wavered. She longed to feel his arms around her, hear his gentle snores and know that she was safe and loved.

She smiled softly. "A few more days and you'll never have to ask again."

Dawn found Grace holding tightly to John's hand as they headed down the sloping gangplank in a pea-soup fog looking for Kenai Charters and their guide Hank Rupp. She clutched a steaming cup of coffee to ward off the early morning chill.

They climbed aboard the twenty-six foot outboard and introduced themselves to the other four passengers, a couple from Seattle and their two teenage sons.

After rigging their rods and placing them into holders, Hank cranked up the motor and they pulled away from the dock. As they approached the mouth of Resurrection Bay the fog began to lift revealing a shoreline of granite cliffs, a secure island rookery for thousands of sea birds. Its sides were streaked white and as the boat slid through the narrow passage between it and the mainland, the gulls and guillemots, puffins and murres swirled overhead in a cacophony of bird noise.

Thrusting into the Gulf of Alaska, the Kenai Peninsula has a spectacular coastline broken by misty, glacier-carved fjords. Porpoises followed the boat, black oystercatchers swooped over nearby tidal beaches, tufted puffins nested on rocky cliffs hugging the ocean, and several bear were spotted along the shore. Best of all, the ocean breeze kept the mosquitoes away.

The morning had been overcast and rainy, but as they motored along, clouds began to part revealing a patch of blue sky overhead. The boat rose and fell on long gentle swells and Grace hoped she wouldn't get sea-sick. Around Aialik Cape, rocky spires of granite loomed out of the fog looking like beehives rising from the sea. Hank studied his GPS and slowed to a good trolling speed. He yelled, "We're at a hot spot now."

Everyone grabbed their rods.

When Grace got the first hard strike she let out a sharp squeal. The fish made a long, powerful run before it threw the hook, but it was a good sign. Minutes later, she got another, and this time she landed a silver. The skipper measured it carefully before he deemed it a keeper. By now everyone was getting hits. It was obvious that they were on fish.

The couple from Seattle was after a trophy fish so they spent the early part of the morning fishing for king salmon. When the tide started to run out the skipper rigged them with feathered lures and they trolled the rocky shore. He said that salmon typically move along the shoreline hunting herring so he cut the motor and they went with the tide. They were drifting over a deep hole, intent on their rods, when a tour boat approached and cut its engines.

Passengers lined the rail taking pictures. Grace grabbed her camera as their guide pointed to a bull orca with a pod of females and juveniles surrounding the tour boat. The whales rolled all around the boat for several minutes, issuing deep gasps as their dorsal fins and blowholes broke the surface, then slowly moved off.

By late morning they had their limit. The fog had burned off and Hank started the motor under a glaring sun to head back to Seward. The men relaxed, basking in the hot sunshine, sipping beer and exchanging fish stories. John snuggled close to Grace and slipped his arm around her waist. His thigh touched hers and he felt her tremble. He gave her a knowing look and leaned down to whisper in her ear. "How lucky can a man be? I'm not only getting me a wife who likes to make love but one who likes to fish as well."

CHAPTER TWENTY-SIX

By early afternoon John was driving north on the Seward Highway stopping often at scenic overlooks to take pictures. As they drove the mountains seemed to draw closer, almost overwhelming them with their sheer majesty. It was a cool, clean-washed May afternoon with tender blue skies and fleecy white clouds. A green haze of tundra grass undulated at the side of the road, whipped by the breeze created by passing cars.

"You haven't mentioned the *Times*," Grace said as they drove along. "Did you get another assignment?"

"Not really. Remember I told you I talked to Ed about possibly doing a piece about the effect of global warming in Alaska?"

Grace nodded.

"Well, it was all rather vague and then I ended up in the hospital. We more or less agreed that if I found anything interesting I would write it up and send it to him." John looked sideways at Grace. "Honey, I've been thinking that maybe I'd like to write a book instead."

"A book? You never spoke of that before. Do you mean a novel?"

"No. Either a compilation of the columns I've written over the years, or an in-depth study of the logging situation in our national forests. Or maybe an article about the decades worth of marine debris fouling the coastline. I don't know. I've just been turning ideas over in my mind. It seems to me that living up here, relaxed and close to nature, would be the perfect place to do something like that."

"I think it's a wonderful idea, John."

He grinned sheepishly. "I think all this wild Alaskan beauty is bringing out the artist in me. I'll admit I haven't been the same since I stood in the middle of that cathedral of landmark trees in the Tongass."

"That really affected you, didn't it?"

"It did. The Alaskan Audubon Society is proposing that the Forest Service set aside as off-limits the top fifty percent of undeveloped watersheds still open to logging. There is a growing public awareness that we need to do a better job of managing our ecosystem—not just here but worldwide. It's somewhat like looking in our rearview mirror. We can see that no forest has ever been just a repository of trees. It's a whole vibrant structure where creation continues to unfold." He frowned. "Don't let me get on that soapbox. I'll bore you to death."

"No you won't. I'm interested. I thought your article in the *New York Times* was wonderful. What was it you said about paying the loggers to stay home?"

John chuckled. "The Forest Service manages the sale of all of the cut timber but many of the logging sales it puts up for bid have no takers. In one year it spent thirty million dollars overseeing timber programs and sold only seven hundred thousand dollars worth of lumber. According to my calculations that's a loss of well over twenty-nine million dollars. For the two hundred jobs the loggers claim to have been lost the government could pay each man $146,000 a year to stay home and let the rain forest alone."

"Of course, that won't happen."

"Of course, it won't. But honey, it's just one way of illustrating how foolishly our government uses our tax dollars."

Grace grabbed John's arm. "Look . . . over there on your side. An immense herd of caribou."

Bandit spotted them too and began to bark. John pulled over and stopped.

The mass of animals was traveling as a slow moving wave, eating on the go, their antlers bobbing up and down in the tall grass. "Aren't they beautiful?" Grace exclaimed. "There must be close to a hundred. I've been studying about them. Both sexes carry antlers, although the males are bigger."

"That figures," John quipped. He reached behind him to grab Bandit's collar. "Calm down, fellow."

They continued to watch the caribou for several minutes before moving on.

"Let's talk some more about that book you want to write," Grace said.

"Any ideas?"

"You could write about senior love."

"What about senior sex?"

"Well. . . ."

John laughed. "I still have a lot more research to do on that subject—and I don't mean the kind you get from a book." He thought abjectly of the untried device in his luggage—now waiting for his wedding night.

"I think we better change the subject, Mr. Hathaway."

"Okay, then, how about a book on the migration of salmon? That's a fascinating subject. Do you know that the females travel thousands of miles to lay their eggs in the exact place they were born? Then they die."

"I think you have a one track mind." She lifted a Thermos from the floor and unscrewed the lid. "How about a cup of coffee?"

As they sipped hot coffee Grace consulted the map she kept folded into squares, naming each small town they passed through: Wasilla, Trapper Creek, Talkeena.

Their morning fishing trip had delayed them but by switching drivers they were able to take advantage of the lengthening daylight hours and arrived at Denali just before dark.

Grace had phoned ahead explaining the reason for their late arrival and Marvin was waiting for them with the Eagles Nest van. The restricted Denali Parkway was still officially closed for the season and they did not yet have a Big Bear Lodge decal for their own van so they were forced to leave it at the Visitors Center.

Lois greeted them warmly, but seeing how exhausted they were she gave John a key to his cabin and showed Grace to her room.

The lodge kitchen smelled heavenly when Grace joined Lois in the morning. She was busy at the stove, sausage links sizzled and coffee perked, the aroma of hazelnut making Grace's mouth water. John was already there, sitting on a stool at the counter, a cup cradled in his hands.

She sidled over to him for a kiss. "Good morning, sleepy head," he said rumpling her hair.

"Morning"

John laughed as he turned to Lois. "I'm still learning about my girl. She isn't at her best the first thing in the morning."

Grace yawned and Lois handed her a steaming mug of coffee.

"We were just discussing the wedding plans," Lois said as she began to lift eggs onto their plates. "I've received the one-day permit and talked with park officials for approval to have the ceremony at Reflection Pond so everything is all right on that score. The park road is still officially closed for the season but lodge owners have the right to use it. I think we should drive over to the pond today and pick the spot where you want the ceremony to take place."

"Did John tell you my family is flying up for the wedding?"

"Yes. He said they'd arrive in Denali the day after tomorrow. I'll send Marvin in with the van to pick them up. She heaped sausage, eggs, and browned potatoes onto a platter. We have Cabin 7 cleaned and ready for them. Have you looked over the final copy of the wedding vows I sent you?"

Grace nodded. "They are lovely, Lois. Just what I wanted."

"I agree," John said around a mouthful of food. "Grace showed them to me. Um, these sausages are fantastic." He winked at Grace. "I hope my promised wife is as good a cook as you are."

Over breakfast, they discussed what they should do next. Grace wanted to touch base with Mrs. Ross and see the cabin she offered to rent them for the summer. John was anxious to get the decal she had promised them for their van so he could retrieve his car and their luggage. Lois was busy getting her cabins open and cleaned but was willing to loan them the lodge van to drive to Big Bear.

Mrs. Ross greeted Grace with what could only be a look of relief. After being introduced to John she showed Grace where she would be working and reviewed the description of her duties. She would start as a Guest Service Representative, or GSP, in the Naturalist/Guide position ready to answer guest's questions and help them as needed. As time permitted she would train as a guide. After checking her CPR certification and commercial driver's license, and filling out the necessary employment forms, Mrs. Ross handed her the key to the available cabin and sent them on their way to examine it.

Grace had asked for seclusion and they were delighted with the cabin they were given. It was nestled on the fringe of a forest of spruce and alder, secluded from the worries and activities at the main lodge. The fragrant cedar cabin had two spacious rooms and a tiny kitchenette with a private bath and shower, television, telephone, a free standing fireplace and cozy furnishings. Floor to ceiling windows in the back opened to a large deck with a view of nearby Moose Lake. It would be perfect.

"Thank heavens we have electricity. If I am going to write I need an outlet," John said as he followed her out to the porch.

"And it is heated. It can get pretty cold at night early in the spring."

John stood behind her with his arms around her waist. "Ah, but now I have my own personal furnace—someone to cuddle with. You are all the heat I need."

She glanced over her shoulder to look up at him. His eyes, softly brown and serious, met hers. He turned her just enough so that their bodies touched. They stared at one another ravenously embracing in the sunlight. She could barely breathe as his hands framed her face and he leaned down to kiss her. It started out soft and tender then flamed until she began to worry that her legs would collapse beneath her.

"We'd better stop before this gets out of hand and I throw you down on that bed in there," he said gruffly. "I may not be able to wait for my wedding night." He grinned. "Speaking of which I may have a surprise for you."

John woke the next day with a vague sense of foreboding. Something was wrong. He cocked his head. Was it a sound that had roused him from a deep sleep?

There, he heard it again. A long howl—followed by another howl, then furious barking.

He glanced around the cabin. It was cold and dark. And empty.

He jumped out of bed, fully awake now.

"Bandit," he yelled. "Bandit!"

As if in answer the distant barking grew more anguished followed by a series of hair raising wolf howls.

John yanked on a pair of jeans and ran to the door. His stomach sank as he realized it was ajar. Apparently he had not closed it tightly and Bandit had poked it open. John padded into the yard in his bare feet calling, "Bandit . . . Bandit . . . Bandit" over and over again.

The dog was gone. And John's heart sank when he realized where he probably was.

The barking and howling had stopped momentarily and John stood in the cold dawn uncertain what to do. Sound travels long distances on the flat tundra and without noise he did not know which direction to take. Or what he could do if Bandit had decided to join a pack of wild wolves.

He went back into the cabin and started to dress—his mind a whirlwind of emotions. He had no gun. Grizzlies were a constant threat in the wilderness and he had planned to buy a rifle but had not yet done so. It was foolhardy to go after a pack of wolves without protection of some sort.

He was trying to decide what to do when there was a tap at the door. He opened it to find Grace in pajamas and a housecoat with a worried look on her face.

"I saw your light," she said. "Is anything wrong? The sound of the wolves howling woke me, then I heard you calling Bandit."

"He's gone. I'm going out to look for him."

"The barking has stopped. Maybe he's on his way home."

"Or injured . . . or dead." John ran his hand through his hair. "Damn this Alaska and its *call of the wild*. This is twice now. He never ran away in New York."

"Don't blame Alaska. He may be after a female, again. Maybe you should have had him neutered," she retorted.

"I know. I just never had the heart." He grabbed his bomber jacket and started toward the door.

"I'm going with you."

"In your pajamas?"

"Come up to the lodge and get the emergency backpack Lois keeps at the desk. It has first-aid supplies, a blanket, a knife, and an air pistol. I'll throw on jeans and join you."

"No! It's dangerous out there."

"Don't argue. I know where the wolves den." She tugged at his arm. "I love Bandit, too. You may need help, John."

•   •   •

Grace and John hurried across the tundra on a barely discernable trail toward the river bed where they had encountered the wolf last September. Grace knew from her wilderness tours that a pack denned in an abandoned fox den on the rocky cliff just beyond. She and John did not speak, each lost in their private fears.

They were climbing a low ridge when John extended his hand for her to stop. A soft whimper permeated the stillness. He began to run toward the sound, Grace right behind him.

"There," John shouted as he headed toward a yellow heap beside the trail.

Bandit lay still—a trail of blood behind him.

John hunkered down and lifted the dog's big head. Bandit's eyes were closed, his muzzle covered with blood, one ear hanging by a flap. John ran his hand down the sodden, bedraggled fur of Bandit's neck. There was a deep gash with clotted blood.

"He's still breathing, thank God," John said.

Grace knelt and began to stroke the dog's head, whispering his name softly, tears running down her cheeks.

John pulled the nylon blanket from his backpack. "We'll have to make a litter and carry him. He's heavy, do you think you can manage?"

"Of course. But first maybe you should take that roll of wide bandage and try to pull the opening in his neck closed."

While Grace lifted, John did the best he could with the bandage. Bandit opened his eyes and feebly licked her hand. They spread the blanket on the ground and pulled the whimpering Lab onto it. "On the count of three lift your end and keep the blanket as taut as you can. We must hurry. Do you know where the closest veterinarian is?"

"I have no idea, but Lois will know."

Together they trudged up the trail toward the lodge. Bandit lay still as death.

Lois met them at the door and after an agonized look at the mangled Lab instructed them to deposit him on the kitchen table.

"The closest vet is in Denali but Marvin is part Indian and very good with animals. His mother was a tribal shaman. When needed he tends to the pets of our guests. I saw you coming with the litter and called him. He should be here in minutes." She had no sooner spoken when Marvin came bursting into the kitchen carrying a black satchel.

He immediately went to the injured dog and after a quick evaluation began to lift supplies from his well-worn bag. He examined the membranes in the dog's mouth and checked Bandit's pupillary responses.

"The membranes in his mouth are white, indicating a large loss of blood, his pupils are dilated and his heart sounds are abnormal," Marvin commented expertly. Deftly he sprinkled a powder into the wound on his neck. "He will need surgical attention. You must get him to the veterinarian in Denali as quickly as possible." He pressed a poultice to the wound. "Keep pressure on this so the wound does not start to bleed again."

"Do you think he's going to die?" Grace whispered, a sob catching in her throat.

"He is hurt very badly," Marvin said. His broad face softened with compassion. "I will chant the healing prayer of our people. Go now, you must be quick."

There were no cars on the road and John, his face grim, drove as fast as he dared. Grace sat on the floor in the back of the van, cradling Bandit's head on her lap, her hand pressing the compress tightly to his neck.

"Turn here," she called up to John as they reached the Denali rail terminal. "Doctor Gruen's office is in that strip of shops."

Lois had called ahead and the veterinarian met them at the van where he took immediate charge. He carried Bandit inside and placed him on the examination table. After removing the poultice and gently prodding the wound he said, "Your dog needs surgery. I must place him under anesthesia and it will be five or six hours before we know anything definitive. I suggest you folks go home. I'll call you this evening to let you know how he is doing."

John swallowed dryly. "I think I'd rather stay close by. I have a cell phone in case you need me."

"It really isn't necessary. Some cell phones don't work here. It would be easier to reach you at the lodge. I understand your concern Mr. Hathaway and I promise I'll call you if the need arises."

Grace took John's hand. "He's right, honey. Let's go home."

John drove back to Eagles Nest, his eyes stormy, his lips compressed in a tight line. Neither of them felt like talking and the drive was made in silence. As soon as John reached the lodge he parked the van and went in search of Marvin. He didn't explain why.

An hour later Grace saw him striding out of the utility room with a rifle tucked under his arm. Marvin was apparently arguing with him but John kept shaking his head.

Grace had been trying to read one of her textbooks. She threw her book aside and ran after him.

"What are you doing," she cried.

"I'm going to kill the wolf that maimed my dog," John barked.

Marvin protested. "They are protected. You'll be arrested." He tried to wrest the gun from John's hands. John pushed him aside with amazing strength. "Don't try to stop me," he snarled, with a keep-your-mouth-shut look.

Grace stood straight and tall, her hands clenched into fists hanging stiffly at her side. Her face was still, but her eyes narrowed, raking him. "Wolves are highly territorial and defensive. Bandit was wrong, not the wolf. The male was only trying to protect his family."

"Territory be damned. Are you defending the bloodthirsty beast for almost killing Bandit?" John cried.

"It's true," Mr. Hathaway," Marvin interjected. "The urge to defend his territory and his female is strong.

"I don't give a damn what their rules are—that wolf almost killed my dog."

Grace grabbed his arm. "Wolves are not wanton killers. They have the most highly developed form of social organization in the entire animal kingdom. The wolf was only trying to defend his family against an outside aggressor. It was his right and his territory. Besides, wolves don't kill their adversary, they fight for dominance. Bandit was badly mangled but he was allowed to return home."

"I don't need a lesson in wolf behavior." He looked at Grace with blazing eyes. "I don't believe I know you. I thought you loved Bandit. I knew you had a thing for wolves, but this goes beyond my understanding." John's lips were pursed with suppressed fury and he began to back away from her.

"And I don't believe I know you. Nothing is ever settled with a gun. Never. Oh, you can kill the wolf, easily enough. He hasn't learned to mistrust humans and doesn't know about high-powered rifles." She ground out the words between clenched teeth. "Stop and think about the right and wrong of the situation, John."

"And, if Bandit dies what is that?"

"A terrible ending to something that should never have happened—as much your fault as the dog's. If you had had him spayed before bringing him into the wild this probably wouldn't have happened."

John rested the butt of the rifle on the ground and leaned on it as though the air had gone out of him. He stood motionless, his eyes fixed on the horizon, his face a snarl of agony. "I love him, like a child," he said, struggling to control his quavering voice.

Grace stepped up to John and gathered him in her arms. He heard her sob. The rifle dropped to the ground and Marvin, who had been standing quietly a few yards away, picked it up and moved away.

No words were necessary. They had met the crisis and survived it.

CHAPTER TWENTY-SEVEN

Dr. Gruen phoned them shortly after nine P.M. to say that Bandit was awake and doing fine. He said he would like to keep him for twenty-four hours until he was sure he was stabilized. John agreed saying that they would be coming to Denali tomorrow to pick up family members at the train terminal and would see him at that time.

The next morning John was eager to check on Bandit, but Grace wanted to stop by Wonder Lake on their way to Denali and pick the spot where they would have the wedding ceremony. Bandit's adventure the previous day had disrupted their plans and the wedding was set for the next day. The permit was dated for May 14th so they had to go forward as scheduled.

At the lake John pulled off to the side of the road and parked. With their arms around each other's waist, she and John walked to the edge of the lake, lost in each other, consuming the scenery. An array of spring flowers, white anemones and red dwarf alpine rhododendron bloomed amid patches of snow on the floor of the valley that seemed to roll toward infinity. Reflection Pond in Denali has to be one of the most beautiful wilderness areas on earth, Grace thought as she closed her eyes and leaned against John. Patches of purple lupines spread across the high mountain meadows as though applied with an artist's brush. And before them, the face of Mt. McKinley, the greatest single pitch of rock in North America, glimmered in mesmerizing perfection in the still waters of the lake. They were both caught up in the moment, forgetful of their recent conflict. Insects chirped around her and a soft breeze ruffled the water. A red-tailed hawk circled overhead, and a large long-tailed jaeger, a bird of prey, dove down toward its quarry on the tundra like a kite gone out of control.

Grace broke the serene silence. "I never fail to marvel that out of the millions of people on this earth we found one another. I'm sure you could have had your pick of dozens of women, after Mary died. Why me?"

"Why you? Because you're good to be with, Grace. I love what you've done with your life. And you're funny and sweet. You're what I need—someone to talk to and laugh with and someone to hold on to." He smiled. "Why me?"

"Because you are strong and gentle at the same time. I've never heard you criticize a person for their shortcomings. You are interested in everything around you, and I see a love of nature that you are not even aware of."

He lifted her hair and kissed the back of her neck. "Who can explain love, Grace," he murmured.

When Bandit greeted them with a bark Grace almost wept with joy. The dog was on his feet and his tail wagged slowly as he ambled over to nuzzle John's hand. He looked comical. His ear had been sutured in place protected by a large bandage.

"I can't thank you enough Dr. Gruen," John said, shaking the doctor's hand. "I was afraid we lost him."

The doctor smiled proudly. "He is doing remarkably well—still a little listless but that comes from the anesthesia. You can pick him up tomorrow."

John frowned. "We may have to send Marvin, the guide from Eagles Nest, to get him. Grace and I are getting married tomorrow."

"Well, congratulations."

John settled the doctor's bill and he and Grace walked across the street to wait for the train from Anchorage.

"There's Ben," Grace squealed as her son descended the iron steps. Grace rushed into his arms and he greeted her with a hearty bearhug and kiss.

"Where are Emily and the children?" Grace asked, looking around in confusion.

"I had to leave them home. Because of snow days Ted's graduation was postponed until June. We didn't want him to miss all the parties and excitement of the last weeks of school and Kelly is studying for college finals." He looked chagrined. "It was a last minute decision. Emily used it as an excuse to stay home. I promised the kids they could come out for a visit later in the summer."

"I'm disappointed," Grace admitted, "but I'm glad you came." Susan won't get here until tomorrow, just in time for the wedding. She is flying all night and will rent a car in Anchorage. Grace continued to scan the people still descending from the train. "I'm looking for my friend, Shirley."

"She's in the first-class coach." Ben glanced down the track. "There she is now."

"Shirley," Grace cried as she spotted the tall figure of her friend. She ran to greet her and they embraced warmly. "I can't believe you actually came."

"Lord, I can hardly believe it myself," Shirley said.

John strode toward them and Grace proudly introduced him. She did not miss the look of admiration on her friend's face.

"And, this is my son Ben. You know him don't you?"

"Indeed I do. We saw each other on the plane and had dinner together in Anchorage last evening."

Ben looked a little flustered.

"I put the decal on our van so we are free to leave for Eagles Nest anytime," John said. "Ben I know you are staying there, how about you Shirley?"

"I have reservations at the Princess Lodge."

"Then, why don't we take you to the lodge first and we can all have dinner together." John said.

"Sounds good to me," Ben commented. "I'm starved."

As they walked up the hill John pulled Grace aside. "I have a surprise. George is in Anchorage. I didn't want to tell you he was coming because he wasn't certain he could get away.

"Oh, John, how wonderful."

"He just called me. He would have been here today but the flight was over booked and he got bumped. He's renting a car and should be here tomorrow." John beamed as he reached out and folded Grace's hand in his. "He will be my best man."

"My son will give me away and your son is your best man. We are truly blessed." Grace said softly.

And that night as they all sat chatting on the restaurant's outside patio Grace gave a gasp and pointed to the sky. The aurora borealis flashed across the heavens in an eruption of colors. Long tails of red, yellow, and green whipped across the night sky. Multicolored sheets rose and fell in an intricate dance. It was extraordinary and everyone sat speechless, awed by the beauty.

The wedding day had arrived at last. By late-afternoon the clouds that normally cloak Mount McKinley had dissipated as though God knew the importance of this day. It was beautiful spring weather. McKinley rose behind the lake, a still cathedral of rock and ice reflected in intoxicating beauty, its alpine whiteness tinted a lambent blue, lavender and gold. Willows and aspens were bursting out with new buds. Clumps of grasses and sedges, patches of lichens and mosses and a wide assortment of flowering berry plants carpeted the ground. Crickets chirped, squirrels chattered, birds sang. New born baby lambs followed their mothers on the steep sides of the mountain, watching the vehicles and gentry assemble below with impunity.

Susan helped her mother from the car, handed her a spray of yellow, long stemmed arctic poppies and placed a crown of forget-me-nots and dogwood blossoms on her short-cropped gray hair. Grace wore a soft, ivory-cream crepe de Chine dress, simple in-line with a round neck, and a single strand of pearls that had belonged to her mother.

Ben took her arm. "Ready, Mom?"

"Ready."

With a firm grip of Grace's arm Ben walked her to the edge of the lake where Lois, John, Susan and George waited.

Marvin, with a big grin on his face, led Bandit to stand beside John, handsome in a crisp navy-blue suit with a white carnation in the buttonhole. Despite the solemnity of a wedding ceremony everyone began to laugh. Bandit wore a large, plastic, Elizabethan collar on his head. It resembled a funnel with the end cut off, intended to keep him from scratching the white bandage still wrapped around his head to secure his ears. He looked slightly indignant but wagged his tail enthusiastically.

Marvin stepped to the side to join the small group of well-wishers—Mrs. Ross from Big Bear and Shirley.

Ben stopped in front of Lois and Grace handed her flowers to Susan. Shafts of afternoon sunshine dappled the bride and groom.

"Who gives this woman in marriage?" Lois asked.

Ben answered, "I do." He placed Grace's hand on John's arm, and stepped aside.

Lois opened her bible and smiled sweetly. "What a blessing for us to be here this afternoon with this couple to witness their love and joy as they make their marriage vows. Thank you for choosing such a spectacularly beautiful site for your wedding. And thanks be to God for the gentle breeze and perfect weather. As the Psalmist wrote: 'This is the day the Lord has made, let us rejoice and be glad in it.'

"In preparation for the marriage vows, let us turn our minds and hearts to the most important requirement for a truly successful relationship . . . love. As Saint Paul wrote to the Corinthians: 'Love is patient. Love is kind. It does not envy, it does not boast, it is not proud, it is not rude, it is not self-seeking, it is not easily angered, it keeps no record of wrongs . . . it always protects, always trusts, always hopes, always perseveres. Love never fails'."

Lois bowed her head. "Shall we pray?

"O Lord our God, may you give Grace and John the ability to nurture and rejoice in the love they share this day. May you bless their marriage always and grant them your peace. Amen.

"And now, John and Grace, please turn to each other and take one another's hand. John repeat after me: I, John, take you, Grace, to be my wife and promise to honor and love you from this time forward. I promise to cherish you in times of trouble and celebrate with you in times of happiness, so help me God."

Grace repeated the same vows, and they exchanged the rings that George handed them. Then Lois concluded the wedding ceremony: "As authorized by the State of Alaska, I pronounce you husband and wife. John you may kiss your bride."

After they exchanged a deep, reverent kiss a radiant Grace took one of John's hands.

"I would like to read a poem written by a very dear friend, Margaret Sponsler. She sent it to me when she learned that we were getting married."

Grace withdrew a folded piece of stationery from the pocket of her dress and gazing tenderly into John's eyes began to read:

"What is this love we now have?
It is not the love of youth

"The love that excited us and encouraged
us to step into the stream of life.

"The love that encouraged us to be good
children to our parents, good parents
to our children.

"The love that supported great friendships
troubled times, helped us establish
spiritual and moral values.

"All this was the love of our youth.

"What is this love we now have?

"It came to us out of loss, loneliness
and sadness.

"It came to us quickly and brought the
laughter and sparkle of new life.

"It took the frayed edges of our lives
and wove us whole again.

"It comforts us when days of the past
come creeping into our present.

"It gives us new experiences to make memories
of our time together.

"It give us courage to set our children free,
knowing there is someone here for us.

"It is a touch: a look that says, Come give
me your hand. I will walk the slower pace with you.

"And we say, Thanks be to God, for he has given
us a love for our youth, and a love for now."

This lovely poem would link them in their new life like no
ceremony ever could.

THE END

ABOUT THE AUTHOR

In addition to this book, Dody Myers is the author of five historical novels. She blends historical fact and real people with fictional characters to put a human face on our past.

Myers and her husband, Dr. Ainslee Gruen, currently divide their time between Chambersburg, Pennsylvania and St. Simons Island, Georgia.

Visit her online at www.dodymyers.com

CPSIA information can be obtained at www.ICGtesting.com
Printed in the USA
LVOW041519171112

307593LV00001B/83/P